Anywhere But Vernon

Jaelyn Banks

Contents

CHAPTER 1

Colin looked down knowing this season of denial was finally over. There, among the final notices and collections letters was the proof needed to hammer the last nail into the coffin that was his life. All it took was one word in bold red letters for him to realize everything he strived for was now beyond recall.

EVICTION

In a way, it was a relief. He didn't have the money to pay anyway, and he was tired of lying to the landlord. A clean cut was always the easiest way out. At least that's what his latest girlfriend told him. Colin's life was mostly fine three years ago. He had just arrived in East St. Louis truly believing this would be a new chapter in his life and that the dead-end job, bitter ex-girlfriend, and violent loan sharks would stay in California where he left them. Within three weeks he had a delivery job, a cheap, but pest-free apartment, and he met Shery. She deemed his relatively mediocre life as worth something, and for that he was grateful. But not being able to hold up the charade, even if it was longer than most, she regarded her own worth as more and therefore left. "At least we can make it a clean break. No messy back and forth, no calls…I'm out, Colin." That was two months ago.

Colin had let himself fall slightly into disrepair since then. His dark brown hair went from fashionably long to shaggy, falling over his ears. The whites around his green hazel eyes were constantly bloodshot due to stress, lack of sleep, and terrible seasonal allergies that had to go untreated this year due to finances. With no one around to impress, his posture became more lax, causing his shoulders to round. This gave his 6'2" slight build frame an arthritic look. He did, however, keep up with shaving and never let his stubble last longer than 2-3 days. His strong, stubborn chin matched his strong, stubborn personality, and, being one of the few vain qualities he had, he liked to show it off.

Now, sitting in his unkempt clothes, in his small unkempt apartment, on an almost broken foldable chair at the too-small, round, foldout table overflowing with bills and loan shark threats, 34-year-old, recently unemployed Colin Warrington had absolutely nothing left to hold on to.

Well, that's almost true. Colin still had his dog Dually. A mostly medium sand brown American Pit Bull Terrier with a white ring around his nose, a white stripe down the center of his face, and a white tummy that loves to be rubbed. Dually is the best canine companion anyone could hope for. Dually has seen Colin through his last three relationships. Realizing Dually was the only consistent source of companionship in his life made the vet bill three papers down the stack of bills and other notices piled on his counter cut him deeper than any other. The truth was, that Dually is old. Now past his 12-year life expectancy, Dually has been more under the weather than not. And with neither wanting to let the other go, the vet's advice, as well as the bill, remained ignored.

"We have to get out of here, buddy. I just don't know where." Colin says this less to inform his beloved dog than to himself. With the need to come back to reality, Colin pours himself a second cup of lukewarm, bitter coffee, sits down on his creaky chair, and contemplates the next steps he needs to take.

"Anywhere but Vernon."

This was a habitual saying Colin usually defaulted on when asked where he wanted to go or where he wanted to be at any given time. But now, hearing himself through desperate ears say the phrase out loud, he bid the question, *why?*

Rubbing his face, Colin arduously pulls up his first recollection of the phrase. It was a record-cold September in Wisconsin. He had to be around middle school age, standing in the entrance to the kitchen while his enraged father flitted from surface to surface, willing himself to not act upon his emotions. Darci, his mother, left more of an imprint on someone's mind for her body than her intelligence. This was not the first incident of his mother unwittingly being taken advantage of, physically or monetarily, and his father was doing everything in his power not to spend time in a cell over it.

Once calmed, Colin found his father over the sink in their small kitchen rubbing his face with cold water and saying to his only son at his feet, "We have to get out of here, buddy."

"Where, Dad? We have nowhere to go."

"Anywhere but Vernon, son." Colin remembered the phrase feeling funny to him and he scrunched his face to remember if or where he had ever heard it before. "Where's Vernon?"

"Vernon is nowhere son, and nothing but bad luck." After a moment of pensive silence, his father turned to him with emotion in his eyes he couldn't quite hide. "Okay Buddy, find your sisters and get those suitcases packed."

His sisters' suitcases remained as empty as his parent's marriage. It was no surprise Colin was the only child who wanted to stay with his father, nor was it a surprise his mother not only allowed the separation of siblings but encouraged it. He was the youngest of three children by a good eight years, his older twin sisters being the result of his mom's physical impression upon his father and his father being too good-natured of a man to walk out on a pregnant woman. If Colin wasn't the physical result of his parent's marriage lasting as long as it did, he would have wished his father's life free of the woman long ago.

Not a full year went by until what little contact Colin kept with his sisters disappeared. It wasn't that he and his sisters didn't share a sibling bond, they just didn't have as much say in the matter. Darci, playing the victim as an abandoned wife, never again lacked the sympathetic company of a man, nor his fortune, so why would she need to stay in touch? As far as either of the Warrington men were concerned, Colin was now, and has henceforth been, an only child.

Colin's father William (Bill if you knew him longer than a few months) was, in all, a good man with a strong work ethic. He tried his best to provide for his family, but the world doesn't always reward those who work the hardest. Despite sacrificing many personal dreams to take care of those he loved, with little to no gratitude, the Warrington family could never get a step ahead.

Since that September, many years ago, it's been one town of misfortune to the next. There were no jobs for an electrician with an extra mouth to feed in Albuquerque, New Mexico back in 1992. That led them to Texas where the volatile spring of '94 destroyed their home along with many others in a tornado outbreak. Hoping to find a haven from violent weather, the Warrington men then turned to Reno, Nevada where a crippling snowstorm in '96 once again destroyed the place they dared to call home.

Every time the Warrington unit was forced to find a new home, his father's answer as to where was always the same, "Anywhere but Vernon" and Colin never thought to question him on it. Vernon or not, they always ended up where the luck was bad. The only thing that made his father's passing back in 2002 easier was the knowledge that Bill finally had some sort of peace.

In addition to looks, Colin inherited his father's vigorous work ethic as well as his bad luck. Despite all he did, how much he fought and sacrificed for those he allowed close enough to label as loved, Colin was unable to make ends meet, therefore falling behind on most bills. He was not a person anyone would describe as lazy, wasteful, or freeloading, instead, they would remember him as being rather stubborn, just like his chin. He was in fact too stubborn to ask for any help, not from pride but shame. His reasoning was, why burden friends or loved ones with his inevitable fate of just not *being* enough?

He no longer had a girlfriend. He no longer had a job. Hell, according to the last thing he read he didn't even have a home anymore. Other than a pile of debt, and loan sharks he could no longer emotionally face, what Colin *did* still have were his suitcases, and, knowing he couldn't stay any longer, Colin's curiosity decided to find out just what bad luck his father was running away from in Vernon. It couldn't be any worse than the luck he already had.

CHAPTER 2

"Okay Dually, we need a map." Colin had no clue where Vernon was, and once Dually was leashed and relieved outside, they headed off towards the nearest gas station about a block away. The only other clue Colin had to go off besides the familiar phrase was his father's old Michigan ID he once stole to buy liquor to impress a crush in high school. Being so similar in looks, this was a plan that should not have failed. However, that incident was as successful as his life allowed.

Colin didn't have any spare money to buy a map but that didn't stop him from looking at one. Being so determined to find Vernon, and not seeing it listed on a regular map, Colin had to look at a very detailed atlas. Giving up being discreet, he even enlisted the gas attendant's help in finding someplace that could very well not exist. Even then it took an agonizing eighteen minutes of tracing lines and dots on the most magnified maps available before the tiny name he was searching for stared back at him from the page. Vernon, possibly the smallest town in Michigan, was real after all.

Leaving East St. Louis behind without a forwarding address or any possible way for his loan sharks to find him was a risky game. At least in California, everybody owed somebody something, so nobody wasted too much time tracking down those they couldn't find. But East St. Louis was not exactly known for treating those who crossed them well. The only hope for Colin is this once-perceived fictional place to help him elude those he owed long enough to either forget about him or presume he was dead.

Being strapped for cash, Colin would have to avoid toll roads all the way to the middle of Michigan and that would add extra drive time. Acknowledging this, no more time was wasted, and just over two hours from locating his next place of refuge, Colin throws the full suitcases, along with any other belongings worth pawning, into the back of his abused, chipped, and rusty red '97 Pontiac Sunfire.

Dually being just as anxious to leave did not exactly sit comfortably with Colin. He was always a mild-mannered dog who enjoyed consistency in his every day. But the faithful dog, being allowed the full front seat on this new journey, had seen this routine before and therefore must have considered it to be "consistent".

The drive northeast from the "Gateway to the West" could be summed up as dull. With only a quick nap in a popular gym parking lot, Collin found himself, with barely any gas and even less cash, navigating the Michigan roadways late the next morning. Missing his exit off I-69 twice, Colin finally found Gunther Road and began his quiet drive through the town he believed to be fabricated most of his life; bound and determined to call Vernon home and keep it that way.

Rambling down Gunther Rd. drew much more attention from the locals than his car deserved. Their unnatural staring was, in fact, so distracting that Colin found himself at the end of town realizing he couldn't remember a single thing about it. Even with all his concentration he could not recall a single store, house, yard, or even road sign.

"What the hell just happened?" Unsure where to go or what to do, he turned right just before a bridge and railroad crossing and into a park that barely lay inside the city limits in the hopes of coming up with the next plan of action.

Dually was also overdue for a much-needed respite. The park, upon first observation, wasn't anything spectacular and thankfully empty. It contained designated locations for the residents to play some favorite local sports, a single covered patio with three weary, green picnic tables that have long been chipped with time and usage, a playground for children that could only be described as a hoard of death traps, and an abundance of the state's most intrusive pest, the mosquito. But still, it was better than no park at all. And with the parking lot being set far back from the main road, with everything it has to offer laid out before him, Colin found himself quite taken with this little plot of land.

From what Colin could discern from the atlas graciously donated by that gas attendant, and how quickly he drove from one end of town to the other, one could easily walk this village from end to end, zigzagging on a lazy afternoon, and still be home before dark. Having nothing to spare but time, that was exactly what Colin decided to do.

Digging through the remaining contents of his back seat, Colin extracted a sturdy leash, a heavily used, unmarked, brown baseball cap, his just about empty wallet, and his beloved watch with which to barter.

The watch, a vintage LECOULTRE Men's 14K gold hand-wind dress watch, was in amazing condition for never leaving the arm of its previous owner. With only minor scratches on the back, a semi-faded face cover, a minor band tear near where the black leather strap touched eleven, and the letters KB professionally engraved under the 6, it was Colin's only remaining possession of any value. Not knowing its true worth, it was, in fact, worth more than all combined possessions he had bartered with along the drive, Colin foolishly hoped to get at most $200. Although ignorant of its monetary value, he instead held onto it for its sentimental value and, finally arriving at his destination, hoped the parting with his father's last gift would only be temporary.

Colin's main objective was not food. He was no stranger to skipping meals and knew his limits. He would be fine until breakfast tomorrow. What Colin needed was to become a new, if not socially distant, member of this community, and that meant residency. After pointlessly locking his car, Colin walked the length of the park back to the main road.

Starting at the beginning of the two-lane street, Colin had the eerie sense of stepping back a few decades in time. Every home he passed had a historic air about it, from

colonial front columns and vintage colors to the wrap-
around porches and spired roofs.

The only thing to assure Colin he was still in the
2010s were smaller houses awkwardly jutting in different
directions from all the additions. This architectural design
seemed to plague the state, bringing smaller homesteads
and businesses to more comfortable square footage.

Nearing the end of a third pleasant residential block,
Colin found himself standing at the beginning of what must
be the town center. With the sun keeping to the south,
Colin made his way from west to east through town,
keeping to the right side of the road. For a town this size,
there was a considerable amount of foot traffic. Thankfully,
the stares he first received had stopped and other than the
occasional "aww" at Dually, people, for the most part,
ignored him.

The first building that made up the main strip
surprised Colin so much he stopped and gave a throaty
chuckle. To his right was the local flower shop, bursting at
the seams with vibrant, odorous plants. No surface, hanging
hook, outdoor metal table, or sidewalk square was spared.
Quickly glancing up at the blooms illuminating the length
of the road like a runway, he then turned his attention back
to the 600 square foot cinder block building that proudly
proclaimed *Living Color* in the half-obscured window.
Next to the shop name and common window sticker décor
was the standard Be Back Soon sign indicating the shop
owner would be out for the next 15 minutes. Noticing
Dually getting a little too rough with a nearby potted plant,

Colin stepped into the road to pass by so as not to break, and consequently pay anything.

Sitting slightly behind and to the left of the flower shop was, what Colin assumed, was the only bank for miles. Looking closer he realized it was instead a credit union. Good, he thought, I might actually be able to have an account. He was not going to set his hopes too high. Cash was always safer for him than credit.

A flashing red light in this intersection was the only electrical means of directing traffic from what he could see. Wondering if the other crossroads bore stop signs and wondering more if he had obeyed them in his recent drive through town, Colin checked for the non-existent cars and continued his hike.

Half of the next block was walled by the classic two-story brick commercial buildings one sees in most small towns. They were very well maintained, consisting of an abundance of arched windows, drip and crown molding that were the classical terra-cotta buff which delicately offset the recently applied bold red paint. It was no surprise to see these buildings made up the more governmental part of town. There was the public library, the welcome center and city government office, the post office, an insurance agency, and a real estate office.

Standing to admire this impressive-for-its-town-size professional center Colin was next subjected to pure architectural chaos. The hodgepodge buildings were almost in competition to draw the most attention. The sweets shop across the way, emitting its sugary aromas, was the first to draw his eyes. The obnoxious canary yellow, single-story building designed to look like a house from the front had superfluous, if not gaudy, gingerbread in garish raspberry pink. One brief look reminded Colin of poor Hansel and Gretel, taking a little of the sweetness out of the air.

Attached to the sweets shop was a dark brown cedar plank storefront with a flat white roof precariously supporting a wagon wheel. It was more than twice the width of the candy store and appeared to be two shops in a shared space. The first window, in dainty white cursive, said the single word Leather, and the second window, past the door, held the single word Fabric in a sloppy bold print. Thinking this to be the only clothing store in town, Colin regretted his limited attire.

Next was possibly the most unusually shaped of the three storefronts. This one sported a faux cone-shaped roof and the entire front looked like a giant turret, leaving Colin with the impression of a relocated medieval tower. Although it boasted a new coat of vulgar violet-purple paint around the overly large bay windows and lower walls, a vacancy sign sat in the window.

Looking at it all, Colin's eyes were assaulted by the vibrant colors of storefronts and flower-lined sidewalks that denied the late spring chill with their full summer blooms. Fully annoyed, Colin was sure no town this size should be allowed to emanate such obnoxious cheer, even if it was May.

Peeling his eyes away from the chaos, Colin became aware of what lay next to the vacant unit. Made up of white cinder blocks like the flower shop, it was the tiniest law enforcement office possible. Not even sure if a sheriff and deputy western jailhouse was still legal in The States, Colin quickly took note of the few cars parked in front in order to avoid them in the future. Too bad. He would have liked to take a closer look at that black '67 Corvette.

The mini police station shouldn't have worried him, but it did. Needing a different view, Colin turned his attention to what stood on his side of the road for the first time. He was surprised to see that it was taken up by only two vendors: a large drug-grocery-hardware store and a corner café. The all-in-one store took up 80 percent of the block and was colored a deep forest green. It sported a large vintage neon sign which proudly flashed "Roy's". If he wasn't close enough to see in the window, the name would have given nothing away as to what lay inside. At least now he knew where to get dinner when, or if, the time came.

The corner café's subtle beauty and quiet demeanor cast a much-needed calm over Colin's visual overload. As if it was taken right out of a French picture book, with the name "Katie's" elegantly painted in the main window in gold, this coffee with cream, off-white trimmed eatery with a decorative wrought iron fenced outdoor eating space made all the other town shops pale in comparison.

Not knowing why his eyes were drawn upward, Colin noticed that above the last quarter of Roy's store and all of Katie's café there was a typical Michigan Addition painted the same coffee with cream color as the café and even had a matching wrought iron veranda. Assuming it was either additional storage space or the café owner's living quarters, it did strike him odd that the convenience store would allow "Katie" to build on top of their store as well.

The café smelled wonderful. Dually pulled Colin closer to the door, but with only a few bucks and much more to see, Colin headed off again in search of his new home.

Passing the next crossroad, this block was home to two rather large churches that mirrored each other, parishes included. It seemed rather odd to Colin to think that a small town the size of Vernon could support two churches that size. But not being a religious man himself, what would he know?

Moving on.

Following the parishes were identical large, paved parking lots. The only difference between the two sides of the road was, on the side he was walking on, there was a well-developed fire garage that sat on the last third of the parking lot. Looking inside one of the open overhead doors, Colin could see two pumpers, one EMS unit, and a type 6 wildland fire engine.

The only reason Colin was so knowledgeable about fire trucks was thanks to a house fire that ruined his sophomore year. After that, he was obsessed with firefighting but eventually decided not to pursue it as a career. Colin was no stranger to pain and felt it wrong to make a living off being the hero to other people's tragedies.

Colin stood at the end of the business section with nothing but houses before him. Every house had the same look, with the exception being one. The multi-family, historic, mini-mansion across the intersection looked to either be a museum, hotel, or both. The nameplate "Brigham" over the entrance gave nothing away as to its identity.

A quick look down the side streets revealed the main road was for the more financially successful people, so turning left he zigzagged his way a few streets north. The homes became less stately-historic and more economic-modern the further from Gunther Road he went. Besides the ever-shrinking homes, there were only two things north of the main strip. The first was a large building that hosted both elementary and middle school, yet with separate entrances. The second, at the very northernmost point of town, isolated and tree-shadowed, was the cemetery. Colin felt no desire to explore there.

With the north side of town thoroughly looked over, Colin circled around back to the main road. Starting once again at the park where his car was sitting, he began exploring the southern half of Vernon after pointlessly making sure no one messed with his vehicle.

Starting behind the bank and flower shop, the blocks south of the red professional buildings consisted of a miniature lumber processing yard that sat alongside the incredibly slow-moving creek. This formed the westernmost border of the town. Sawdust assailed his nostrils, reminding him of a brief period he spent at a lumber mill in Lyons, Oregon. That was a physically demanding, yet good, job. Maybe they were hiring.

The lumber yard shared this side of town with only one other business. Located east of the yard and behind the fire station, Colin assumed it was a mechanic and auto body shop until he saw it up close. Now that it was in front of him, Colin saw this place fixed more than cars. At least, he hoped these contraptions were fixed.

The place was littered with every machine imaginable. Vacuum cleaners, sewing machines, a snow blower, and a hodgepodge of car parts were scattered around the place. None of them, however, looked scrapped or discarded. Instead, they gave off the appearance of being on display as yard decorations, just by a terrible exterior designer. There were even some small, impressive statues built from what Colin concluded were spare parts. A sign made from patchwork metal over the module home-turned-office read Brigham Brothers EST 1963. That's the second time he saw that name.

Though fascinated by the display of machines, Colin kept on walking; determined to find a place to stay before his stomach defeated him. A few more streets hosting small homes boasting flowers not quite as colorful as the city center, and a second, underdeveloped park with a few attached fields just about to give a hint as to what they were growing were all that lay to the south of town. These homes, even smaller than the ones to the north, were still void of any sign of vacancy. Not even a for-sale sign dotted a single yard. Aggravated and now discouraged, Colin could not help but wonder how the downtown realtor could ever stay in business. Surely, this real estate magician was not *that* good.

By the end of their town walk, Colin noticed Dually's labored breathing and decided to head back toward the convenience store for an early dinner and a chance to trade in his father's watch. Maybe one of the workers knew of a place to stay nearby or if anyone was willing to board him in this small town. The quickest way to Roy's meant having to pass the corner café again. Colin knew Dually had to be as hungry as he was and, feeling sorry for his beloved pet, Colin regretted tying Dually to a lamp post outside between the store and the café.

CHAPTER 3

Roy's was the largest business on the main strip and quite a nice set-up. To the right of the entrance was a sort of mini-hardware store. Tools for simple home improvement, lawn work, light mechanical jobs, cars, and even a few small appliances lined the corner walls and covered 4 stalls and racks. There was also a sign to let customers know anything not found there could be ordered. Colin thought that might come in handy and made a mental note.

The back corner behind the hardware section was designated for recreational equipment. Camping, biking, hiking, water sports, gardening, outdoor games, and sports gear were astonishingly compacted and organized in an easy-to-locate manner. Colin knew from a high school job that it was no easy task organizing so much stuff. Whoever designed this side of the store should get a promotion.

Again, a sign stated whatever was not found could be ordered. It didn't mean much to him this time. He wasn't much of an outdoorsy type.

The left half of the building was a grocery store with three checkout lanes, an office, and a bathroom near the front. Not as impressive, but still put together well for the amount of space it was allotted.

Navigating the aisles, Colin was greeted a little too brightly by all three -floor workers and even a few locals doing their daily shopping. Without using a handbasket, he grabbed an off-brand box of cereal, a loaf of bread, a small jar of peanut butter, a bag of apples, and the cheapest bag of dog food on the shelf. Then, doing some quick mental math, he put the cereal and apples back before getting into the check-out line.

The cashier, Brad according to his name tag, was either not one for checkout conversation or literally had nothing to say to Colin beyond the earlier, "Hello!". That was unfortunate. Colin knew how awkward he could be when striking up a conversation, but this was no time to be self-conscious, so he inquired about the owner and whether he could have a meeting. While Brad tried to work that out, Colin slipped outside and ate two makeshift peanut sandwiches. It was rather difficult, given he had no graceful way to spread the peanut butter. While giving Dually a meager yet sustaining pile of food he was asked back inside, ushered to the small square office, and seated in front of an impeccably organized oak desk. Thank goodness he didn't get much peanut butter on himself despite the lack of cutlery.

The office was not by any means large, but the number of documents, charts, files, and personal knickknacks the owner was able to fit inside this space was amazing. With everything labeled, color-coordinated, and from what he could tell, in chronological order, Colin supposed anything could be found in this office with precision in a matter of seconds. Mystery solved as to who organized the right half of Roy's convenience store.

A man of average height and build walked into the room and seated himself behind the desk. Introducing himself as Roy, the man finally looked up with his blue-grey eyes and quickly assessed Colin. Taking in his too-long hair, wrinkled clothes, and scant food purchases, pity could first be registered on the man Roy's face. But before he gave Colin a complex, Roy's look of pity turned into something closer to determination. Colin didn't know it yet, but that awkward conversation with Brad was about to pay off.

"What can I do for you, son?"

Colin didn't like people calling him "son", but not wanting this friendly store owner to find any fault in him, Colin kept that opinion to himself. This was a time to impress, not criticize.

"I'm sorry for interrupting your work sir, but I figured a man who ran one of the biggest businesses in town could help me. I'm looking into moving to town and I need to pawn something to help keep me on my feet and put towards a down payment on an apartment or room for rent." Seeing Roy glance again at his small grocery bag, Colin quickly added, "And I'm looking to get a job as soon as possible to pay the loan back, with interest. Please, I couldn't tell you why, but I worked so hard to get here and I'll do anything if it means I can stay."

From the moment Colin opened his mouth, Roy tensed behind his desk. It was subtle, but there. Not the kind of tense one sees in a dog before it bites, or an animal before it runs, but the kind a person gets when hit with a revelation. Colin wasn't sure which of the three he would have preferred.

"Of all the places in the state, you wanted to come here?" Roy surveyed Colin with new eyes that made the younger man quite uncomfortable. Leaning back in his chair, Roy folded his hands and continued studying Colin. "All right, I'm at least willing to look at what you've got. If it's worth anything I'll pay you a fair price for it and negotiate payments for you to get it back. I'll also put out a good word around town for a job if you find yourself having some trouble."

"But why? You don't even know me. I mean, don't get me wrong, I would really appreciate that, but-" Colin was cut off more by the look Roy was giving him than his response.

"Son, let's just say there's something familiar about you. On top of that, I've been around so long I'm an excellent judge of character."

This was a little hard to believe. Colin knew he wasn't the best judge of age, but the man sitting across the desk from him could not have been any older than 60. To be a self-proclaimed expert judge of character seemed a little arrogant, but again this was a time to impress not criticize, so Colin sat there and silently nodded his head in agreement. "Let's see what you have."

Colin sat forward, took off his watch, and passed it to Roy. The moment it touched his hand, Roy stared at it without moving for some time. Then he lightly fingered the watch face and turned it over, glancing up at Colin several times during his examination. Feeling slightly uncomfortable by how long it was taking, Colin shifted in his seat and broke the older man from his daze. Roughly clearing his throat, he handed the watch back, eyes locked on Colin the whole time. "I can't take that from you."

Of course not, thought Colin, allowing the pain to show. He just couldn't take it anymore. Colin never wished to part with his watch; he just wanted life to be kind to him for once. Colin set the watch down, leaned on the desk, and rubbed his face, letting out a groan.

Dropping his hands, Colin pleaded, "Please Roy, I've got nothing left. If I could, I would show you something else, but I don't have anything left. I've held onto that watch for as long as I can, but I'm desperate now. I'll take anything for it."

Roy interrupted with a quick raise of his hand, "I didn't say I wouldn't help, I said I couldn't take that from you. I'll give you a cash advance without that watch as a pledge, BUT there are two things I require of you first."

Was this man for real? Colin was going to get help from a stranger *and* keep his watch.? It is always risky to agree to terms before hearing them; for all he knew Colin was about to agree to a kidney transplant. But the older man had not given Colin any reason to distrust him so far, so…"Name it, sir."

Locking eyes again, Roy laid out the negotiations. "First, you need to agree to be a man of your word. Saying you'll do something and following through with it are two different things and if a man can't be trusted to keep his word, then he's not welcomed around here."

He made it sound like he owned the town, but Colin wasn't about to tell him that.

"I will, sir. I'll keep my word."

Nodding his head as if conducting a business deal, Roy continued with an even voice, "Good to hear it. Second, you'll need to work for Katie."

"Wait, hold on. Katie? As in the café Katie next door?"

Roy looked surprised by this question. "So, you've been there already?"

"No sir, I just…I'm not so sure they'll hire me. I mean, wouldn't it make more sense if I worked for you? After all, you're the one helping me out." Giving out a light laugh, Colin couldn't help himself, "This is a joke, right?"

Roy just stared at him to show how serious he was.

Colin muttered under his breath, "I guess not."

"Look, I want you to go see if you can work for Katie because the only available place in town happens to be above her café. The entrance is accessed from the parking lot out back, however, *that* door opens into a foyer where you can also access my store and the café. The café opens well before this place, and unless I knew you were already up and working when she's there I would refuse to even think about letting you stay, even if she *could* lock you out of her side. So, if you can get a morning shift there, I'll give you $400 now and the first week free."

Colin nearly choked on his spit. "$400?! I, how…" This was happening all too fast. Shaking his head, he took a deep breath to steady his stampeding thoughts. Not seeing anything wrong with these terms, there was only one thing left to say. "How could I ever repay you?"

Chuckling a little, Roy stood and said, "Like I told you, we'll work out the negotiations pending on how your quest with Katie goes. She just got back from her afternoon break, so head on over and come back when she gives you an answer." Colin stood up, but Roy had one more thing to say before getting up himself, "Hey, um, don't let her off too easy. Non-locals can scare her sometimes." Standing, they shook hands on the matter, but before letting him go, Roy suggested a quick trip to the bathroom to clean up would go a long way.

CHAPTER 4

The normal café patron would first notice the sweet smell of freshly baked confections or the bold aroma of coffee, followed by the elegant design and layout of the place, setting the mood as foreign and romantic. Next, they would hear an acoustic version of a favorite song coming through the small speakers hidden around the room, giving an overall warm, familiar, and alluring ambiance. Hitting those senses was impressive, but what brought the whole package together was Katie. Always dressed in today's fashion with a retro twist, and wearing her trademark carnation red lipstick, the café owner was the most important part of the place and always ready to welcome patrons in as if she were welcoming the most esteemed of guests into her very own home. Of course, things never happened to Colin in the typical way, and he was no normal café patron.

Hearing the door chime, Katie turned from her conversation with a regular and excused herself. Seeing the unknown, tall, and somewhat disheveled man nervously taking in his surroundings, Katie approached to welcome the newcomer like she would anyone else. However, the closer she came to this stranger the more Colin could feel his presence unwelcomed. The emotion in her all-too-amazing eyes could not be hidden, and every step said something different. In her first step, they showed curiosity and confusion. In the next, they looked flustered, as if she recognized him and could see every sin he ever committed. In the third step, the slightest hint of grief flashed before turning into pain, and by the fourth and final step, she had no mastery over the tempest that brewed beneath the surface. She fumed at him, and he hadn't done anything wrong. Well, that she knew of… yet. What was it about these locals and their staring judgments.

Instead of her usual cheerful greeting, Colin received one of the most out-of-character welcomes possible. "Who the hell are you?" she demanded. Colin glanced from her to the customer she was speaking with earlier. The only response he could think of was, "Hi?" The elderly lady put her cup to her lips and turned, giving them some false illusion of privacy. Thank goodness she was the only customer currently in the café.

Realizing her mistake, Katie tried, oh boy did she try, to recover from her social blunder by using a more appropriate greeting. "I'm so sorry about that. How may I help you?" Too bad it came out a little too late and a little too flat.

Somewhat put off by her more than offensive greeting, Colin was still aware his new residence would be determined by him getting a job here. Here. Of all places. Without much of a choice, he quickly decided not to let her first impression determine the outcome for the rest of his stay in Vernon and, not wanting to beat around the bush, he went straight into his mission.

Brushing his feelings off, Colin tried to play the cool card in hopes of calming down his potential new boss.

Taking a quick breath, he dived in. "My name is Colin Warrington. Roy next door sent me over. He said there was an apartment of sorts on top of the store that he's willing to let me stay in for a while, but since it also has access to your café, he said in order for me to stay there I need to help you out around the café."

"You're… Bill's son?" Hearing her say his father's name unnerved him, and it showed. How could she possibly know Bill? He never came to Vernon, at least not in Collin's lifetime. She didn't look anything like him or his sisters, so a secret family was out of the question. Confused, Colin asked, "How do you know my dad?"

Seeing a wall go up, that question went ignored. Instead, Katie went into a mini, yet private (so as not to disturb the older woman who was obviously listening) interrogation. "Why the hell did Roy send you over here? Omigod, I can't *believe* him. How did you even find Vernon!? And why would you want to stay here in the first place?"

Despite her being obviously attractive, her short and slightly spiky, deep red hair should have been a hint of her fiery personality underneath. Her most attractive feature was her big eyes of deep blue bursting from the center and fading into an almost silver gray. However, Colin found her nosy attitude and downright weirdness a bit of a turn-off. If this woman was always so strange and curt then it was no wonder she only had one customer. Even if she did wear well-fitting jeans, a soft, green, lightweight top that hinted at some curves, and had full lips painted that attractive color…okay he knew how she must get *some* returning customers.

Colin furrowed his brow and, slightly offended, said, "No offense, but I don't think that concerns you."

The woman retorted, "Well, no offense, but you thought wrong. I don't need any help, especially not yours, so you can go back to Roy and tell him to forget it." And with that, she turned away to play nice hostess once again.

Damn it! He was so close to having this work for him. Why can't she just give him a chance?

Seeing no other way, he *had* to make her see how desperately he needed this. Willing to do almost anything but literally beg, he grabs her attention with a slightly raised voice that carries throughout the room. "Please! Please don't turn me away. I can't bake, cook, or even make drinkable coffee, but I'll do *anything* handy around here." She stopped walking but still stood with her back to him. Now it was his turn to come to her. "Or…or you can teach me! I'm not too bad of a learner." He lied. He was too stubborn to want to learn anything. "I need a place to stay and I don't have any money. I offered to put this down as a pledge, but Roy wouldn't hear of it. That's why he sent me here. Because if, for some reason, you're not okay with me staying, he's not either."

Katie didn't owe a single Warrington anything, and she knew that. Everybody in town knew that, and oh, what a scandal this would be! So why she turned around for what was supposed to be her last look at this stranger, the modern replica of a man the town forgot long ago, she couldn't tell you. If it was anyone's guess, it was to give this man a piece of her mind.

However, when she did turn around, the watch held out in his open hand caught her attention and stopped her tirade in her throat. No, it wasn't a shock, it was a gut punch that sent her taking a literal step backward as decades of emotion slammed into her chest.

Her eyes again. If reading them before was effortless, this time it was downright glaring. Torment. Before she could even gain control over herself, Colin hastily pocketed the watch and turned to excuse himself. Whatever made him think this town would be any different? What was he trying so hard to prove to himself?

Katie was nearly hyperventilating. This was a Tuesday. Tuesdays were supposed to be the most uneventful day of the week, and this was nothing short of eventful. Her mind blank from thoughts flying too fast to grab, she stopped Colin just inside the door with the word neither of them expected to hear. "Wait!"

Colin didn't miss the slight catch in her breath, and she didn't miss how much effort was needed to whisper, but her words finally came, "Why do you have that?" It took him a second to realize she was talking about the watch in his pocket. A watch that had been his father's long before he was born. A watch that not one, but two people now, seemed to have recognized in the last hour. A watch that might finally be living up to its reputation of bringing good luck?

Colin could already tell. His chances of getting a job with this cat of a woman were gone. If he wasn't so desperate, that thought would have brought some relief, but he was desperate. He was also so tired of hiding his emotions, thoughts, and dreams… she didn't understand, and feeling his fate was already sealed, he decided to no longer hide. Too bad. The only thing that decided to show itself once that wall was down, was his anger.

Colin turned towards her, his full 6'2 frame straight and taut. Boring into her eyes, the only gentle part of him was the hand that held his watch as he briefly chronicled its past.

"I've had this since I was 24. There was never a day my dad wouldn't wear it. I don't know where it came from, but he said it gave him good luck." Looking down with a bitter sigh, Colin continued. "Too bad the luck's been broken on it ever since I can remember." When Colin looked back at Katie, some of the fire went out, but there was still ire. "It's the only thing I have left of him, and I would do anything if it meant I could keep it." With a scoff, he added, "Hell, I even tried to get a job with you. Some luck." And with that, Colin was out the door.

Roy was staring out the front window of the store, trying to not look nosy and failing spectacularly, when he saw Colin walk up and angrily untie Dually from the light post. A glance in his direction and a shake of his head told Roy all he needed to know. That stubborn daughter of his. How long will she stay bitter? He gave a parting wave and turned away, not seeing Katie tentatively approach him from behind. "Don't go," she cried.

He heard her, but making sure he didn't imagine it, he turned around. Dually betrayed him. With an excited wag of his tail and a quick nuzzle, Dually was much more interested in this newcomer than Colin thought he should be. Succeeding in stealing her attention for a few seconds, Katie quickly stroked his ear before looking up at Colin, not quite meeting his eyes. He didn't know what she had left to say to him, but disinclined to be the first to turn away, he waited for her to speak.

A few seconds passed before she was able to meet his eyes. Her voice faltered, "I didn't know he was gone. I'm really, truly sorry to hear that." Colin thought she was done, but before he could accept her condolences she added, "I didn't think he would keep the watch, let alone wear it." This woman was confusing beyond measure.

Clearing her throat to collect herself, she stated in a no-nonsense manner, "I don't need any help," A little nicer, but still in a way that made him feel patronized, she added, "but you do. You can go inside and tell Roy you start tomorrow. 4 am. Not a minute late or you're fired, got it?"

The emotional yo-yoing dumbed him down temporarily. Running a quick hand through his hair, a shadow of a smile turning up the corner of his mouth showed all the gratitude he couldn't verbalize. Then he understood what she had just said. "Wait, 4 am? What's there to do at 4 am?"

Thinking it took him long enough to catch on, she had her own little smirk. "Show up for work and you'll see." She went to turn but caught herself first. "Oh, and knock before coming in the back door. I don't appreciate being scared and you wouldn't be the first person I've injured because of it." After that quick warning, she turned and was inside her own establishment before Colin could ask her anything else.

Knowing better than to believe an item could actually be good luck didn't stop Colin from pulling out his father's watch and wearing it the rest of the day, taking glances at it now and then for more than just to look at the time. For the first time in his life, Colin wondered what story lay behind this little wristwatch. He had always looked at it as an extension of his father, not even thinking it had to come from somewhere. Then his mind went to Katie's response to seeing it and made a mental note not to wear it around her at work. Work. That single idea brought Colin his first authentic smile in months. With that, he entered the convenience store to tell Roy the good news. Hopefully, Roy had an alarm clock he could borrow as well.

CHAPTER 5

The apartment entrance through the convenience store was in the back left corner and made to look like a second supply closet that remained locked to all patrons and most staff. Through the door and to the left was a straight stairwell that went up between the two stores and ended at a landing. It was wide enough to not make one feel claustrophobic or be a health hazard, but just barely. The landing tried to make up for it. It was more of a foyer than a landing and even hosted a couch that miraculously made its way up those stairs.

Stepping through the door brought Colin into a tight hall with two doors opposite each other. The one to his left offered a small bathroom with a half shower, pedestal sink, and toilet that would make any seasoned Tetris player proud. The door to his right was a furnished bedroom with only enough room for a queen bed and an antique six-drawer chest. Until now he had not thought about furniture or appliances.

Stepping back into the hall he made his way up to where the living room branched to the right and a set of French doors leading to a dining room and miniature kitchen were on the left. Seeing that all material needs were taken care of, this was both amazing and disappointing. Then the cold hard hand of reality slapped him. Shaking his head, he voiced what both men in the room knew to be true. "Roy, this is great, but I can't afford this place. I thought it was an empty studio space or a storage room, not a fully furnished apartment."

All the math manipulation in the world couldn't come up with a way to pay for this place with the café job alone. Roy, however, decided not to share that bit of information. "I'll tell you what, son. Don't worry about that for the next few weeks. Once you get some money coming in, we'll make a deal that works for the both of us."

"That sounds like a mob invitation," said Colin tentatively.

Roy's guttural laugh couldn't be contained. It really did sound like a mob boss sinking his claws into some unsuspecting victim. But that wasn't what this was.

"This place is sitting here empty anyway, so we both might as well put it to some use. That's all I meant by it. Take stock of what you're going to need, and I'll see you down in the store."

If this was how Vernon would be, constant highs and lows, no middle to stand comfortably on, Colin couldn't decide if his father was right to stay away, or if the two of them should have come back to this place a long time ago.

Shopping was uncomfortable. Colin never found it easy accepting other people's generosity, and this much generosity was more than he'd had in a while. Not wanting to take advantage, and not wanting to owe the full $400 on top of rent, Colin retrieved a few bathroom supplies, means to properly provide for Dually, and an alarm clock. His

peanut butter sandwiches and waste-not-want-not attitude
would get him through for now.

The biggest snag was Dually. He was housebroken
and used to living in an apartment building, but all the ones
they'd been in over the years had working elevators. The
stairs proved to be too much for the canine, and since he
could not stay in the storage area at Roy's and no one dared
ask Katie if he could move in over there, Collin was on
carrying duty until a more permanent solution could be
found.

Once Dually was comfortably on the couch, Colin
hastily made his way to his untouched car at the park and
drove it over to the small parking lot behind the businesses,
leaving it in a space marked Employees Only. It took only
two trips for him to move his meager possessions upstairs.
He was thankful no help was offered for this task.
Everything he owned was haphazardly thrown into this
pathetic little car, and Colin didn't have the energy to
assure his new landlord the apartment would stay in
pristine shape. Especially since he really couldn't guarantee
that, and the man had a thing about keeping your word.

The only thing Colin had left to do was get some
sleep. If he was going to be fully awake, clean, and dressed
before 4 am, he was going to need all the sleep he could
get. After Dually was let out one more time and two peanut
butter sandwiches were devoured, Colin lay in bed at 8 pm
in vain.

Thinking he would rather use this time than waste it
in a strange room, going to bed ridiculously early to work

for an even stranger woman, he instead took an appreciative shower and decided to clean up his appearance a bit more than the earlier bathroom trip allowed. His work was far from professional, but his previous mop of hair was now tamed back, and his nicer shirts were de-wrinkled from the steam of his shower. Colin looked in the mirror and every bit of his father looked back at him. The only difference was his chin. He had a much more stubborn chin.

Passing out around midnight and snoozing his alarm, twice, Colin was left with 13 minutes to frantically throw on the clothes he wisely laid out the night before, have another begrudged sandwich, and run Dually down and back up the stairs after doing his business, before panting at the closed door that would open to his new life. Trying to slow his breath and calm his pulse a little, Colin glanced at his father's watch to see that he had made it to work with only a minute to spare. Not wanting to risk the wrath of his new boss, he drew a hand through his shorter hair to control it and rapt on the door.

CHAPTER 6

Katie's thoughts woke her earlier than usual this morning and not being one to waste her time, she was at the café a full 45 minutes early. She could tell by the dark windows above that Colin was not even awake yet and wasn't quite sure what to make of that.

At a quarter to 4, all was still silent upstairs. She had been vacillating between a sense of relief and disappointment. Knowing he had not personally wronged her, she still wanted nothing to do with this man. Was she curious about who he was, how his life had been, where he had been growing up and such, and, mostly, what had happened to Bill? Yes. But distance was the safer option for both of them, and a safe distance is where she determined to keep this Colin Warrington.

The shuffling footsteps upstairs snapped Katie out of her rumination and made her realize she, in fact, was more relieved than disappointed by the silence, and was in no way prepared for the man coming down the stairs. No matter how much she wanted to satisfy her curiosity, Colin had to go with a desire to never come back.

This resolve did not sit well with her. Under any other circumstance, she was a very hospitable woman. Being mean wasn't in her character and it wasn't fair to the poor man. She could tell just by looking at him that the world had beaten him up and won several times, but again, distance.

Katie stood at the back door listening to his coming and going on the other side. Looking at the clock, praying for the minute hand to go just a little bit faster so she could justifiably fire him, Katie heard his knock at the door just before the changing of the hour. Hesitating, she bounced on her heels trying to work up the strength to let him inside.

Colin, unsure if he had knocked hard enough or if this was a sign that he was fired, decided to knock again with a little more force.

After quickly unlocking and opening the door, Katie stood holding onto the knob and did nothing but stare. Nothing prepared her for this. With his hair cut and face flushed from running up and down the stairs with his dog, Colin stood there at his full height wearing a solid black fleece and olive-green cargo pants, a nearly identical picture to his father's old Michigan ID. The biggest difference between the two was Colin being a good 10 years older than his father's photo and his chin. What a prominent, stubborn thing it was. If she looked closer, she would have noticed his eyes were greener than Bill's hazel did, but no one else would have known that.

Standing there, victim to another awkward stare-down, Colin was unsure what to do. "Hey" was the lamest thing he could say, but it worked to get her to snap out of wherever her mind had gone.

Distance. Distance! was all her mind could scream. Heeding the warning, she cleared her throat and in a very not-nice tone stated, "You were seconds from being fired."

"Yeah, I was pretty worried about that when you didn't open the door. I slept like crap last night and sort of cut things last minute. I'll be here sooner tomorrow. What happened to your hair?"

The short red locks were gone, and in their place were long, touch-me, chestnut brown tresses that gently fell on her shoulders. They perfectly complimented her mesmerizing blue eyes, which were the first things he noticed this early in the morning.

"Oh, um, that was…a wig." She said so with little conviction, hoping his sleep deprivation would mask the blatant lie. "The woman at the hair salon is my friend, and I let her pick one out for me yesterday."

Thinking he believed her, she still felt him taking in the change of appearance a little too much. To get his attention, she gave Colin his own look-over and said matter-of-factly, "You're going to regret your choice of clothes."

Looking down, Colin couldn't have known what Katie did. Wearing all dark clothing would attract baking particles in the air. Of course, this ignorance gave him the sense that she would nitpick anything he wore. So, whether it was a good choice or not, she would say he was dressed in the worst possible attire. This put Colin on the defensive.

"Well, I thought you would appreciate me wearing the only clean clothes I have instead of none at all. And since you weren't exactly forthcoming on what all this job entailed, how was I supposed to know what to wear?"

True. "Yeah, you have a point there. Next time, short sleeves and pants that can't stash kitchen equipment would be preferred."

"Got it. So, why are we up at this godforsaken hour?" Stepping aside, she let the now-irked Colin in. Like the convenience store, the door to his apartment was meant to look like a locked broom closet, minus the broom and mop sitting instead in the wet station next to it. To his right was the back entrance that led to the parking lot and straight across from him was the employee bathroom.

Leading him to the left, Colin was able to take in Katie's attire without her noticing. Today she was wearing maroon, cotton, high-waist shorts that ended just above her knees and a white with black polka-dot, silk collared shirt. It was a button up and a sapphire blue tank peeked from underneath.

With her hair longer than yesterday's, she swept up the mass of wavy brown into a messy bun. She secured it with a retro '60s hair scarf the same color as her undershirt before she entered the cooking area.

She did not stop in the kitchen to show him around, but he was surprised by what he saw in the brief time it took to walk through. Colin had worked in a kitchen before, but only as a busboy, and was confined to the washing sections. Never being an actual baker, he didn't quite know what to expect. He did know one thing though; for the amount of space she had, her set-up was impressive indeed.

Along the wall adjacent to the employee restroom was the industrial dishwasher as well as a full washing station for dishes that needed to be done by hand. Above the three washing basins were metal racks to drip dry the larger pots, pans, and baking sheets. Following this around, the entire exterior wall was composed of three large windows that could open at the top for good air circulation.

In front of the windows was a low, movable metal workstation. The top was cleared off, except for the plastic wrap machine on the left side to seal baked goods. Underneath were two shelves perfectly filled with mixing bowls and larger measuring cups of all shapes and sizes.

Left of this rolling metal stand, in the northwest corner, was an industrial-sized stand mixer that was larger than any Colin had seen. Along the wall opposite the wash station, from right to left, there was a unit of three ovens stacked on top of each other. Next to them was the bread oven, then a space wide enough to hold two 16-tray bread racks. After that came an oversized fridge-freezer, then the door that led behind the café counter.

Along the last wall was another oversized fridge, several shelves holding baking utensils, and a second rolling station that looked more like a dresser with a butcher block top than anything. In it were all the aprons, towels, hair nets, gloves, and pretty much anything else needed to clean or cover something. All were meticulously labeled.

A large metal island in the middle provided most of the prep and workspace. Quickly taking all this in, as he tried to match Katie's half-time marching pace, Colin was impressed indeed.

Stopping just before the doors, Colin nearly collided with his boss. Thankfully, he was able to recover from this sudden stop before she turned around and explained his working conditions. Her lips were the same attractive color as yesterday. "Your hours will be identical to mine. That means you will be here from 4 to 9 every morning and then from 1 to 6 every afternoon. The only exception is Sunday when I go to church, and Monday when everyone is required to be here from 5 until we're done."

"What? Why do I have to have exact hours as you?" he demanded.

"Because I don't trust you, you live above me, and I'm your boss." She said this a little too smug as she crossed her arms. "Show me you can work under these conditions, and I *might* be able to change your schedule around."

"But that doesn't leave me the option of getting a second job somewhere else. I was hoping to work at the lumber processing plant too."

"They aren't going to let just anyone work for them. If you don't like this, you can go back upstairs, pack your bags, and leave. Now, if you're done complaining, let me tell you a little about what we do here."

Not seeing much of a choice, Colin took a wide stance, folded his arms over his chest, and nodded.

"We make everything from scratch. At least the baked items. All our meat, produce, and dairy are delivered and prepped in the late afternoon. Every few days we have different specials. It just depends on the demand and customer feedback. For example, today I will be making ten dozen different berry, multigrain, and chocolate muffins, five dozen chocolate eclairs, and our cinnamon chip loaves, as well as our everyday quiche, croissants (chocolate and regular), fruit tarts, cinnamon rolls, turnovers, macaroons, and cookies. There are two baking times: morning and afternoon. The specials are all done in the morning and the everyday items are done after lunch. Since everything is made fresh, what is not eaten today fills the shelves until the afternoon bakes are finished and what is left over is put in Roy's store."

Colin's face reflected the shocked awe he felt. Once he was able to compose his thoughts, Colin asked, "How in the world do you get all of that done?! And who eats all of it? There's, what, 1,000 people in this town?"

"788 actually," she stated matter-of-factly. "And even though they are all *very* supportive of my bakery, it's the nearby gas stations that purchase and sell most of the daily specials. It's a good way to get my food out there without necessarily bringing people here. Did you get a good look at the dining area yesterday?"

Still working out how he was supposed to help make so much food every day, Colin mumbled, "No, not really. I was a bit distracted."

Forcing a scoff to cover her amusement, she murmured in believable irritation, "Okay, follow me."

Leading them through the double door next to the oversized fridge, they emerge into the café beside the counter. The long counter took up the entire length of the room. Half of it was a refrigerated display case filled with only labels for now. The second half was extra bar-style seating. Behind it was a full coffee bar and a large chalkboard menu listing the coffees, teas, specials, sandwiches…he didn't really read it all. But from what he did read, the prices were good. While he was looking at the espresso maker, thinking he could really use the pick-me-up, Katie reached down to switch on the empty display case, starting the cool-down process.

"How come you don't leave it on overnight?"

Katie paused halfway up. She didn't look at him fully when giving her answer. "It's an antique I'm not quite ready to part with. I don't want it to die."

Turning away from the display case and coffee bar, Colin saw the café had three elegant cream-colored tables large enough to each sit four people comfortably. Two couples tables sat along the parallel inside walls, sporting the same color and design. A wood bar and six stools looked out the oversized front window, and although it was still too early for the sun to be up, Colin knew outside the door was a wrought iron lined sitting area with two matching iron tables surrounded by three chairs each.

The walls were the same coffee brown color as outside and supported pictures of colorful landscapes that looked to have been taken over different decades. Colin assumed they were all of the French countryside, but there was no evidence to support this theory.

Colin's gaze then swept over the entire place and, after a deep breath he said, "This is a great place," Katie could tell he really meant it.

With a small smile of her own, she replied, "Glad you like it, because you're staying right here." Katie began to walk back towards the kitchen and called over her shoulder, "I have a lot of baking to do and since I don't know or trust you, or care to do either of those in the foreseeable future, you will be out here and away from me the entire time."

After she was a few steps away, Colin followed after her calling back, "But wait, I'm supposed to be working!"

Katie stopped and turned to face Colin. Without skipping a beat she said, "Oh, you will be, just not with me. The display case takes about twenty minutes to cool. Once it's at 42 degrees, get the food out of the far fridge. Everything is properly labeled, so there should be no excuse for getting the placements wrong." Cringing a little on the inside at how belittling she sounded, it was all Katie could do to ask for forgiveness. Being a natural morning person, she could not use that as an excuse. There was just something really irritating about having another Warrington in her café. Especially one that was so much like his older counterpart.

"And for the other two hours?" All right, there were a few differences between the two men. His sarcasm was not lost on Katie, and the next bit came out all too easy, and just as sarcastic.

"I'm glad you mentioned that. You're new here so you have fresh eyes. Look around, and fix anything you see needing fixing or cleaning. You said yourself yesterday you can't even make drinkable coffee, and without a food handler's license, you couldn't help me in the back even if I wanted you to. The only positions left are go-for boy and cleaning." Katie paused to take a breath and then thought of something. "Do you know how to use an industrial washer?" Nodding his head yes, for he had many jobs just like the one he apparently had now, she continued, "Good, you can bus too. Now, I really need to get going on those eclairs." Without another word she disappeared through the double doors, leaving Colin alone.

CHAPTER 7

"Colin!"

It was not his name that sent a chill down his spine, but rather the manner she said, or rather, yelled it. Only bad things happened when people yelled his name. Jumping down from the chair he was using to change a lightbulb, Colin frantically burst through the kitchen door. Looking around and seeing a hundred different ways Katie could injure herself, she was found standing at the center island, completely unharmed yet a bit startled by his violent appearance.

"Um…" she shook her head slightly to clear her thoughts, "it's been more than twenty minutes. You should start filling the display case."

Not realizing he was holding his breath, he let it out in a big huff. "What did you have to yell at me for then? Dammit, I thought something happened! Geez!"

"Well instead, something *didn't* happen. The display case did *not* get filled." She masked her alarm with anger quite well. She didn't think he would be so concerned.

"Yes, I know. I was trying to fix a lightbulb that was out and didn't think a few extra minutes in the big fridge would make your food inedible."

That was not a correct response. This time, not even having to feign irritation, Katie snapped, "I also made a pot of drinkable coffee if you want some, and I wouldn't have *had* to practically scream your name if you had heard me the first three times I called for you!" With that said, she began to take the food out herself.

A closer look around showed she had indeed made a pot of coffee, and two mugs filled nearly to the brim sat on the metal cabinet that looked out the window wall. He had honestly not heard her call for him from the kitchen. Feeling the blame was all on him, he decided to try and make it up as best he could.

"Let me do that." He said, stepping up to take the chilled pastries from Katie. She looked hurt but quickly schooled her emotions. "I'm sorry for snapping at you, it's just…the only time I hear yelling is when something bad has happened, not when someone's calling me for coffee."

"I was calling for you to do your job," she said a little snappy.

"Yes, but you were also being nice. Thank you," he said humbly.

Damn, this man and his way of making her desire less and less to be catty, especially when he said thank you. But the guise had to stay. "Make sure you get the labels right." That was all she said before turning to finish filling up the rest of the muffin tins and dotting them with lightly floured fruit and crumble.

Colin went back and forth, filling the display case in silence. It wasn't until the case was filled and reviewed that he allowed himself the cup of caffeinated goodness. If she baked as well as she made a cup of joe, her attitude had nothing to do with her café success. He would gladly pay her asking price as a daily customer. At least he would consider it if someone else was working the bar.

Striving to do as much cleaning work and repairs upfront as possible, Colin noticed he was going to work himself out of a job by the end of the week. Slowing down to make sure that didn't happen was a temptation. A fleeting one though. His morals and work ethic wouldn't allow him to dwell on it for long.

Continually going to the back for either cleaning supplies or tools in the cleaning closet didn't seem to bother Katie. She was so concentrated on her job, that Colin would have been surprised if she even remembered he was there. How fast this little woman could bake amazed him. The seemingly impossible task of creating so many specials in the morning only now seemed possible. Not wanting to seem like he was stalking or paying any more attention to her than necessary, these thoughts as well as his desire to stay in Vernon were kept to himself.

CHAPTER 8

There were two other morning workers who arrived about ten minutes before opening. A married 38-year-old mother of two named Bree Truman whom Colin respected and felt immediately comfortable around. She is the main "waitress" of sorts. She oversaw the register, handled any special customer orders, and made sure the patrons in the dining area were generally waited on. And there was Justin Dunsworth, a 21-year-old college student who worked the coffee bar and all things drink-related. Justin did not seem the friendliest person in the morning, but neither did Colin, so his standoffish body language wasn't too bothersome. At least it was good to see a Millennial still willing to work to make his dreams happen.

By the time they arrived, Colin had filled the display case, set out the plastic-wrapped goodies on different countertop shelves, bowls, and plates, replaced two lights, tightened the legs on seven chairs, and made sure there was not a cobweb or dust ball to be found. Not a bad morning's work on only three cups of coffee.

Despite herself, Katie was impressed by his ability to spot the little things. She didn't know that her ability to create and assemble no less than a hundred different baked goods in only a few hours was just as impressive to him. Too bad. If she didn't desperately desire him to leave, they could have made a good team.

The first customers of the day must have been regulars since at six o'clock, they walked in together and sat at the back bar, right where their pastries and coffees waited for them. These two men, around their early thirties, seemed to be in deep conversation and a bit too interested in the newest employee.

Standing there, unsure if he should be helping out Bree or coming up with something else to fix, Colin entered the kitchen and waited for a good stopping point to ask Katie what she now expected of him. But a baker of her skills doesn't have a good stopping point, and after an awkward minute passed, there was nothing to do but dive in.

"Hey, Katie? Now that people are arriving, do you want me to wait on customers like Bree?"

Her head popped up from the cinnamon rolls she was icing. Her deer-in-the-headlights look reflected her blank shock. Knowing exactly who was sitting at the counter, Katie shouted, "No, stay away from the customers!" She was at the door in less than three steps. Looking out the circular window she asked, "Did they already see you?"

None of this sat well with Colin. Did she find him unqualified? Did she suspect he would drive away customers? Did she not want him as a source of gossip in this bizarre little town? Two of those were, in fact, true, but she didn't give him any time to ask.

"I have a ton of dishes that need to be washed before this afternoon's baking. You get to the dishes and anything Bree brings in while I make up the order forms for next week.

"Arnie is one of my gas station delivery guys, and he'll be here in about 10 minutes. Help him load the truck when he gets here. Once you're done with all that, let me know and we can take off a little early."

That sounded better to Colin than waiting on customers he didn't know and hearing gossip about him behind his back. He also wouldn't mind getting off before nine and getting some actual sleep. That, at least, was his thought before looking at the unbelievable amount of washing he was required to do. "Oh, and Colin?" He turned his eyes from the dishes to the woman who obviously took pleasure in his dismay, "With the food deliveries, anything you drop or mutilate will be taken from your check."

With a steady flow of morning customers, Colin did not finish the dishes until just after 8:30, but an extra 30 minutes was an extra 30 minutes he would gladly spend sleeping. The delivery goods were placed in the truck unscathed, thankfully. Arnie was a man who emanated simple, country living. Not in a derogatory way, but this somehow made Colin realize just how far away from a populous municipality he was.

Katie did all the ordering over at Roy's since they both benefited from sharing a delivery truck sent from the nearest large city. Only three times did she peek in to check on Colin's progress. Her expectations were beyond unreasonable and criticizing his "slow service" with much too much attitude made Colin wish she would keep her messy hair and frizzled brain on the other side of the door.

Colin knew if he saw his new boss again before he saw his pillow, he would say or do something deserving of unemployment. He took off upstairs to get some much-needed sleep. However, Dually was there anxiously waiting to be let out, and Colin put his own needs aside to tend to his best friend.

Out back, Dually was taking much too long to find the right spot to get the job done, and the bang of the back door jolted Colin out of a zoning-out he didn't even know he was partaking in.

"What the hell! Thought you could just leave your post without letting me know. I'll sack you for that!" Her voice was fiery and eyes ablaze. Colin didn't know what he did, but she was pissed.

"Whoa, hold on! You said if I got all those dishes done, we could take off early. I got them done, I'm off early. And since you seemed to be knee-deep in orders, I thought you would like to *not* be disturbed." Colin threw up his hands in an attempt to mediate, but it was all in vain.

"And again, you thought wrong, didn't you?" Realizing anyone in the nearby vicinity could hear her, she instead lowered her voice to a venomous low. "But why wouldn't a Warrington just take off without saying anything." Storming back inside, Katie locked the door in hopes of making him go through the grocery store to get back upstairs. But, she considered, he was only out there, instead of upstairs sleeping because of the dog, so she silently unlocked the door. That was how Colin's first morning ended.

CHAPTER 9

What was that supposed to mean? How did this town know his dad? Or was it another Warrington? That didn't make sense…he was asked if he was Bill's son. And the likelihood of another Bill Warrington in such a small town was near impossible. Colin wondered, what did Bill do wrong? These questions haunted Colin all the way up the stairs and into his bedroom. This made his extra 30 minutes of rest disappear along with another hour before he gave up on his fruitless pursuit for rest and made himself yet another peanut butter sandwich.

Nowhere near ready for his afternoon shift, his alarm screamed him into consciousness. He did not know when or how he managed to fall asleep and did not have much time to think about it before once again descending into his new form of hell in the shape of a kitchen. That reality TV title now made so much sense to him.

Katie had not thought about where to put Colin during the afternoons. Still wanting to keep him from the customers yet wanting him in the kitchen with her even less, she conceded to letting Colin bus tables, keep the floors and outdoor space clean, and play go-for boy to Bree and Justin. The nosier café patrons were morning people anyway.

If this was meant to keep him busy, it grossly missed its mark. That made him an even easier target for a seasoned yet spry woman, with short white hair and a determined look that strained her already pinched facial features, who walked right up to him and, in the most business-like way, introduced herself as the town mayor: Mrs. Minton.

"Well, a Warrington if I ever did see one. I understand why she wanted to keep you out of sight from the regular morning crowd. They can be such a nosy pair, but I was here yesterday when you came in seeking employment and she couldn't keep you from me if she tried. Not being one to judge, I am rather surprised you stayed. Now tell me, are you just passing through, or have you thought about making one of our neighboring towns home?"

This would have been a strange introduction to Colin if his last 24 hours hadn't happened. Also, she was the mayor. Wasn't it her goal to have the town's best interest in mind, which included (he would think) population growth and more local jobs? But then he remembered there were no residential vacancies and chalked it up to her willing him to still work in town even if it meant he could not physically live in it.

Ignoring the coffee Justin handed her without needing to order, Colin sensed this woman would not abandon this conversation even if it meant a lukewarm drink. And no true coffee drinker accepted a lukewarm drink. Not sure why this made him feel so uneasy, Colin quickly said the only thing he could think of. Too bad it sounded as lame out loud as it did in his head. "I'm not really sure."

Mrs. Minton pinched her already tight mouth in such a way she seemed to have lost all resemblance of lips. It was clear, this was not at all what Mrs. Minton wanted to hear. "What? Well that just won't do, will it? I can't work with 'not really sure'; it leaves too much to the unknown."

Seeming to forget Colin was the main topic at hand, Mrs. Minton began a rhetorical spew. "Did no one think to send you to me before just giving you an apartment? And with the Brighams of all people! Don't get me wrong, I'm a very reasonable person to work with, but do you know how disastrous this could be? But, well, how could you, this being your first time to Vernon and all?"

That was startling. He knew there really wasn't much evidence to go off, but Roy Brigham appeared to be more honorable than this woman was implying. Feeling a sense of loyalty towards him, Colin would have given this woman a piece of his mind. However, he was unable to do this because 1) she was the mayor, and he did not want any problems with a government official, and 2) he was still working and relied on this job.

Employment. Being employed by Katie was, indeed, the injunction placed upon him, mandatory for residence. Why, then, should this burden not also be his scapegoat? "Well ma'am, Katie is really the one who determines if I stay or not. Maybe you should bring this up with her."

That did the trick, for Mrs. Minton's head began to swivel, immediately looking for the proprietor.

His victory was short-lived. "Boy, you don't know how right you are. Get her for me."

He didn't really have to be asked if he could label that a request. Colin sauntered to the kitchen and, after a few seconds pause, locked eyes with a confused Katie. All he had to say was, "Mrs. Minton" for Katie to narrow her eyes at him in the most condemning way. Clapping the flour off her hands, she passed him with a look just as determined and pinched as the woman he just left.

After her freak-out this morning, leaving the kitchen was not an option. Not that insurrection hadn't passed through his thoughts at least once since then. But caving to such adolescent behavior was beneath him. That, and even with all the caffeine in the world, Colin didn't have enough energy to think of rioting, let alone follow through with it. Therefore, the afternoon dishes were tended to, and not quickly lest he be found idle.

CHAPTER 10

It was some time before Katie returned. She went straight to baking again without even a sideways glance towards Colin. Some would think her behavior rude. He just felt awkward. There was no point in washing any more dishes until the end of his shift, so Colin went back to the front to help Bree and Justin with the trickle of customers.

That's when the dance began. Katie would come out to mingle or restock the non-perishable items in the front display case, Colin would head to the kitchen to wash some items. Katie would pull the refrigerated foods and store them in the back fridge, Colin would go to the front and make himself busy.

This suited them both fine, for the most part. Every time he returned to the café, he found something to add to his list of repairs and improvements, hoping to prolong this job if possible. But every time he headed back to the kitchen, left with only his mind and a meager number of dishes, his thoughts would wander to his new employer.

Anyone who looked at Katie would describe her as a "looker". But to Colin, her feminine figure and, let's be honest, overall stunning appearance, could not compensate for her waspish character. She was beautiful to watch but seemed more dangerous the closer she came to him. And he better not metaphorically swat her away, lest he wish for a painful sting.

It was only when all the dishes were caught up and his extensive repair/cleaning list was finished that he could stop and observe Katie with her customers. No, not just her customers, everyone else but him.

She smiled in a way that wrinkled her eyes in the corner. When someone talked, she locked eyes with them in full attention and didn't criticize or scoff at what they had to say. Her voice was more singsong than snap. And she acted as though she had all the time in the world. No deadlines, no demands, no go-go-go attitude. Even Mrs. Minton, who somehow had the time to come back for yet another unordered cup of joe, was warmly welcomed by Katie.

Epiphanies, like the reality punches they are, can hurt. She *only* hated him, and he had no idea why. He had done this woman no wrong and yet, over some phantom deed or another, she constantly berated him.

The only logical conclusion was his father must have done something terrible for the whole town to not just remember him by name, but fully hate him over it. And whatever it was must have been directed to this particular individual for her to treat the "criminal" son in such a manner. Maybe Vernon wasn't such a good idea after all.

That teeter-tottering ride was becoming sickening. Up: he goes back to his wonderful apartment to find his meager needs provided. Down: Showing up for work five minutes early earns him another criticism. Up: Roy continuously checked up on him, making sure he was clothed, and fed, and seemed to genuinely care about him.

Down: His work around the café was either insufficient or too much. If he wasn't accused of being idle, he was accused of trying to change her entire store. Up: The bakery hours worked well for him once he was used to waking up early. And Bree was an awesome co-worker. She even introduced him to her family and shared a meal with him more than once. Down: Another day working for Katie.

Then there was always Katie in general. She was even cordial to people Colin knew were strangers. But Colin? Absolutely nothing, nothing he did was good enough for her. Even when his actions exemplified perfection, there was a snarky comment. And he was no fool. He knew most of them were faked.

In just over a week Colin was pretty fed up with his Jekyll and Hyde boss. Colin could hear some of the customers whisper about "Bill" or "Warrington's son", yet no one flat-out talked to him or asked who he was.

Well, that was mostly true. There was always Mrs. Minton, who was not subtle in asking if he was coming or going, and more often than not emphasized the going. She even prodded about what misfortunes brought him to her small town. Not wishing to lie, but also knowing women like her were usually the town gossip, he simply stated he had heard of the place over the years and wanted to see it for himself.

Mrs. Minton usually ended their interrogations by hinting his father and the Brigham family had known each other. He meant to bring it up with Roy over the few times they've met, but he never hinted about knowing his father and it wasn't exactly a conversation he was ready to have. Especially if his father *had* wronged the town in some way.

It turned out Katie's first morning customers, Charlie and Jack were The Brigham Brothers, her brothers. He found that out after his third morning. They were easily more pleasant than their younger sister, however, he wasn't sure how much socializing they would be doing. If Katie treated Colin in such a way in person, he could only imagine how she spoke of him behind his back. Or worse, how she spoke of his father.

It was that very thought that brought all the teeter-tottering to an end one day, just over a week after Colin arrived in town.

Their afternoon shift had just ended, and the two of them found themselves alone in the kitchen together. A little more irritated this evening than usual from playing her double life, Katie was beginning to tire from the glances Colin kept stealing at her whenever he thought she did not notice. Trying all she could to ignore him, she couldn't, and before saying goodbye for the day she turned to him expectantly and the staring competition began.

He breaks the silence first. "So…"

"What," Katie asked confused.

"Are we gonna do this all day?"

Katie gave a small wave of her hand in dismissal and said, "Of course not, we have to go home at some point."

Colin didn't appreciate the joke, if it was one. "You know what I mean. This. You and me. I've seen how you are with everyone else around here, so this really sucks. If you don't want me here, fine, I'll leave. I'll go *anywhere but Vernon*. But you at least owe me the answer to one question"

Her staring continued, silently waiting for him to get on with it. "My father was a good man. He worked hard all his life trying to take care of me and my sisters and was never given anything to show for it. Do you know what he called this town? The source of all his bad luck, and he vowed until the day he died never to come back."

Colin didn't know how much hurt and anger he carried inside until he began to speak. Being both pained and relieved, his emotions started getting the better of him. "So, since I can't ask HIM about what happened anymore, I'll ask the only person who seems to have a problem with him or me. What the f-" Colin cleared his throat, and started again, "What the hell did my father do to make you hate him so damn much that I must pay for his sins?! Huh? Because that question has been plaguing me every night since I got here."

Not understanding why she would look down, mute, Colin mistook it for stubbornness, setting him off the rails. "Tell me dammit! Because I love my father, but this place…you...are making me question everything. Who he was, what he had done, and I can't stand it! And I don't want to hate my father without a damn good reason."

Still looking down, Katie can't help but ask, "Did he really wear the watch every day and call it his good luck?"

Huffing, Colin can't believe his ears. Why, out of all the responses in the world, would she ask that question? He was the one needing answers tonight, not her. "Yeah, but he never saw it. He never had a single lucky day. At least not in my lifetime. And you didn't answer the question."

Obviously struggling for words, she lamely said, "He never came back. I hate him because he left and never came back."

That didn't make any sense, and he said so. "That doesn't make sense. I've been with him my whole life, and he has never been here. Not in my lifetime at least. So you don't even know him! What, are you adopted? Are you his secret love child or something?!"

"Oh, no, nothing like that." Katie was a bit shocked at such an assumption.

"Okay then, if not, how the hell do you know my father?" Colin could feel his blood pressure rising. This woman could be so aggravating!

"I can't tell you."

"Why not," Colin demanded.

"Because you won't believe me, and more people are involved than just me," Katie stated matter-of-factly, and turned to put her things away.

Colin lost his temper and growled, "You're killing me! Just tell me who you are and why you hate him so much!"

Katie turned back to him and spat back, "I don't! I love him!" That was the last thing she wanted to come out, but it did. Chalk it up to riding this emotional roller coaster, needing to come clean, or whatever you want. It still didn't change the fact that she never meant to confess her feelings. Oh crap, what was she supposed to do now?

Bewildered, Colin sputtered, "I'm sorry… what?"

Too late. Time to come clean. "Well, I mean, I did."

"You loved him? As in, you had a relationship with him?" Colin put his hands on his head in disbelief and began pacing the room while Katie tried to get his attention. Talking over her, Colin said, "Wait, we're screwing my dad?! Oh my god, what the hell!"

Katie finally yelled over his rantings. "Yes, NO! I…" she sighed, realizing how screwed up this all sounds. Of course, he would freak out, why wouldn't he? "Those questions came out really close to each other. Let me explain… It was a very *very* long time ago."

"You're, like, not even thirty! My dad's a cheating pedophile! What the f- argh!" Colin cried out in frustration.

Understanding that her apparent age would make everything harder for him to wrap his mind around, his anger could be excused. But still, that pushed assumptions too far. Feeling a little upset over this last statement, she decided to take a more direct approach to this whole thing. "Okay, okay, stop it. Now, you have it all wrong.

I...I've..."Katie was having a hard time forming her thoughts and Colin was too impatient to wait.

"Well, what is it!?"

Katie swallowed the lump in her throat and said, "I haven't seen Bill in forty-five years."

CHAPTER 11

"Oh yeah, because that makes *perfect* sense." Colin couldn't keep the sarcasm out of his voice even if wanted to. Katie stood there, silent, staring at him with eyes that reflected all the discomfort Colin felt. "Oh, I see it now. You're a crazy lady and my father had good reason to stay away. Goodbye." Colin tried to swiftly sidestep Katie, but she was able to block his path to the stairs. "See, there, right there, is why I didn't want you here! I tried to tell you, and even said you wouldn't believe me! But you just had to push and now…well, now you can't leave." She took a deep breath after this outburst and continued, a little less frantic, "At least, not yet."

"Crazy to creepy in under a minute. Great job." Colin said.

"You're more than welcome to go. I've been trying to get you out of here since I saw you, but you're so damn stubborn."

Without thinking, another of his father's sayings slips out. "Swearing is unattractive on a woman."

"Yeah, I know, okay! I'm the one who told him that."

This took everything to a whole new level of freaky. His dad said that phrase all his life, instilling in him the ability to control his tongue. Okay, at least mostly controlling it, keeping the worst swear words at bay. It also kept him from some unsavory women. At least, he thought, it did until now. "You know you're a freaking lunatic, right? This doesn't add up… none of this adds up."

The tell-tale signs of mental dismantling were not exactly new to her, and Katie understood that if she didn't handle this right, some real damage could be done. She couldn't do that to him. Well, she could. But she couldn't do that to Bill. And if she was being honest with herself, she owed Colin for all the crap he'd gone through on her behalf.

Peeling off her catty façade, she addressed Colin in her normal tone. The stark difference grabbed Colin's attention more than anything else could. "I know none of this makes sense. If you promise to not go anywhere until I make two phone calls, I will tell you everything. All right? Can I do that?"

"Who are you going to call?"

"…The other people involved."

His curiosity must have gotten the better of him. Knowing he should turn around and hightail it out of there, he still couldn't help the word "Okay" from slipping out of his mouth. That was something else about Colin. Sometimes, he was too curious for his own good.

Kathie pulled out her cell phone and began to dial, glancing up at him often to make sure he kept his word about staying still. The person on the other end answered, and without ceremony all Katie said was, "I need to tell him…….yeah…..okay, tell the guys," and hung up.

Not feeling at all comforted from his standpoint, Colin blurted out, "Oh *that's* reassuring."

Katie's features softened slightly. She could understand his reaction, so she calmly replied, "It's so I don't have to make more than two calls," She began to dial the second number. It didn't ring more than once before she started talking. "Hey, it's me. I need to tell him. ....Well I'm sorry, it's not exactly like I *wanted* to. He was insistent and let's be honest, he would have found out soon anyway…"

Getting a little short with whoever was on the other end, Katie sighed and cut off the other voice. "Yeah, well this isn't exactly a cakewalk for me either, okay? Can you have everything ready by tomorrow?" Seeing his unfavorable reaction to this comment, Katie holds up a hand to reassure a freaked-out Colin and calm him by mouthing the word 'papers'. Her reassurance was a little too late though, with the worst of possibilities having already flashed through his mind. "Okay, after we get off in the morning."

"Like hell, I'm working tomorrow!" Colin didn't mean to blurt that out. The hypothetical outcomes of tonight were bad enough without his big mouth making things worse. After being given a pointed look, he began to pace the small but snug kitchen.

"Okay, thank you," was all Katie said before hanging up. Bracing herself to tell her story yet again, Katie took a deep breath and began.

"My name is Kathleen Brigham. I am 26 years old, and I have been dead since 1967".

After a short, yet nonetheless awkward pause, Colin blurts out, "So that's it? You're telling me you're dead?"

"Well…yes, but…. I must say, that isn't the usual response I get." Another pause sat between them, nearly unbearable for them both. "There is more."

Colin threw his hands up in exasperation and, with a slight, manic laughed, said, "Oh, of course there's more, goodie. Isn't there always more to a fairytale? What, can you fly now? Turn invisible too?" Sarcasm dripped from every syllable, telling Katie he didn't believe one word she was saying.

As if talking with a small child, Katie calmly said, "Colin, I'm not trying to deceive you or make light of anything. I was born in 1941. My parents, Roy, and Helen, as well as my brothers Charlie and Jack…and my sister, Nora. We all died in 1967 together in a house fire."

Raising his eyebrows with an awry smile, Colin answered Katie as one would speak to a three-year-old telling you their mother was pregnant. "Aww, you have a sister?"

Exasperated, Katie couldn't take Colin's blatant reaction to such a big anymore. She shook her hands at him and nearly stomped her foot, trying to get him to see the magnitude of her situation.

"Colin, please! Why won't you take this seriously? I mean, really. I've had all sorts of reactions over the decades, I've even been shot at, but this?!"

"You've been shot!?" Colin dropped the patronizing act.

The noise level gradually rose with every back and forth, like the sound of waves crashing as one walks steadily towards the shoreline. Good thing Colin waited for the end of the day to bring this up. He could only imagine Katie's reaction if customers overheard. However, this meant the conversation ceased to be formal and began to transform into a shouting match, with both determined to outspeak the other.

"Stop getting off point. I am trying my hardest to tell you how I know Bill, and—"

"Don't call him that," Colin spoke over her.

"It's *my* name for him, so I'll call him that if I freaking feel like it!"

"Stop!"

It is Colin who came out of the shouting match victorious. Throwing up both hands in a gesture of surrender, Katie ceases to speak at all. With both now panting, they allow the conversation to proceed at a more civilized volume.

"Just stop it, all right? You do *not* know my father. You are just a bitter woman who is trying to hurt me now more than you already have. You and your family are *not* dead, and I am *not* an idiot. I will also be gone first thing tomorrow, so thank you, Miss Brigham, for giving me a reason now to say, 'Anywhere but Vernon', because I will never, *ever* be coming back."

"Fine. You want proof I'm not lying?" Katie picks up a paring knife from a nearby drawer.

Backing away in shock, with his hand outstretched Colin condemns himself for allowing things to get this far. "Whoa, Katie! Put the knife down and get away from me. I don't want to hurt you."

Bracing herself, Katie barely cuts the outer part of the pad on her left hand. It was not enough to cause any serious damage, but a cut that would take some time to heal, nonetheless. Katie immediately rinsed the knife and put it in the industrial dishwasher for sanitation. Turning back towards Colin to show him the cut, she briskly says, "I'll see you tomorrow" and turns to leave the café through the front.

Colin yelled "No you won't!" after her but is not sure if she heard him through the double doors. He hastens to the back-stair door and fumbles the key a few times before unlocking it. Taking two stairs at a time, Colin quickly gained entry to his apartment and hastily collected all his belongings. After making multiple trips to haphazardly throw them into his car, it was only at the end of this exhausting emotional expenditure that he realized he still had as little money as he arrived with and not enough gas to get to anywhere he would consider a reasonably safe distance to crash for the night.

On top of it all, Katie said he wasn't allowed to leave yet, and after the way she behaved earlier he thought it safest not to see what else she could do with that paring knife.

Going upstairs to, at the very least, sleep in a bed before he found himself out on the road again, Colin looked around the apartment and couldn't help but feel strangely attached after such a short time. Roy was very good to him.

His mind went back to his first night here. Colin found a large storage container outside his door with a note written in a feminine script that said, "Other stuff you might need". After unloading it he had a half-full refrigerator, washed clothes in the closet, toiletries he forgot to get the other night or was almost out of re-stocked in the bathroom, and an invitation for him to join Roy and his wife, Helen, for dinner two nights later.

Helen was to thank for the box. Roy introduced her while he was purchasing his original supplies, and she must have eyeballed his shopping cart. Medium-built with thick, chocolate brown hair, she emanated the same warmness as Roy and if Colin's disheveled appearance bothered her in any way, she didn't show it. Welcoming was the word he would use to describe her.

He and Dually went to the dinner, surprised to see the large multifamily complex across the street from the fire station housed the entire Brigham family, giving each of them their own unit. Not knowing there were still families with such close relationships, Colin was both impressed and a little weirded out.

Roy and Helen were in the first downstairs unit. The home was cozy and comfortable, the food was great, and their sons Jack and Charlie joined in on the festivities. The only one missing from Taco Night was, to his great relief, Katie.

Jack and Charlie delivered a one-of-a-kind food bowl for Dually the next morning. It was designed from spare parts littering their shop. The craftsmanship was outstanding. It could have been considered a masterpiece if sold in a shop somewhere. Colin was now debating bringing this touching gift, knowing it would only serve as a reminder of a place he was apparently never meant to know about.

There was also Bree. Colin had just met up with her husband Henry and their boys at the semi-dilapidated park the other day. It took a few trips, but the park wasn't nearly as bad as he originally thought. That didn't mean it couldn't stand to have a makeover.

Henry was a good man who was loved and respected by his family, and the two boys were the sort of teenagers you enjoyed being around. The mayor, Mrs. Minton, was still a bit nosy for Colin's liking. Nevertheless, she was at the café every day and tried her best to say hi to him; always sneaking in a way to ask a few more questions. Even Justin had just started to warm up to him, revealing his desire to own his own graphic design business once he finished college and saved enough money with the barista job.

Speaking of jobs, Colin even had himself a job interview at the lumber yard in two days. Of course, he still had to help around the café in the mornings, as per his rental agreement with Roy, but he really wanted the lumber yard job and was willing to do anything to make it work.

He was confused, weary, and literally concerned for his well-being only an hour ago. Now, he was just mad. Why must the only psycho woman in town have to be his boss? Why must she make his work life miserable, make up lies about his father, then flip around and start acting all nice just to make up more lies about herself and others? Then she had to end it all by scaring the crap out of him with phone calls and a paring knife!? If that wasn't enough to thoroughly piss him off, she never even answered his question. "What the hell!"

Colin did some mental math. Did she really expect him to believe she was 71 years old? That is so stupid! But then recalled her first reaction to seeing him. His father's saying, "Anywhere but Vernon." Her reaction to the watch. Everyone's reaction to the watch.

The watch.

Taking the wristwatch out of his left pant pocket, Colin thumbed its face. Never questioning the letters before, he looked at the bottom rim where, right under the six, the professionally engraved initials KB glared back at him almost as hauntingly as their owner's eyes.

A cold sweat broke out on Colin's brow. Flying down the stairs and straight to Roy's office, he was disappointed to find it closed abnormally early. Going out the back, he headed for the brothers' shop. It, too, sat eerily vacant. His nerves were starting to get the better of him. Turning towards the Brigham house to confront them all, Colin thought better of it and instead went to the only other person he was sure had some answers, Mrs. Minton.

The lights were still on in her office, and like a bug, he made a line straight for them. Mrs. Minton is afraid of very little, including bugs, but a sharp rap on her door sent the older woman out of her chair a few millimeters before she was able to recompose herself. Scolding herself to know better by now, the first thing out of her mouth, once the door opened, was, "I told her you wouldn't believe a thing."

"Are you kidding me, you too!? How do you, of all people, expect me to believe such a cock-and-bull story?"

"Well, I must say, that's the quickest anyone came to me after getting a call. Exactly what "cock-and-bull" story did she tell you?"

"That she's dead."

Mrs. Minton cocked an eyebrow and asked, "And you don't believe her?"

As if he were stating the obvious, Colin blurted, "Hell no! Why should I!?"

Mrs. Minton didn't reward his outburst with an answer. Instead, she sat back down in her chair and studied him for a little bit. The people in this town are very good at that. "Colin, you and I don't owe each other anything, but as a town…acquaintance, may I ask one thing of you before you leave?"

"How did you know I was going to leave?" asked Colin.

"I'm very good at my job."

"I don't think anyone is in a position to ask me for a favor right now."

Mrs. Minton thought about that for a second before saying, "That's fair, but if you could, don't leave until tomorrow."

"Tomorrow? I want to get the hell out of here now."

"And where would you go, exactly? I'm very aware of your current financial predicament, and you haven't paid your debt yet."

Colin's mind began calling her a most inappropriate name before being interrupted with even more unsettling news.

"I need you to stay until at least noon. I have some legal documents for you, but they are quite old and I need to update a few clauses. It's been a while since we've needed someone to sign them." Her uptight, pinched features took on a softer, haggard look.

"Wait, you're the person she called?" That explained the long hours she was putting in. "I should have known. How can you have any part of this? I mean, isn't it your sworn duty as a government official, or whatever, to keep your town protected and in order?"

The haggardness fled, and a new emotion sparked in her eyes. She was insulted to the point of fury. Colin immediately regretted his thoughtless statement and waited for Mrs. Minton to collect herself, hoping what she decided to say would not sting too much.

"To answer your two questions, Mr. Warrington, yes, I am the person she called because it IS my sworn duty to make sure my town is taken care of, and that starts with making sure YOU don't leave without signing these papers that I will now be spending most of the night drawing up. Now, since these people took some pity on you for God only knows why, giving you a home, food, job, and community, I would say the least you owe *them*, before putting them all in very real danger, is allowing them a chance to explain their situation.

Rising from the chair to her full height, Mrs. Minton unceremoniously marched Colin to the door, and, staring him down, she ended their conversation with, "Now get out. And the next time you come banging on my door, demanding information just to insult me, buy me dinner first!"

And with that, Colin found himself once again outside. With nowhere else to go but "home," Colin remarkably failed at making the evening resemble any form of normality. I Dually tried though. After lugging him down and back up the stairs, Colin surrendered to an invigorating, lukewarm shower in some feeble hope to wash away the stress and memories of the evening. Only when the warm water was gone did Colin, all too willingly, collapse on the bed and drift into a deep, dreamless sleep.

CHAPTER 12

A series of three knocks on the door woke Colin the next morning. The shower must have worked somewhat. Forgetting what had transpired the previous evening and worried this meant he was late for work, Colin rolled over to locate his watch and check the time. It was six in the morning; he was late for work and now out of a job. But that wasn't what bothered Colin. Once Colin felt the weight of the watch in his hand, he couldn't remember why it made him feel so apprehensive, so uneasy.

The second, more urgent, series of knocks commanded Colin out of bed, yet the door opened before he got there. At six in the morning, he found the entirety of the Brigham family standing on the apartment landing, coffee in tow, waiting for an invitation to come in; Katie tentatively shifting from foot to foot in the back of the group. At the sight of her, confusion fled with his drowsiness, and last night's events raced in to take its place.

Instead of accusations, threats, or questions hurled one after another, he simply held up the watch and, in a voice that resembled acceptance more than denial, said, "You're KB."

"Yes." Her steady gaze and everyone else's silence told him nothing more.

It could have been argued Colin wasn't in his right mind. That he was in mental distress, working under lack of sleep, or felt physically threatened by all their presence. And if anything happened warranting a lawyer, that's exactly what he would tell them.

However, going against every warning his mind was screaming at him, Colin retreated into the apartment, silently granting them entry, and accepted what he hoped was a cup of liquid sanity from the oldest Brigham brother. Silently waiting for everyone to settle into the small apartment space, Colin took the last seat on the couch that was, thankfully, the furthest seat from Katie.

Looking at each Brigham in turn, except Katie, Colin again could not believe how attached he had become to them over such a short period of time. Was he so starved for affection that it didn't matter if the youngest in their clan confessed to being dead if it only meant he could stay with these people, or was there something more to it? Then Colin remembered it was not only her she claimed was deceased. Colin addressed no one specifically, "Tell me everything."

With coffee in hand, the hot vapors permeate the air like their vexed emotions. His request was not a simple one to fill. On one hand, they have all told their stories before and were somewhat familiar and excited to share this aspect of their lives. But Colin so far had responded unlike anyone before, and they were unsure how to proceed.

Roy was the first to clear his throat and address the situation. "Katie said she spoke-" an irritated look from Colin helped correct that description "Uh, Katie said some words were exchanged last night regarding our…situation."

At this they waited, breath held, to see how Colin would respond, for this moment would indicate their future standing with Colin and how to proceed with their new friend. They were also abruptly aware the room was filled with six people, all armed with extremely hot liquid.

Looking them all in the eyes again, including Katie this time, Colin stuck to the facts. "Katie told me she's dead. That you're all dead." The tone in which he said it was so flat, they began to look to each other for answers, hoping another was able to decipher his emotions.

Colin might have been looking solely at Roy, but it was understood he was addressing the entire room as he let out a deep sigh. "I'm not crazy, and from the short time I've spent around you all, I know you're not either." With this statement, the room breathed a collective sigh of relief. He wasn't going to fight them. He wasn't going to yell. And he didn't accuse them of being crazy. As far as starts go, they were off to a great one.

Giving up on forming any cohesive thought, Colin decided to just start talking. "I don't believe in ghosts. I can't believe in ghosts. Ghosts aren't real! So how *can* I believe you?! But there's the watch, and the engraving, and you all somehow know my dad…." Not wanting to ask, but needing to satisfy his curiosity, Colin addressed his boss for the first time, "Katie, let me see your hand." She held up her hand, showing no sign of injury or self-inflicted harm. "Figures. You don't know this, but I saw you burn your arm a few days ago. When I tried asking about it the next day, I saw it was gone and you yelled at me to get back to work."

All surprised at her actions, it was Helen who voiced what they were all thinking. "Kathleen, you yelled at him?" There was that slight reprimand in her voice only a mother could pull off.

Hearing it, Colin laid on the sarcasm, enjoying the shame on his "sweet" boss' face. "Oh, she's been a real peach all week, insinuating my bloodline is solely made up of cheats, liars, and bums."

"That's beneath you." This time it was Roy who spoke up with an icy glare towards his daughter. It's one thing to be shamed by your mother and another to be scolded by your father, and Colin chose to hold his tongue regarding Katie's treatment of him after that.

Looking down in shame, like a child caught doing something wrong, she mentally reviewed her treatment towards Colin over the past week and knew they were right to be disappointed in her.

"You should have said something, Colin. We have plenty of practice dealing with Katie and her temper tantrums," was Charlie's contribution to the morning so far. Jack just sat there, still surprised that his sister had treated Colin, Bill's nearly identical son, in such a way. At last, Katie spoke up, desperate to defend her situation. "I just wanted him to leave before all of this happened. And…and he looks so much like Bill." Katie looked at Jack when saying this, gaining a sympathetic nod from her brother.

Colin didn't know the weight of their exchange. Not wanting to get off topic, Colin decided to do some other prying. "Katie said something about a house fire. Is that how you all… died?" He felt stupid letting those words come out of his mouth, but there was nothing for it. Despite his firm belief that ghosts were still *not* real, he couldn't ignore the fact he was sitting in an apartment with five people self-proclaimed to be dead. "What the hell," he thought, "I might as well get some background information."

Taking on the role of storyteller, Roy took a quick sip of coffee, reminding everyone they too had the hot, heavenly drink, and began. "It all started about 80 years ago. Helen and I became some of the first hundred or so residents of Vernon in the early 30's. Married with a baby girl and no jobs in Lansing, we landed here where property was cheap, and we could be part of a developing town. It was easier then, building something from the ground up than trying to fit into something that was already established. My father, Walter, owned a good-sized farm between Lansing and St. Johns, and with his knowledge of the land, he was able to produce more crops than our family could ever eat. That's how I was able to start Vernon's first grocery store with little startup cost."

"Dad," Charlie interrupted, "I don't think we need to go *that* far back" He knew it was easier to get straight to the point. "It's simple, Colin. There was a house fire in 1967, we were all home for it, and we all died."

"But there is more to it, right? I mean, you're here, your house is here, and the whole town must have known you died if there was a house fire. So, why is it you guys, out of billions of deaths before and after nineteen sixty…seven, are the only ghosts I've heard of?"

Roy picked the story up from there. "Yes, there's more. We were not the only ones who died in that fire, nor were we the only ones who came back. We're just the only ones left."

"Left? What do you mean, left?"

"I'll get to that soon, but first, the fire. It happened and no one knows why. The town officials back then said our bodies were taken to Owosso, but after a whole day and night passed, we were all missing and the house was back, perfect as if nothing had happened at all. Every one of us woke up in our beds--or couch in Jack's case--and nothing was different or out of place, save a message written on the common area wall. 'Don't leave her'."

Colin wanted to ask more about the message but wasn't given the chance. Jack cleared his throat, and everyone turned to him. Colin became aware of the man's stiffness for the first time and knew whatever he had to say demanded his full attention. "The why, the how…after knowing for two minutes you have about as much insight as we do after 45 years. But here is what we do know. We are dead, which means we do not age, sustain injuries for longer than a day, or reproduce. We are the only ghosts left that we, or anyone we know, are aware of. And our weird existence is tied to the house."

Colin didn't quite understand and asked, "Tied to the house? What do you mean? And what happened to everyone else?"

CHAPTER 13

Roy really enjoyed his role as a storyteller. Once again, he picked up the conversation, adding a little history to it. "Our home was built as a boarding home with enough room for our family as well as housing up to four smaller family units. Think of it as a mini long-term hotel or bed and breakfast, but the renters had to keep their units in working condition and feed themselves. The first, and still only one, of its kind in Vernon."

Colin didn't have the heart to interrupt and explain what an apartment complex or fourplex was. By his tone, Colin could tell Roy was very proud of their home and "modern" way of living, and right now simply wasn't the time to burst his bubble.

"There were three other families besides us, the Henderson's, Lewinski's, and Markel's. The whole town was in a panic when we all reappeared, showing up for work, school, friend dates… It was chaos. There was an emergency town meeting, and everyone was ordered to remain in Vernon until we could figure it all out.

"Once all this was declared an act of God, nerves began to calm, and pews began to fill. However, it was still a long time before any sense of normality came. The first day back at school, one of the Lewinski kids had a rock thrown at him during recess from another student who was too afraid to let him come close. The poor kid was in bad shape, but come next morning he woke up without any sign of injury"

"Just like Katie's hand," Colin thought out loud.

"Yes. That was the first time we realized we were waking up in the same condition we went to bed the night before the fire."

"Like Phil Conners?"

Charlie smirked. "Where do you think they got that idea? Except Phil died, multiple times, and mostly on purpose. We have no idea what would happen to us if things progressed that far."

"And we don't want to!" was Roy's firm interjection. Colin didn't miss the fleeting glances towards the other Brigham brother. Roy continued, "Since then, there have been haircuts, burns, broken bones, tattoos… nothing sticks"

If he had not been talking to physically tangible ghosts at the moment, Colin would have found this information astonishing. The possibilities. The never-ceasing second chances.

"But this doesn't explain where everyone went. Where are the other families? Do they live somewhere else?"

It was obvious they were uncomfortable with the question. Or rather, uncomfortable giving the answer. Taking time to collect their thoughts, they all shifted in their seats, some taking nervous sips of their coffee while others straightened their clothes. The movements themselves weren't unusual, but they all started and stopped at the same time. If a scientist had observed them, they would have found it fascinating, as if time had synchronized their mental wavelengths on a deeper level than nearly all relationships are capable of. But Colin was not a scientist. He was an average, everyday Joe, and it was eerie.

Leave it to Charlie to tackle a difficult situation. "No. They don't. After their son was hit, the Lewinskis decided to move. They feared for their children's safety, and with good reason. After some well-meaning encouragement from friends and out-of-state family, they packed up a small van with what they could. But once they crossed the town line, well ...poof. Sorry, but there's really no better way to explain it than that."

"They disappeared, or dissolved, or however you want to describe it. As soon as they crossed the city limits, they were gone. The van crashed just on the other side of the railroad tracks by the park. Had the Henderson's dog not beaten us to the crash and vanished before our eyes, I don't know how many of us would have run across city limits without warning."

A shiver went through Helen, "I know the Henderson's loved that dog, the poor thing, but I'm glad none of you crossed the boundary first."

"Okay, so where are the other two families? The Henderson's and Markers?"

"Markel," Charlie continued. "The Markel's were busy trying to leave just like the Lewinski's and refused to believe they just disappeared. I don't know why on God's green earth they thought we would make that up. Their stubbornness to see reason is why that couple is gone. The Henderson's is a sadder tale. All we could get from Mrs. Henderson was they were taking an evening walk, and when they got to the south side of town, along the creek, Mr. Henderson must have taken a step over the town line. The next thing she knew, he was gone. She, too, went missing less than a year later, but no one believes that was a mistake. After that, we asked Mayor Burkley, Mrs. Minton's father and mayor at the time, to mark the town line so there would be no more accidents. We couldn't stand another family tragedy."

"That was a hard year for everyone." Noticing the redness around Jack's eyes, Colin sensed this was much harder for the younger brother than the rest of them. Not sure how much more he could take himself, Colin sifted through the hundreds of thoughts and ideas vying for his attention, one trumped them all. Finally, he said, "I still don't know how this means you're tied to the house."

If Jack's loss was noticeable, their collective loss was solid enough to feel. This time it was Katie who tackled the question. "Do you remember Roy's brief history lesson? That baby girl wasn't me, it was our older sister, Nora. She was with us the night of the fire too and like us, came back when the house did. She owned Living Color, her typical view of a joke."

Colin could see the irony in so many ways. If he knew nothing else about Nora, that was enough to like her.

"In the late 80's, houses in this area were starting to renovate. Additions were made, and electrical and plumbing were updated. Asbestos was a big hit back then." Colin took a look at his popcorn ceiling but didn't interrupt Katie. "The town decided to take on a more modern look, and with our family being one of the originals in the area, we decided to remodel as well. The tenant units were done first since they were so much smaller than Mom and Dad's section. It was difficult, knowing who used to live there, but also cleansing. Next, we fixed up the downstairs shared living space and public bathroom. And you've seen my parent's newer kitchen. Everything was going well and looking great until we got to Nora's room.

It was hard for her to continue, but she did. "She insisted her unit be done first since she would be forgoing having her own unit and staying with mom and dad, but after we pulled out all her furniture, she didn't feel quite herself. The next day we tore out the carpet and repainted all the walls, and she was gone. Not dead again, just gone."

"Are you sure she didn't…leave town?"

"No." Everyone chimed in on this except Jack. Katie continued with tear-lined eyes. "Nora never planned to leave; she loved it here. And even if she wanted to…leave…she would have told us first. Left a sign. This is how we make sense of why we regenerate every day; we're tied to the house."

This new information exponentially multiplied the questions now waving and screaming for his attention. Not only have they all lived a "Groundhog's Day" existence for the last five-ish decades, unable to change physically, but they were also stuck in a house, unable to change their surroundings. How disappointing and limited their life must be. Even if they didn't have to worry about weight, injury, prolonged sickness, or death…what a bleak existence.

Then Colin got a good look at Jack. In addition to the red eyes was a jaw set in anger, a back stiff with resentment, and knuckles white with rage.

Charlie's voice cut into Colin's astute observations, "She will have been gone eighteen years this September."

"Eighteen years?" Looking at the pain on Roy and Helen's faces, his heart truly ached for this family. Eighteen years, and they still hurt this much. "I'm so sorry."

"We had to be sure our theory was correct. The only thing we could think of that caused her to disappear was the house renovation, so we tried something a little different. Like the Henderson family, we too had a dog that came back with us, Chase, who was very old even before he 'died'. He was destined to be forever ill, and to be fair to him, we should have put him down the year before. So, we all said our goodbyes and began updating the laundry room he slept in. Just like Nora, Chase vanished too."

That sounded so heartless to Colin. Looking at his beloved Dually, he could never, ever do such a thing to his dog.

"Is that why there are so many historical houses around here, with all the updated homes on the north side of town, out of sight? To make sure your place doesn't stand out? And is that why everyone distracts people who are passing through, so they don't recognize one of you?"

"Wow catches on quick, this one," was Charlie's praise.

"And you think once her room was torn out, there was nothing original left to regenerate Nora, so 'poof'?" He knew he shouldn't have said that the moment the words were out of his mouth. What was he thinking? They had just opened a wound telling their story and he goes and rubs salt on it. To quickly change topics, he finally brought it all around to what he wanted to know from the very beginning.

"I'm sorry, that was very tactless. And I don't want to belittle your loss, but…Please tell me, how do you know my dad? I didn't know Vernon was even a real place, let alone that he was ever here."

Everyone was grateful for a change of topic. All, but Katie. "In 1965, right out of high school, Bill moved here and worked with me in the café. He became my everything, and I was going to marry him. But the fire happened four months before our wedding."

Suspecting there was *something* between his father and this family, Colin was still unprepared for that. "Oh, um…" He was dumbfounded. "Well, that makes your comments about him last night make a whole lot more sense." Without taking the proper time to chew on this information and how his comments would affect her, Colin's idiocy continued. "Good thing you didn't marry him though, or I wouldn't be here." Charlie snickered at Colin's foolishness, and Katie was shocked into silence.

Then Jack spoke up for the second and last time. "You don't know how right you are." With that, he excused himself and quickly departed the apartment. With a worried look on her face, "Go with him, Charlie," Helen demanded, leaving only Roy, Helen, and an irate Katie.

"I think I'm missing something." Boy, was Colin 0 for 3.

Staring at the door his sons disappeared through, Roy didn't have a ready answer this time, and Katie was too mad to speak even if she wanted to. That left Helen to pick up the conversation. "Jack had a family before we died. They were in the process of moving from Vernon to Lansing. He did all the actual moving since her job required her to stay in town, and since you could take your child to work back then, their son Luke stayed with his mom. Jack was only going to be away from them for a few nights. Nearly everything was boxed up, and he was sleeping on the couch when the fire happened.

"At first, we all rejoiced for him. He came back and could be with his wife and son! But that was before we knew it was literally impossible for him to leave town. Then there was the psychological side of everything."

"Psychological side?"

"Lisa loved Jack deeply. We all know that. They had a beautiful marriage. She even moved back to town with Luke so they could all stay together. But… she couldn't get herself to be *with* her husband anymore. After all, he was dead, and a physical relationship felt taboo, even if he was physically here and as alive as he could be.

"It was too much, for both of them, to be around each other and not with each other. Then there was something else we didn't anticipate. Lisa got older, but Jack didn't. Everyone in town knew what happened, but she couldn't explain to anyone else why she had such a young husband. After years of Jack wanting to be with his wife and Lisa dealing with the fact that, though she loved him and longed to be with him too, he was still dead, Lisa moved back to Lansing. It was an acrimonious separation on both sides.

"Then there was Luke. He was only a baby when the fire happened. They tried to keep Jack's death a secret from him, but little children are perceptive and would ask questions no one felt comfortable answering. He was about six when Lisa finally moved away. It's hard enough explaining a separation to a child, but how can you tell them their father will never come visit? Never see you at school or your new home? That tore Jack up more than anything, knowing he could never be a part of their lives and there was nothing he could do to change that.

"After all that, the worst thing happened. Poor Luke was in an accident when he was nine, and we lost him. Lisa was good enough to have him buried here so Jack could help put him to rest, but poor Lisa. She blamed Jack. She blamed all of us. And she couldn't understand how Jack could come back, but not their son. It broke her. She's buried now, next to Luke and Jack's headstone." Silence punctuated the story's end. Oh, Jack.

"We all lost things, people, rights, over the years" Roy turned away from the door and back to the conversation, "but that boy has lost so much more. Now, I'm sorry Katie. I know I've said it thousands of times, but I am sorry you have and probably always will have a broken heart over Bill. But this man here is right; he's only here today because, as fate would have it, you two *didn't* marry. And that watch proves he always loved you too. Just be thankful this whole thing didn't ruin Bill's life as well."

Feeling free to jump in and hoping to make up for his earlier insensitive comment, Colin thought it right to share his father's side of the story. "I don't think my dad was ever strong enough to bring himself back to Vernon. He cared for people deeply, and if you were the world to him as much as he was the world to you, he would never have been able to face such a loss. I'm sorry too, Katie. You needed him, and he didn't even know you were here."

The only giveaway to the ocean of turmoil churning inside her was her stormy eyes. Everything she felt regarding the man she loved, and the decades of heartbreak she put herself through, just to have his *son* tell her he loved her all along was more than she could handle. Bill was dead. Her undying hope to see him again was all in vain, and she couldn't fight anymore. She was no stranger to pain and grief and loss, and she knew it never really ceased over time. But this wasn't a normal loss, this was her Bill. Out of every possible way of taking this news, rage won out in the end.

Jack and Charlie's departure freed her bottled bitterness. With a pound of her fist, her steely dead voice seemed even more violent than if she were to shout at the top of her lungs. "He rejected me. He never came back, not even to look for my grave. How could he love me and never come back for me?" Even if he were on the other side of town, Colin didn't think he could escape her grief. "He had no excuse. And now he's dead, and I'll never see him again. I can't go to his graveside because I'm trapped here." Unable to control the sobs, she trailed off, almost to herself, "He had no excuse!"

Allowing her to feel her pain and knowing there was nothing they could say to comfort her, Roy and Helen chose to remain silent. Colin, however, could not stand to watch her wallowing in self-pity and let his irritation get the better of him. He was going to give his hysterical, dead but still living, catty with a heart mushier than butter in summer heat boss a reality check. "Are you serious? He didn't reject you, he thought you were gone! And since my dad really *is* dead, now you get to understand what he had to go through."

Katie's shock stopped her crying in its tracks. Helen sucked in a breath that put her at risk of choking, and Roy couldn't stifle his chuckle in time.

"I'm sorry for your loss Katie but come on. My dad didn't abandon you; he couldn't overcome his own grief. And that's not a sign of his rejection; it's a sign of his love. And we were in such a crappy way, he couldn't have made the trip back here, especially once he got sick. Hell, I barely even made it! I wouldn't have known this place even existed if he didn't mention it during life's suckier times, which was all the time, by the way."

Laughing a little, more to himself and his memories than to her obnoxious behavior, Colin let out a fond sigh while thinking over his father's favorite phrase. "You have no idea how much he cared."

Letting his words sink in, the piercing in her heart eased gradually with every shaky breath she took. With more resolve than she's had in years, Katie straightened herself a little and finally looked around the tiny apartment. The tiny apartment that was once destined to be her and Bill's first home was now occupied by his son. After sitting vacant for all these years, the place is now filled with signs of the love of her life. Finally, being put to use in the way it was always intended. Her eyes came around, falling once again on Bill's son.

"I really am glad to have met you, Colin. It really is nice to see Bill's life come to something good." Everyone was unsure where she was going with this and chose not to interrupt while she collected her thoughts. "I'm so sorry for how I treated you; what you've seen is not who I am." It was a lame apology, but an apology all the same. Forgiving with a nod of his head, Katie smiled at his acceptance and cleared her throat again. "So, that leaves only one more order of business for today's…intrusive meeting. Would you like to stay in Vernon?"

This question came as a bit of a shock and frankly, Colin wasn't quite sure if he heard her correctly. Taking a risk and trusting that he had, in fact, heard her right, only a second passed before an emphatic "yes" escaped his lips. He had a new home, a boss he hoped to be much more compatible with, a surrogate family, and a hell of a lot of questions. Also, where would he go?

They didn't stay much longer after that, and their presence was sorely missed once Mrs. Minton showed up with a mountain of paperwork. "Necessities to keep those in 'the know' under control. Lord knows we need another book or movie based on them." Colin thought again about the ever-popular Groundhog's Day as well as some other books he had read over the years and understood where she was coming from.

On top of agreeing to not write a book, movie, screenplay, blog, or even journal entry about the family, he also agreed to never openly promote the town of Vernon. "I am very much dedicated to the health and well-being of my town. It has been deemed safest to keep it a secret, so if you are to ever leave here, I am to be one of your few allowed references for a job or residence." Colin cocked an eyebrow at Mrs. Minton and asked, "And if then you still don't like me?" It was meant as a joke, but she took it all too seriously. "Then you best not try to leave."

He was given 24 hours to look over the paperwork before signing it, and he took that time. Walking the town again with clear eyes, Colin figured everyone here must have signed the same contract, held the same secret, and lived with the same dedication towards the Brigham family. If all 788 of them could do it, why not him?

CHAPTER 14

The next day was Sunday and Colin went straight over to Roy and Helen's house first thing in the morning with Dually in tow. Looking at the multi-family complex, he wondered for the thousandth time since hearing its story how it had come back. How did all of them come back? The historical landmark loomed over the street, the town, showcasing the past and disallowing the city to have any future. Feeling a shiver crawl up his spine, Colin shook it off, not allowing this architectural marvel to be anything more than beautiful in his eyes. It was just a house, nothing more.

If given an eternity to live, Colin thought sleeping in on the weekend would be on their to-do list. That was why Colin was a bit surprised to see Roy answer the front door in full dress attire as if he were going to a wedding. Once ushered inside Roy's unit and found the whole Brigham family present, his curiosity wasn't satisfied until Charlie explained they were going to the weekly church service.

"You guys go to church?" Colin asked.

"Of course, we go to church," came Helen's response from the kitchen where she finished up some potluck items. "In fact, I think the whole town has gone to church since the fire happened."

That didn't make any sense to Colin. Without taking the time to stop himself, he then asked, "But you're dead. How does that make you, or anybody want to go to church?"

Everyone tried to answer this question at once, but it was Roy again who stole the spotlight. "Son, we are dead, yet daily rejuvenating spirits that can interact with the physical world. How can we NOT believe in the spiritual realm? And, given many decades to search for ourselves, Christianity was the only religion that not only made sense of our predicament but also went along with our strong moral codes. We were designed, called to worship, and sent to do good works for God's kingdom, and He has a purpose for us all. Even us dead folk. Now, come, we don't want to be late."

Being roped into a church service was not how he planned to spend his Sunday. To be honest, he didn't catch much of it and couldn't even tell you what the message was on. All he could remember was singing too many songs that ceaselessly repeated themselves and being surprised by biblical jargon that popped up in the service now and then that had to do with blood and farm animals.

Once the service was finished for real--for there were a few times he thought they were done but they were not--a large fellowship picnic was being hosted outside in the oversized parking lots. There, he was able to sit with the Brigham crew as well as Bree's family and Justin.

"I guess it's true," Colin thought out loud, "the whole town really *does* go to church."

It was not until three in the afternoon that Colin was saying goodbye and heading back towards his apartment. He very much wanted to ask a list of questions to Roy and

Helen but found the church potluck an inappropriate setting.

Near the end of the church block, Colin heard his name being called out, and, turning, he saw Katie rushing after him. Seeing her outside the café and fully enjoying herself made him a little squirmy on the inside. He knew why, but didn't want to acknowledge it. Instead, he waited for her to catch her breath and asked if she needed anything.

Still a little breathy, Katie said, "Hey, I'm pretty sure I can guess why you came over this morning, and it didn't have anything to do with church, did it."

"Um, no, not really." Colin didn't even try to hide his feeling of being roped into something he didn't want to do. Though, he couldn't complain about the meal. He'd attend again if only for that.

With a lopsided grin, Katie replied, "Yeah, I figured as much. So, how many questions were you planning on asking? Or were they only for my parents?"

There was no way for Katie to know or understand Colin's shift in personal convictions over the past 48 hours. The Brighams had been telling their story for decades now. It was expected for him to have more questions than they had answers, so she took his lack of response as acceptance, though, in reality, he was successfully hiding his conflicting emotions. In that brief pause, Katie saw how much Colin not only looked like his father but possessed some of the characteristics she appreciated most. He was a Warrington through and through.

After a few seconds, Colin muttered, "How did you know I was going to ask questions?"

She could not help the light laugh that escaped her lips. It was so nice for Colin to hear, but again made him squirm uneasily on the inside. He pushed that disturbed feeling away as quickly as he could. "Colin, everybody has questions when they find out about us. And don't worry, we will answer them if we can."

CHAPTER 15

Colin tried his best to act normal at work the next day but couldn't help feeling there was a neon sign that could rival Roy's, flashing "He Knows" over his head. It wasn't that people were side-glancing at him any more than usual, he just didn't know who was in the know about him staying and therefore couldn't interpret the side-glances as curiosity regarding him personally or curiosity regarding his future plans now that the Vernon Secret was out. At least he knew he could trust Justin and Bree with a few of his questions. They welcomed him into the café cohort yesterday during the church potluck and confessed looking forward to the tension at work reducing with Colin's recent revelation. The problem was, that now that he was free to ask any question he wanted, he no longer felt comfortable asking. After all, this was a rather private affair and at the end of the day Katie was still his boss.

A steady flow of customers kept Colin from doing much talking anyway, so when there was a lull in the crowd Colin made it a point to speak with Bree. She was the closest with Katie and the nicer of his two co-workers. Still nervous over what he was about to do, Colin took a deep breath while his eyes quickly swept the café one last time.

"So… Bree, does everyone here know about…you know." He wasn't as smooth in asking as he wanted to be, but it was what it was.

"About Katie and the family? Yes and no. Locals do, but since we're close to a major highway and get more out-of-town business than you would expect, we tend to keep it on the DL."

"So, no one talks about it? Ever?" Colin was incredulous at the idea.

But all Bree did was shrug at the question. Wiping down a nearby table and heading back to the cash register, Bree said, with a tone that suggested it should have been obvious, "It's kind of old news, Colin. I've known Katie for over twenty years. And they've been dead for, what, almost 50 years now? And it's not like we can freely share the news with others."

Wanting to point out how crazy this all is, Colin continued his questioning. "It is so weird, thinking a small town like Vernon could have such a big secret. I mean, what other towns have stuff like this going on? Are we the only ones? And how does everybody seem okay with it all?

Ceasing her work at the register, Bree turned to face Colin and told him in a motherly way, "Everybody loves the Brighams, even before they died, they were the favorite family in town. And this is just exciting to you because it's new. Don't worry, soon enough it'll be the norm."

Colin knew she meant well, but it didn't come across that way. "I'm not exactly sure knowing I'll get to a point where this is comfortable is comforting."

Their conversation was interrupted by Mrs. Minton's arrival for her usual evening treat. Once Bree was off to retrieve Mrs. Minton's chocolate raspberry muffin,

Colin decided maybe someone more detached would be best to talk with.

This being only the second time he purposefully spoke with the woman didn't make for the smoothest of greetings, but if she was at all taken aback or offended, she didn't let on.

"Evening Mrs. Minton. Do you mind if I sit with you for a little?"

Pursing her lips as if to keep back what she really wanted to say, Mrs. Minton gestured for him to sit down and tersely said, "If this is supposed to be the dinner you owe me, I've already paid and am not nearly hungry enough to count this as a meal."

Surprise registered in Colin's eyes and he muttered, "Oh, right. I sort of thought that was a--" Her pointed stare told him to get on with it. "I was just wondering if you could tell me what it's like for you, knowing and all. How has it changed your life, or maybe made you look at things a different way? What was it like growing up in a town with ghosts?"

Slightly impressed, Mrs. Minton accepted her chocolate raspberry muffin from a silent Bree and slowly took a bite from it, waiting for Colin to show some sign of uneasiness before responding.

"I must say, no one has asked me that before. There are many lifelong residents here in Vernon, but I am one of the few who were around the morning the apartments caught fire. And I was devastated to hear my favorite babysitter had passed away."

"Katie babysat you?" Colin couldn't picture a little Mrs. Minton, let alone Katie following her around, wiping her nose, and tending to scraped knees.

"Ha! Don't be ridiculous." Mrs. Minton's response broke through Colin's thoughts. "Katie, I'm sure, could be a wonderful babysitter now, but I was talking about her older sister Nora. I was so very fond of her."

"I still don't know much about Nora. I'm sorry she is no longer here…again."

"Well, I can't say growing up in a town with ghosts is much different from growing up in a town without. Of course, I wouldn't really know. However, every town has its secrets and this one just happens to be what keeps me in a job."

Mrs. Minton took a few more bites while Colin's imagination went crazy thinking of all the other types of secrets another small town could have. Ghosts didn't seem so bad after all. Not sure what else to do, Colin made to say goodbye and rose from the table.

Mrs. Minton gave a farewell shoo with her hand and turned her full attention to her muffin. Then, before he had walked more than two steps, Colin turned back and asked a tough, yet prodding question.

"Mrs. Minton, do you ever get to talk with Helen or Katie about Nora?"

The shock on the old woman's face made her eyes bulge and seem nearly comical in comparison to her pointed nose.

"Now why would I speak to them about something so personal as that?"

Colin took a heartbeat to think about that, then he shrugged and said, "Because you seemed to care about Nora too. I didn't know if maybe they had you to grieve with or if they had to do that alone."

Turning away again, Colin never saw the pain that replaced the shock in her eyes. If there was one description Mrs. Minton would give the Brigham family, 'alone' was not one of them. But that didn't mean it wasn't true.

CHAPTER 16

In the week that went by after the secret was out, the café had never looked so grand. It's amazing how much better one's workplace can be when you're actually wanted.

It was only 5 am. Up until then, Colin had many questions, but not enough nerve to ask them. His cowardice, Colin decided, had taken enough time, and he had a good ten minutes to waste while the refrigerated display case cooled down. If only he could come up with a smooth introduction to this conversation.

"Hey, Katie." Smooth was not his forte.

Katie just smiled in response. She knew his curiosity would get the better of him sooner than later. Her carnation red lipstick turned up ever so slightly at the corners and it was a sight that both lifted his chest and twisted his stomach. He wondered if he would ever get used to it.

"What is it like, to wake up the same every day? Have you ever wished it would end?"

Oh, he started out deep. Will she ever get used to him surprising her? Her upturned smile flattened with this question, causing him to immediately regret asking it. But it was too late, and he genuinely wanted to know.

"Yes, and no," she said. "That's a little complicated to explain." Setting aside her order form for next week, Katie stared at the countertop while she thought about that question. Colin shifted uneasily from foot to foot before deciding to join her at the kitchen island.

Once he was comfortable, Katie looked up at him but did not catch his eyes. "I spent nearly half a decade heartbroken over Bill. I felt cheated and betrayed and wanted it to end a few times. And there were moments when I was dissatisfied with it all. But those were moments of selfishness and thank goodness they were fleeting. I keep telling myself there has to be a reason why I come back every day. I have a purpose here and even if it is to run a café, I need to do it the best I can. Plus, you know, I didn't lose as much as others."

He didn't need to ask who she meant. Nora and Jack's stories were common thoughts that passed through his mind. Unsure if he was allowed to ask more regarding them, Colin chose some other questions that steered away from grief and pain.

Many of his questions were repeats of past inquiries: How do birthdays work, what do you do in your spare time, do you know any other languages or musical instruments? This line of questioning was only broken by finally stocking the display case and Katie popping the cinnamon rolls that had been rising in and out of the oven. He thought it was amazing how she could do everything quickly and without a recipe.

"Do you have all your recipes memorized?"

Katie nodded. "For all my normal morning treats, yes. But I have my baking book on hand in case I'm having an off day."

"Can I see? I bet after all this time you've been able to perfect them all."

"Well…" She wanted to say no. Her hesitation made that clear enough. Colin wasn't at all offended by it. In fact, he was quite surprised he had even asked. But now that he did, he realized he truly did want to help out in the kitchen.

"I am a bit behind on things, and I *do* have to get all this work done before we end up disappointing our early risers." Seeing he oh-so-much wanted to be a part of the kitchen experience, Katie went to the supply closet and came back with an extra hair net for Colin. Tossing it to him, he asked if she was serious. "Yes, I am serious, Colin. It's called CFR Title 21, and it's not a suggestion." Along with the hair net, he was also supplied an apron after thoroughly washing his hands and pocketing his watch for safekeeping.

"I have all of the recipes and directions in this binder." Where she pulled the giant 3-inch binder with laminated recipes from was a mystery, but there on the center island now sat the secrets to all her bakery success. "I don't share my recipes with people I don't know, so if one goes missing, I'll know exactly who to go after. You got that?"

That last part was said in an unfriendly tone that perfectly matched her no-nonsense gaze. Since this was her livelihood, it was only fair for Colin to be upfront and honest about his baking experience. "I'm not exactly planning on starting a rival business. To be honest, I didn't even ask to help you bake. I don't know how to, let alone want to."

She stared Colin down, then nodded her approval. A few of her recipes had been taken in the past for the very purpose of starting a rival bakery. Of course, being limited to Vernon city limits and in all other senses dead, there was nothing she could do but watch another person become famous with her hard-earned work. So great was her distrust, that not even Bree (as loyal as she was) had seen this recipe binder. But it wasn't the same with Colin. She knew he hadn't come to town to take anything from her, and it felt really good to be able to trust someone again.

"Too bad. I'm the boss, and you still need this job. There's just one very big problem."

Since she said this in a much friendlier voice, he knew she wasn't serious. But he also knew that passing up this opportunity would only lead to regret. "Yeah? What's that?"

"You're going to regret your choice of clothes." Looking down, Colin realized he was wearing dark jeans and a black shirt that would attract baking particles in the air. Of course, he was dressed in the worst possible attire. It was his first day of work all over again. "Well, in my defense, you did put me on the spot." Knowing this was true, and not caring, she started delegating duties.

"After this last batch of cinnamon rolls comes out, we need to start on some special-order eclairs and then the muffins. The eclairs take the longest, so I'll get started on those. I want you to take the largest mixing bowl that fits in the stand mixer and start measuring out the dry ingredients for the muffins. Make sure you increase the recipe by 10."

"Katie, I'm not so sure about this. I mean, I only got my food handlers license on the off chance you would need help. I really don't know what I'm doing." A little out of his element, Colin looked around and thankfully noticed that every shelf and drawer was carefully labeled. Wondering if Roy helped her design this kitchen, or if the same OCD streak ran in the family, he began his search for the measuring cups.

"Don't worry Colin, just follow everything exactly how it says in the book. If you have any *baking* questions let me know." And with that, Katie started flying across the kitchen leaving Colin standing there determined not to look like a fool.

CHAPTER 17

"It's wrong **again**, Colin! What the heck!?" This was the third time Colin attempted to measure out the correct amount of flour, baking powder, salt, sugar, and cinnamon, but for some reason, he could not get it right. He had lost almost the entire morning measuring wrong. "Are you even looking at the recipe!?"

"Of course, I'm looking at the stupid recipe! I'm not an idiot!" She thought it best not to respond to that statement.

"At this rate, you'll be paying me to work here. Now show me what you're doing wrong." Colin, fuming at her condescending tone, once more began to measure out the ingredients. After the first scoop, she stopped him. "Oh no! Colin, you're supposed to measure the cups out flat, not heaped. It's baking 101."

"How the hell was I supposed to know!? I told you I didn't bake! God, I knew this was a mistake." He threw down his apron, tore off the stupid, yet necessary hair net, and stalked over to the employee bathroom to clean up his clothes and his ego. She was right, he did regret his choice of clothing.

Every oven was turned on, giving the kitchen a much too hot feeling for this hour of the morning. On top of that, every particle of flour had clung to him as if for dear life, leaving his shirt with streaks and smudges of white that would not be brushed off.

He heard a knock at the door. "Colin?" He knew it was petty, but he still didn't answer. "Colin, you said you didn't know how to bake, and I didn't take you seriously. This is my business, so the blame is mine. I'm really behind schedule, so I need you to come out and help or leave. I know you today is your first day of work at the lumber yard too, and I'm sure that's been on your mind."

Not feeling like he was really given a choice, Colin came out of the bathroom, grudgingly put on a new hair net and apron, and started to measure the fruit and wet ingredients that would go into the muffins Katie began to work on. At least there wasn't much more than a random eggshell here and there to mess things up.

After that, it really wasn't so bad. Arnie was asked to wait a few minutes while they finished the morning's delivery load, but Katie agreed to do all the dry ingredients until she could show him the proper way to measure, and they fell into a comfortable rhythm, completing the morning's baking early enough to enjoy another round of questions over coffee before going their separate ways for the rest of the day.

Colin over-fantasized about his time at the Mill City Sawmill. It was either that, or he was not as young and buff today as back then. Either way, Colin limped upstairs and begged for his arms not to give way hauling Dually up and down for his bathroom break. After one day he already knew doing both jobs would be physically impossible. He would have to put in his notice first thing tomorrow. He wouldn't even bother with a two-week notice. A box of cupcakes and, "Sorry, I quit" should be good enough, and if it wasn't, it was all he would bother to do. This, too, seemed like a dream he would never see come to fruition. Not knowing why, he wasn't as emotionally crushed over this as he expected to be. His last thought before falling into a dead sleep was, *"At least I still have the cafe"*, and he would have shook his head at that thought if he wasn't already asleep.

CHAPTER 18

"Colin? Colin. Colin!"

A distant thunder rumble turned into a close-by pounding on his door. Hearing his name being shouted, Colin wincingly threw himself out of bed and rushed to the door. The weight of every step was a reminder to quit later. Throwing the door open, he saw a most startled Katie looking him up and down in a scared, most unflattering way. This, paired with her calling out his name, sent shivers down Colin's spine, initiating a visual body search of his own.

Scared for different reasons, it took a while before both were done staring. He was nearly twenty minutes late for his shift and hadn't even made a sound to indicate he was upstairs, or worse. And she was, again, yelling his name.

"Colin, what happened!"

"Kate, what's wrong?"

Blinking at his question, Katie stated, "Colin, you're very late for work."

"What? No, I'm…" Looking down at his father's watch, he didn't even bother to finish that sentence. "Dammit, I'm sorry Kate. Give me ten minutes and I'll be right down." Thankful for having an excuse to turn from her scared-turned-irate expression, he was aware there was still a lot to learn about this woman.

Nine minutes later, Colin burst into the back room ready to help with the daily specials. What he found was Katie baking in such a way he had never seen before. She was a pastry machine on steroids. Colin watched her hands accomplish their tasks as if they had a mind of their own. Flying around the kitchen, Katie didn't give Colin a chance to step in and help, so instead he spent the morning up front as before. She didn't even pour him a cup of the coffee she had made.

Although the refrigerated display case was stocked and the entire place was ready for the first customers of the day, they still had a good hour before being officially open. Thinking of any excuse he could, Colin chanced a second trip into the kitchen. Without saying a word, Colin stood back and took a closer look. Katie was still a baking machine, but her eyes were full of tension, worry, and the slightest sign of tears. There was only one thing he could think to do about that.

"Kate, hey stop for a moment." When she wouldn't acknowledge him, he decided to take a bolder approach. "Kate, if you don't stop baking right now, I'm going to lick a spoon and stick it in the dough."

Fire flashed in her eyes. It reminded him of the first time they met, except for one important difference. There was no faking on her part this time.

"You do that Colin, and it will be the last thing you do in my kitchen, do you understand me!" and with that, she threw off her apron and stormed out the back door to pace the parking lot.

Colin huffed and charged after her. Though it was still the early hours of the morning, he didn't care that the back door slammed against the wall in his haste. Frustrated, he half demanded, "Kate, what happened?! What's wrong?"

"You were late!"

Her voice had a slight shrill to it, but she kept pacing. Colin knew she was holding something back, and he didn't want to play her guessing game.

"No, that's not it. What's *wrong*" Emphasizing that last word made Katie stop in her tracks and let the emotional weight she was carrying fall off her shoulders, drooping them as she did so.

"I thought you liked it here; liked being at the bakery now."

"I do! It's at least much better than when I first started."

She blinked back some threatening tears, but her voice had at least leveled out. Pacing again, Katie continued, "I was getting used to seeing you in the morning. Used to having someone around that," she stopped to search for her words, "that actually cared about my situation."

This was a stall tactic or a distraction he wouldn't allow her to use. Not this time. "Kate, you still didn't answer the question."

Her pacing stopped once more. Taking a clear breath, Katie confessed. "Colin, you didn't show up. You didn't make a sound. I was genuinely happy for you getting the job at the lumber yard like you wanted, so I arrived a little early to make coffee and talk about your first day. And… You probably don't know this, but I can hear every step you take upstairs, so when your alarm went off and you didn't stop it, didn't get up, nothing…. I thought--"

Caffeine-deprived, and tired of her not completely forming her thoughts before speaking, Colin crossed his arms and sighed in an attempt to nonverbally relay he was not telekinetic. Katie got the hint.

"I just got used to having you around, that's all. It's nice to have you here, and I'm finally thinking of you as you, and not as Bill's son. And…"

Uncrossing his arms, Colin knew this was significant to her, but was still not sure why this would make her into some emotionally driven baking monster. Thank goodness he now had extra cupcakes to give to the Lumber Mill this afternoon when he quits.

The impact of Bill's death took a much harder toll on Katie than she realized, for in truth she believed yet another Warrington had passed on without her. But this was never to be said out loud "I thought you had *left*."

Oh. He got it now. At least, he thought he did. Thinking this had everything to do with the fact his father had left town did make sense. Knowing nothing he could say would make things better, Colin went for the bold approach first, whatever the consequences. Marching straight for her, he threw his long, and still very sore, arms around her strong yet dainty frame and hoped they communicated better than his words ever could. There they stood, allowing the world to pass them by for a few seconds. Thinking she was finally calm enough to listen, Colin began to explain what happened.

"Kate, I was so tired this morning I didn't hear anything until you frantically pounded on the door and that scared the crap out of me because I thought something bad had happened to you. I'm relieved everything is okay, but I hate feeling like that, so unless something is really wrong, *please* stop yelling my name."

Katie couldn't answer that. For all she knew, the worst thing had happened. How else was she expected to respond? But again, she would never say that. "Okay" was all she trusted herself to say.

"Good. And take note, I finally found a place I'm not expecting to leave. At least, not if I can help it."

Colin let go of her then and went back inside to answer the oven alarm. Katie stayed outside for a few minutes longer. It was a relief knowing he didn't plan on leaving Vernon, leaving her, but it was a sentimental thought and an empty promise. Katie knew he would eventually leave her, one way or another.

That hug in the parking lot was the first physical contact they shared. It was only a hug, right?

After stepping back inside Katie allowed Colin to help her eat the scones that were made earlier just for them on the countertop. Once the last of the morning baking was in the oven, the two of them shared a pot of coffee and talked about his first, and last, day at the lumber yard and what kind of cupcakes the workers would appreciate the most. By the end of his shift, with a box of cupcakes in his hands, Colin felt something about this connection with Katie was different than any other he had experienced…and not just because she was dead.

CHAPTER 19

There are three main perks of working in a small town with nothing to do. First, you get to know everyone, and your circle of friends begins to expand beyond those you personally work with. Second, with so many work hours and a growing community circle, you don't miss the typical entertainment a larger town offers. And third, since there *are* such limited entertainment choices to spend your money on, and you work so much, you can actually build up a savings account.

Just over two months since Colin rolled into town with literally nothing but a watch to his name, he was financially stable enough to make other living arrangements. After all, he still couldn't afford a place like the one above the café, even with all the small-town benefits.

Determined to do something nice for the man who gave him his big break, Colin went to Roy's perpetually organized office during one of his lunch breaks with an offering. Once in the office, Colin sat back and allowed himself to be overwhelmed by the smell of warm bread and cinnamon in his hands. Roy was enjoying one of the café's reduced-price cinnamon chip mini loaves of bread in such a way only a man whose weight never changes could. The reason the price was reduced: Colin made it, and not very well. If Roy was doing this for Colin's benefit, it was hard to tell, but he appreciated the enthusiasm with which it was received.

The bread was no sooner consumed than the man got down to business. "Okay Colin, now what can I do you for?"

"Well," it was much harder for Colin to talk to him now than he first thought. "I was wondering if I could talk with you about the apartment." Seeing Roy's eyes raise at this statement, Colin assured him that there was nothing wrong with it and that he enjoyed it immensely. "The thing is, for the first time in probably my entire adult life I'm finally financially stable. I live in a good town, I have good friends, and I feel like I'm taking advantage of your hospitality by staying there under our current arrangements."

Roy let an awkward silence fall between them as he mentally chewed on this thought only to break it before Colin could get too comfortable.

"No Colin, I do not think you are taking advantage of me. I would like you to stay where you are."

This could not have been right. There was no reason for Colin to stay there, and both of them knew it. There had to be something else going on. Knowing Roy better now than he did two months ago, he felt free to pry a little more.

"Roy, why did you let me stay there in the first place, and why are you trying to keep me there now?"

Roy let out a sigh. Colin knew that sound all too well. It was a sigh of burden, and he heard it a lot growing up. If Colin hadn't just satisfied Roy's sweet tooth with the interesting mini loaf, he would have dropped the conversation right there. But, seeing there was no way the younger of the two would leave without a satisfactory answer, Roy instead chose to confide in his newest friend.

"Here's the deal Colin. You have no idea what Katie was like before you came to town. Don't go reading too much into it, but she wasn't nearly as light-hearted and happy as she is now and hasn't been for a very long time. I mean, she has always been sweet, hardworking, and a friend to nearly anyone, but now it's…more. She's finally living more." Roy's eyes took on a distant look as he continued.

"You don't know how trapped we are. We wake up here, tucked inside a small town with an eternity of days, never allowed to go out and see the world that is ever-changing beyond the city limits. Helen and I have made our peace with it. Charlie is so much a people person; he always has a friend or two dropping him off the latest invention or stopping by with a new toy and a story to go with it. Jack is still so lost, it's probably safer for him to be bound by our limitations. Thank God Luke and Lisa are buried here, and he has Charlie to always keep him in better spirits. But Katie…

"Son, Katie wanted to get out of town and see the world even before she died. Knowing she never could, never will, took some of the spark out of her eyes. Then there was the whole thing with your father."

Colin shifted in his seat at this comment. "Don't worry, son. I don't blame the man one bit. He didn't know, and how could he? For the rest of his life, he thought he lost her and that was enough of a burden for him. But… The poor girl was forced to have a life but never really lived. At least, not until now." A heavy silence settled between the two men for a few heartbeats before Roy continued.

"Now, I know you two aren't physically involved." Aftershock sprung to Colin's face, Roy laughed before giving his explanation. "Trust me, we're an open enough family after all this time. We talk about everything. But here is the thing, she no longer seems to be pacing, waiting for her escape. She's finally fully present and *enjoying it.* She's enjoying having you here, with her. Nothing else could have made her this way again."

Colin nearly choked, chewing on that thought. And it showed all over his face. Roy simply stood back smirking at how long it took him to process whatever he was thinking. Colin shook his head a little, realizing they had gotten off-track.

"Roy, I still don't know what this has to do with the apartment."

"Oh, come on son, you're smarter than that," joked Roy. "I need you there because Katie is there. Who knows how she would take another Warrington 'leaving' even if it is just down the street?"

"But…you can't expect me to live there forever!"

"No, I can't. But can I at least expect you to talk with Katie about it first? See how she would feel about it?"

Colin smirked at that. "I'm supposed to cater to a seventy-one-year-old?"

Roy shook his head and said, "No, but catering to a friend? That's different. Oh, and Katie's birthday is coming up in September; just in case you didn't know. Do something special for her, will you? You'd think she would stop caring by now, but she's always loved her birthday."

Colin wanted to protest this too, but upon reflection, Roy was only doing something sweet for his daughter as well as keeping Colin from doing any financial harm. "Thank you, Roy. I'll enjoy my place of residence as long as you'll let me."

Shaking hands, Roy says, "Son, I wouldn't have it any other way. Now go get me another cinnamon loaf."

CHAPTER 20

August was not as hot as other places he lived, but my god was it humid. How he could sweat more on a day that was only 84 degrees than he could on a day that was 104 was beyond comprehension. Why any county would put on a fair in the middle of this sticky heat was dumbfounded. Scheduled for the second full week of the month, the weather literally could not have been more miserable. "That's the point, Colin, to give us something to look forward to" was the only reason people would give.

However terrible the weather was, the town was expecting quite a lot of foot traffic next week and most businesses were preparing to shut down in favor of selling their goods at the local booths.

"Kate, are you guys closing down too, or are you going to be baking while Bree and Justin work the booth?" Colin didn't really care who did what work, he just wanted to know how he fit into all the festivities.

Katie cocked her "That's a good question, Colin. Normally I would be back here, or hanging out at Roy's, but I haven't been to the fair in so many years and I want to do things a little differently."

"How so," asked Colin.

"First, I'm going to change up my look a bit and sell my own baked goods. It's been a good decade since I've done that, and I'm ready to again. I'll also try and make some contacts with nearby shops and see if they're willing to carry any of my items. Little places, like coffee and gift shops though. I don't think it would be wise to go much beyond that. I mean, gas station sales are doing great and all, but I think it is time to expand Katie's Café. It's also nice to have another set of hands helping out in the kitchen."

That last statement felt good. Every now and then he would think about the lumber yard and what wonders it would do to his physique, but it turned out baking was physically demanding as well. There was so much whisking, stirring, and kneading to be done every day, and his upper body showed. But more than that, it had its mental satisfaction as well.

But then he thought about it a little more. Expanding her business beyond the random gas station would do wonders for the café, but it was also risky. Keeping secrets confined to a small town was easier when you didn't purposely expose yourself.

Only fear could drive him to purposely run into Mrs. Minton, and fear did just that. He might have been in town for three months now, but Mrs. Minton was still someone he chose to avoid. Between his shifts, Colin stopped by the city council office and found Mrs. Minton in her office behind her desk. It looked like business as usual.

Mrs. Minton knew this was no social call, so the skeptical squint she gave him was not met with offense. However, she still had her daily business as usual and made it a point to get right down to business.

"Mr. Warrington, I have an hour for lunch, and I don't plan on spending it in my office. So, unless you plan on taking me out on a proper date, I suggest you spit it out. What do you want?"

"Oh, um. Well, Mrs. Minton, I was just wondering how the fair was going to affect…everything." Colin was cut short with the most unamused look. Obviously, a woman like this would have all her ducks in a row.

"Mr. Warrington, you think I don't have all this planned out? I'm not the only person in political authority that knows about the Brighams, you know. I just thank God those other city council members know and love Roy, Helen, and the rest as much as our town does. Don't worry, all media will be monitored and edited, and thankfully the passers-by don't pay much attention to the people behind the stands, just the goods on them."

Still not completely convinced, Colin lingered a little longer in her office. "But Mrs. Minton--" "Mr Warrington, no offense, but I've been doing this for a very long time. I think you could have a little more faith in how I run things. Now, if you will excuse me, that lunch hour is ticking away." And before he knew it, he was standing alone in her office. Seeing that talking with her would get nowhere, Colin decided to leave a little message instead. With the sticky note left on her desktop computer, Colin suspected he might have poked a hornet's nest, but did not care. He was not going to lose the closest thing he had to a family over a silly town fair.

Colin made it through his second shift, but everyone could tell he was a little distracted and instead of their usual invitation for him to come over for a drink or idle chit-chat, his co-workers bid him farewell instead.

Still thinking about what he wrote to Mrs. Minton, Colin meandered back to his apartment, and, upon entering, was not at first aware of what was wrong. His concerns over the fair were shoved to the side once he realized Dually wasn't at the door to greet him as usual.

Calling through the apartment, Dually was found curled up on the cool bathroom floor and struggling more than usual to catch his breath. Knowing he couldn't let his best friend suffer much longer, Colin sat down next to him, unable to do more than affectionately hold Dually and tell him how good of a dog he was.

CHAPTER 21

Katie was always in bed by eight; a feat not easily done by the average person when the summer sun refused to give way and allow the sky to darken. However, years of routine solidified her habit and there was no one left in town to know her to be any different. This is why she was first skeptical of, then worried about, the knock on her door around nine. If it was some kid playing a prank, they would have given up after the first round. If it was something more serious, they would have had some sound of urgency to them. Then her mind went back to that morning when it was *her* knocking on someone's door, and her thoughts automatically went to Colin. Why was she so afraid he was going to leave? Or worse, die?

Before she was even to the door, her phone rang, and the ID read Colin. That couldn't have been right, he was supposed to be in bed as well. "Colin? What's wrong?" was the only thing she asked, and the silence that met her on the other end of the line punctuated her fear. Rushing to the door, she didn't even bother to look through the peephole before wrenching it open.

There, on the ground was Colin holding a limp, lethargic Dually. Burying his face into his furry friend's neck, Colin was wracked with sobs as the iron grip of reality squeezed his chest, threatening to never let him breathe again.

It was hard to understand him through the gasps and his face was still hidden in his friend's fur, so "Kate, he's dying. He's dying and I don't know what to do" was more understood than heard.

Slowly lowering herself to the floor next to them, Katie placed a hand on Colin's shoulders and soothingly said, "Colin, I don't know what to do either. I can see if a vet can come out, but… he's very old, Colin. There's only one thing they can really do to help."

Colin finally raised his head, but only to stick out his chin and say with bitterness, "Well, good thing I brought him over here. Maybe I'll hang around and see if he comes back tomorrow."

Sympathy fled after that comment. "That's not funny." Standing up, Katie chastised, "Do you have *any* idea how terrible that is!?"

He flinched at her stinging words. He did know better; he just didn't care at that moment. After a few seconds, his anger subsided and hers along with it. "I'm sorry Kate, I didn't really mean it. I just say things that…" he could barely get the last part of his sentence out before another wave of emotion crested, "that make it easier than feeling pain."

Believing it was due to the tasteless joke, Colin was even more upset with himself, if that was even possible when Katie turned away from him and stepped back inside her apartment.. "I said I was sorry, Kate. I didn't mean it."

Colin's contrite voice gripped Katie's heart. Turning back to him, with her hand out for support, Katie shushed him softly and said, "No, it's not that. Come on in before anyone else hears."

Colin had never been to Katie's apartment before. He never had reason to, and if he had stopped to think about anything other than Dually and death, he wouldn't have even been there now. But pain that is more than physical can make one do some strange things. This was just one of them.

If Katie was upset about a dog shedding on her once trendy couch, she didn't let on. Dually had fallen asleep within ten minutes of coming inside and Colin was too exhausted from it all to do more than sit next to him and stare into the cup of hot tea meant to cheer him up.

More than tea was made during those ten minutes. Two calls, one to a vet nearby and another to Bree. The vet was on her way over from Lansing. After asking some quick medical questions, the vet began to gather the necessary medical equipment for the unsavory job and said she would be there within the hour. Unfortunately, there was no guarantee Dually would even last that long on his own. Katie quickly told Bree what was happening and asked her to make a sign stating the café closed for the day. Everyone understood death, even a pet's, left a heavy loss, and no one would hold a grudge.

CHAPTER 22

Katie was tired, and not at all ready for another ghost talk. But as she stood there, waiting for the vet to arrive, with a hot mug of her own, she couldn't help wondering if this was what Bill looked like when he grieved her. Did he too lose a little of the spark in his eyes? Did he bottle up all the questions, all the hurt, and silently crumble from the inside? Could she do something to save Colin from this? No. Death affects us all. Dually was going to die, and even though that would be the end for him, at least Colin would know it would be the end. No more laboring for breath. No more guessing when or how it would end more holding on just to not hurt someone you love. The Brighams didn't get such luxury.

"Do you want to talk about it?"

Colin didn't answer for a long time, and Katie began to wonder if she even said the words out loud. Then Colin answered, "Yes, and no. Not really." Colin finally looked at her, but his eyes went through her; focused instead on some spot lost out of sight. "He's not coming back, is he? Even if he dies here in this house?"
There was no hesitation in her words. "No, I'm sorry he won't."

She didn't even look away when she said this. There were others who came to this house, looking for some redemption from physical death, but they never found it either. Some condemned the family over it. Others said,

"Well, we tried," and moved on. But Colin didn't need to
know all of that, she concluded. He will need to make
peace with this in his own time.

"You know, I've talked about this so many times
with others. Coming back, being tied here and to this
house… I'm not so sure I can call it a blessing."

Colin nodded. Never before had someone nodded in
agreement to her statement, especially one so close to death
or losing a loved one to it. But of course, Colin surprised
her. How could she expect anything different? Then, he
took surprising her to the next level. "I understand, you
know. Probably more than most would. You must feel
so…so stuck being alive, but unable to live. Like you're not
allowed to go beyond these walls."

She couldn't be it. And she didn't keep the surprise
off her face. He did understand. Colin continued,

"But maybe that's a good thing too. For all you
know, the house is keeping you from becoming a scientific
experiment from some soulless government officials who
would do God-only-know-what to you, or something."

Her bug-eyed response would have been comical
under different circumstances, but since it was a joke and a
far-fetched one at that, she recovered quickly.
"Hey, it was just a thought," said Colin, putting up a hand
in defense, "nothing is secret out there anymore. It's
actually a little scary how you can find out everything
about almost anyone with the right search words. In fact,
that's one reason I had such an easy time signing all those
papers Mrs. Minton threw at me once I moved here.

There's no way I want others to find out about you and take you away."

Dually stirred on the couch, grabbing their attention and bringing up emotions neither of them wanted. For Colin, it was death. For Katie, it was something more. Something she never considered before, and it scared her.

This was some scary news. Maybe the house *was* protecting them. But that didn't mean she wanted to be a slave to the town of Vernon. Surely there could be a way for her to travel and experience life without having it displayed for all to see. Or, as Colin said, displayed for a soulless government agency to find.

Could it be that the town line, the house…all of this was to protect them from worse fates than death out there? Katie had not been to the movie theater since the '60s, but plenty of movies had found their way into town and she certainly couldn't say she knew the world anymore. And she had tried.

She went on her computer nearly every night, looking at millions of people living their lives. She saw beauty and devastation, wholesome acts and despicable violence, feats of greatness and defeat. But she would never, could never experience it. Here was a woman of adventure imprisoned in a Michigan town that was small enough for someone to walk the entire length in one lazy afternoon.

"I guess I can't help you either." Colin's small voice brought Katie back from her thoughts. He had seen her zone out for a little. Get that far look in her eyes of someplace she would never go. During those few seconds, he did a quick look-over of her apartment. The layout didn't interest him in the slightest. After all, he had other things on his mind at the moment.

Katie noticed his interest in her decorations. "They're everywhere I've wanted to go or wanted to experience. Friends and townsfolk have taken them for me over the years on vacation or work trips, but one day I want to see them for myself."

"Wow." Colin said, "I've grown up all over this country. I never thought I would consider that a good thing until now. I know you've been stuck here forever, but at least you know you have a home. All I've had over the last twelve years was Dually." Gripping onto his loving dog, Colin was once again lost in a sea of pain and uncertainty.

Only once had he experienced death and dying, and Dually had been the only thing to get him through it. How was Colin supposed to let him go, and what did he have to help him through the loss this time? A secret ghost family in a virtually unknown town?

"Kate, I can't do this. What am I going to do?" Colin's voice cracked along with his heart. Burying himself again into Dually's furry neck, he didn't even hear Katie's response, "I don't know Colin, but I'll be right here for you." There, Colin stayed until the very end.

Less than an hour later, the vet arrived, and Vernon, Michigan, a nameless dot on a map, became Dually's final resting place.

CHAPTER 23

The next morning, neither of them knew how to act around the other at first. Colin didn't say a single word after the vet came and put Dually to rest.

The café was closed, but Katie didn't bother telling Colin that. She wanted him to get up and out of the house instead of hideaway, and this was the only way she could think to make him do that.

Colin came downstairs a few minutes earlier than usual. He didn't compensate for the amount of time it usually took to take Dually out in the morning. Once downstairs he became very determined to lose himself in baking. That was to be expected, and Katie couldn't fault him. That was one of the beauties of the café. Katie made the same baked goods week after week for decades, yet there was still something wonderful about making something beautiful and delicious, something that brought people together or became a source of comfort on those hard days that demanded a dose of cream, fruit, or chocolate. And this was certainly one of those days that demanded the healing power of food.

The first two hours went by, and Colin had said nothing more than a weak "morning". His coffee mug was still full two hours after being poured and cold now. Colin asked why Bree and Justin were late for their shifts, and when she told him, Colin just stared at her. After a few awkward moments, Colin asked to speak with Katie out back. She didn't expect it to be a pleasant conversation.

The two were barely out the door when he turned around, eyes raw and jaw clenched. Baking helped some, but the pain of loss is something that cannot be masked or pushed aside for long before gaining total control. Unable to begin, it was up to Katie to break the silence, but he cut her off before she could offer any condolences.

"Colin, I-"

"It's not fair."

This was not the first time someone had lost a pet or person they loved and wanted to curse a Brigham for their immortality, but it hurt so much more coming from him. Hanging her head low, she was waiting for the verbal punches. Thank God Colin was more like his father than just his looks; he had Bill's integrity as well.

"It's not fair, Kate. Did you know Dually was sick for a long time? He had a mass growing in his lung, and I've known about it for a while now, but I let him suffer because I couldn't let him go. And it's not fair because I would let him suffer all over again if it meant I could have him back."

That was the most honest, heartbreakingly selfish thing she had ever heard, and it was beautiful.

"Does that make me a terrible person?" Colin couldn't keep the desire to be validated out of his voice. Seeing her friend hurt brought her own tears to her eyes. Blinking them away, Katie sniffed and softly replied, "No,

Colin, it doesn't. It just means you lost someone you really, really loved."

Colin focused hard on the cracked surface of the parking lot. It was the same parking lot he carried Dually to every morning, afternoon, and night. How could he be here, standing in his usual spot, without Dually while the rest of the world went on around him, and no one else seemed to care? No one else, but Katie.

Colin couldn't understand. "But, how… How can you see so many people you know, and love, die and not be consumed by it? How are you not bitter, mean, and self-isolating?"

"You're talking to the wrong Brigham if that is what you want."

And she was very serious. He just described her brother Jack to the letter and only those who have never lost a loved one could blame him. Katie could sense a wall coming up, and for a brief second, she allowed herself to imagine a Colin who had slipped as far as her brother. The image was startling.

But the Colin she knew wouldn't slip so far. He just couldn't. Or rather, she wouldn't let him. "Kate?" Colin's question didn't penetrate her thoughts at first. "Kate, I never knew how hard it could be for you, for any of you, and I am so sorry."

Would this man ever stop amazing her? A second time he reacted in a way no one has ever done in this circumstance. She was prepared for yelling, personal property damage, curses, damnation, and threats, but an apology?

"How do you guys do this? How do you handle the responsibility of living when everyone else is destined to die?" Colin was finally able to look up at her. His question was unlike any she had ever encountered outside of her own thoughts. However, over the years, Katie began to realize two things were certain. First, there is no easy answer to that question. And second, when she had to come up with an answer, it would change every time. "My answer won't be good enough for you, Colin. I know that isn't what you want to hear. But, if what you said was true and Dually was as sick as you said, it doesn't make you a terrible person for wanting him back. I can tell you over and over he's no longer in pain, but I know that won't take the sting of losing him anyway. All I can say is where he is *is* better and I'm sorry that takes him away from us, for now."

She said "From *us* for now", but they both knew there would be no "for now" for her. Just Colin. That undid him.

Over the decades, that private back parking lot became no stranger to grief, but the raw emotion and tears shed that morning was so genuine it could be felt for days to come.

Not wanting to unburden all of his emotion with an audience, Colin asked for some time alone, and there he spent the rest of the morning lamenting the loss of his dog as the world, one that didn't seem to care about one person's grief, one that had to continue on or it never would, one that knew nothing of another's pain or joy, carried on around him as it always had.

CHAPTER 24

August continued hot and muggy, and the county fair drew closer. Mrs. Minton had and had not responded to his sticky note. The only response she offered him was in the form of a sticky note of her own which read, "Have a little faith." Even with it left unsigned, he knew it must have been from her, for who else would have handwriting so neat it looked like a computer had typed it?

The Friday before the fair was here, and there was a lot to cover. The café was going to be open with only Justin stationed at the counter taking coffee orders as well as any catering and future-order requests. Being married into a big-time 4-H family, Bree would be busy for nearly the whole week, but would still be able to help cover the stand for a two-hour lunch break. There were a few other fill-in workers who would help set up and tear down the stand, but other than that it was up to Colin and Katie to keep the booth going.

Colin was able to see the layout for the fair before everything was set up. It looked like the fair started just on the other side of the church and parsonage property line. The entire road and vacant parking lots were to host all the carnival rides and games. The street branching north was for the vendors and food, and the street to the south was where all the lawn games and seating were. Right in the middle of the intersection was a makeshift pavilion to serve as the entertainment center and for announcements.

One could almost hear the shouts of happy children and smell the deep-fried fair food just looking at the place. But, for one more night, Vernon remained quiet and peaceful.

With the first day of the fair finally here, Colin got up at the normal time and headed downstairs at 4. He was met with a note on his side of the door:

Colin, I will be a little late every morning of the fair. Please get started but do NOT make the coffee. You haven't mastered that skill yet. ~Katie.

Having his coffee skills questioned, Colin swiftly put on a pot only to dump it. Kate's evaluation was right. An hour into the morning baking, Colin was still un-caffeinated and quickly falling behind schedule. Hearing the parking lot door open, he shouted over his shoulder, "Oh good, I still need to get these special-order cupcakes frosted and I haven't even started on the cream puffs. And do you know where the…"

His sentence trailed off when he turned and found a young stranger standing before him. It took Colin three or four seconds to realize that the stranger was actually Katie.

Her long, chestnut brown, wavy locks were dyed a nearly black brown and were cut short and flipped out at the ends. Her dark blue eyes with centers that starburst electric blue were now a bright, yet still realistic, green thanks to colored contact lenses. Even her signature carnation red lipstick was swapped for a neutral tone, causing her more fair skin tone to take on an almost tanned look. To top it all off, she was not wearing a single article of retro clothing or accessory.

She was a completely contemporary woman now. If he hadn't known who walked in the door, he would have never recognized her. Only her body shape and size would have given her away. There was nothing she could do to hide that from him.

"Kate…what did you do?!"

"Gee, thanks," she snorted before saying, "Not quite the reaction I was hoping for."

Colin closed his slightly hinged mouth when he realized he was staring, but there was nothing he could do about it. This surprise seemed to have rattled his brain. All Colin could think to say was, "It's just so, um, different. Like it's not even you."

With the most 'Duh' expression she could muster, Katie couldn't keep the smirk from her voice. "That is the point, Colin. Do you like it?"

In fact, he did. Very much so. Not because she looked more appealing, but because she didn't look like a woman whom he associated with being dead. The change of appearance was already playing tricks on his mind.

"Yes, I do. And a new look needs a new name. Who are you going as?"

Katie shrugged at the question and said, "Just Katie. I am supposed to promote my café, remember? If anyone asks how I could have established the place so long ago, I'll just say my grandma did and I'm named after her. I mean, like you said, I don't look like *me*, so I shouldn't have to worry too much about someone recognizing me."

"Oh." Colin was surprised at how simple her explanation was and how easily anyone would believe it. "That should work. But can I ask something else? Can I please have coffee now?"

Laughing her sing-song laugh, Katie side-stepped Colin and went straight into making coffee. For how distracted he was by her new look, the two of them quickly caught up on the morning's orders. The cupcakes, it turned out, were a gift to the local salon owner, Ashley, who was willing to get up early every morning to do Katie's cut and color. She would still get paid for her time, but nothing says thank you like fresh baked goods. Forgetting she would Cinderella back into herself tomorrow morning, Colin didn't at first realize how much work would have to go into keeping this charade up.

Boxing up the food to take to the booth, Colin had the hardest time keeping his eyes off Katie. Being able to cut the tension with a knife, Katie decided it best to talk in the privacy of the kitchen rather than in the middle of the fair. "Colin, what do you want to ask now?"

Colin flushed and looked down at the muffin he had accidentally double-wrapped. Undoing his mistake, he said, "I'm just still a bit shocked by the new look, that's all, and I'm not sure what to think about it. Why did you pick that get-up?"

Katie dampened her smile and explained, "Oh. Well, a few years ago Ashley was going through her hair training. She needed quite a bit of practice before anyone whose hair *didn't* grow back would let her touch them. It took a while, but by the time she was done practicing on me and the family, she became a very good hairdresser. This was one of the looks I liked the most, and if I could keep it, I would."

Finishing up with the last muffin, Colin murmured, "Well, even if you were given a choice, I wouldn't change a thing." Accepting the compliment, or at least taking it as only a compliment, the two of them continued decorating and loading their wagons with goods for the fair until Arnie's delivery truck came for the usual delivery items.

Despite him finding Katie's normal appearance to be beautiful, Colin kept finding himself stealing a peek at the new Katie in the kitchen. The smirk she gave him the second time he was caught was meant to be humorous, but he didn't like how her makeover was making him more and more nervous the longer they were in the confining kitchen. Thank goodness the whole week was promised to be a busy one.

Ready to transport their baked goods, Colin and Katie stepped out into the bright morning with their pull-wagons, courtesy of Roy, and about half of the treats they hoped to sell that day. Seeming to have appeared from thin air, the block just to the east of their front door had been changed into the picturesque, small-town fair just like Colin imagined. The street was littered with miniature carnival rides they had to maneuver through, but at least the rides were stationary for now.

The north street where the food vendors and booths were set up was the most crowded section, due to all the setup. At first, Colin didn't like that the bigger food trucks were first, between the booths and carnival rides, but then he realized this was on purpose. It allowed those selling goods and wares the ability to converse with the customer, whereas with most food trucks a simple point does the trick.

Since Katie was more particular about the placement of items, Colin took some time to wander to the south side, past the lawn games, where the more fair-oriented games were located. Anything from goldfish in a bag to a panda the size of a middle school child could be won through feats of strength, expert marksmanship, and sheer dumb luck. Being on the competitive side, Colin knew it was only a matter of time before he would be back with a pocket full of small bills.

Amazed by all this little town seems to do, Colin was not surprised to hear this little fair would be bringing no less than four hundred non-local families to their small village every day. Not a bad number for a town that, according to Katie, only had 788 residents.

Arriving at their booth, both Colin and Katie were glad to see they were situated between an out-of-towner selling organic produce from his family farm and The Sweets Shop. Being a full-fledged local now, Colin had been in the candy store numerous times, always amazed by the owner's creativity and childhood charm. The Hansel and Gretel exterior was just that, however, the inside was a confectionery dream with no witch to be found.

Marcy, the most personable chocolatier as well as the owner of the store, was to monitor her stand in the mornings before one of her employees took over, allowing her to enjoy the fair with her family in the afternoons. After needing some time to get over the shock of Katie's full body change, Marcy was delighted the two of them could participate in the festivities. The two women spent most of the set-up time in hushed voices, swapping stories of when Katie used to babysit her and all the shenanigans she would get into. This was made even more humorous, as Marcy was easily in her early 30's. As interested as he was in hearing snip bits of the past, Colin couldn't keep from glancing over to their other neighbor.

A handsome man around his late 20s and at his peak physical state, the tall, dark, broad man with a hint of an Italian accent to their left was Shane Mariani. For not being able to speak with him much before the fair crowd converged on their little town, Colin still gleaned quite a lot of information. Shane's family had moved to a large plot of land near the northern border of the state, and he followed county fairs around to help supplement their family's income. That Shane instantly had an eye for Katie was obvious, and Colin couldn't tell if Katie was truly ignorant or just playing the part. Neither encouraging nor discouraging his more than flirtatious conversations with her between customers, Katie simply stayed the same generous and kind person she was.

There was no hope for it, Colin was jealous. Or was he simply being overprotective? Either way, Colin did not like Shane, despite how nice of a person he was to everyone. Whatever feelings Colin had towards the other man turned into guilt really fast. Katie was not his to claim. No man would claim her, for who would have a dead woman? Startled at his own realization, Colin was able to understand a little more the depth of pain Roy told him about. How she must have felt when Colin's father never returned to Vernon.

By the time Bree and one of her sons came to relieve Colin and Katie for lunch, Colin was quite fed up with Shane and Katie was quite fed up with Colin. Jealousy didn't look good on him. There was only one thing for them to do, go for a walk and see the sights.

Since it wasn't that big of a fair to see, they were already on their second circuit before Colin began to forget about their "macho" neighbor. It didn't take Katie quite as long to forgive Colin. Enjoying the sights, she couldn't keep the wonder from her voice. "Wow, it has been a long time since I've been to the fair. They come here every year, and I think I was tired of having to hide or keep an eye out for anyone who would recognize me."

Colin chanced another side-glance at her as they passed the fair games, reminding himself again to bring some money tomorrow and show off to Katie. "Your own mother wouldn't recognize you. Shoot, you even scared the crap out of me in the kitchen this morning."

"Then how did you know it was me?"

Thinking back on how he identified her solely on the build of her body, he thought it best to fudge the answer a bit. "I knew the only person who had a key was you. And you're short."

Not fully buying it, she led two of them to the food stands to finally get some lunch. After dining on Cajun cuisine, funnel cakes, and ice cream scoops the size of baseballs, the two found themselves at the pavilion where an announcer proclaimed a people's food choice award was to be given out Friday evening along with a plaque and a $500 reward.

"Oh, that could be so good for my café!" exclaimed Katie.

"You're a shoo-in to win. I mean, who doesn't want to see their favorite babysitter take home such a grand prize?" Colin's smile reached his eyes, and he realized he wasn't so upset anymore. Although that could have something to do with the ice cream he was still working on.

Katie playfully hit him on the arm and said, "That's not funny. And I'm not sure I could beat The Sweets Shop anyway."

"Yeah, I think you're right. You might as well throw the towel in now."

Seeing his sarcasm as a challenge, Katie took it upon herself to enter both her and The Sweets Shop into the pool of competing food vendors. But Katie knew she wouldn't win. She never won. Too much publicity. But Colin didn't need to know that.

Satisfied with her actions, Colin stretched his over-stuffed body as if he was just about to do some heavy lifting and said, "Now that you have a healthy dose of competition in your veins to go along with all that food, let's head back. I think our lunch break is already over."

Katie thought he sounded a little high and mighty like he had just saved the day. Well, she couldn't have him going back to their stand with such an inflated sense of self. Putting a hand on her hip, Katied replied, "Okay, but we still need to talk about Shane later." That seemed to do the trick.

So she knew. *"Of course she knew,"* he thought, *"it's not like I was exactly covert about the whole thing."*

Walking back to their stand in a lesser mood, Colin thought Shane seemed a little too excited to see them approach. With a toothy grin and a slight lilt to his words, Shane called to them while they were still a few stands away. "Oh good, you're back! I was wondering if you could help me with something." Not missing the fact Shane was only speaking to Katie, Colin cleared his throat when they finally reached their stand and gave him a look Colin hoped could be taken as intimidating. Shane gave Colin a single nod and nonchalantly said, "Hey, Colin." Nope, it didn't work.

Looking back at Katie, Shane said, "So, you two live in town, right? It's the strangest thing. I usually stay wherever the fair is, but there are no hotels nearby. Do you know where the closest place to stay is?"

"As a matter of fact, I do." Katie's overly-happy response surprised both of the men; Shane in a good way and Colin in a devastating one.

Colin and Shane unitedly asked, "You do?"

Katie gave her award-winning smile, but before she could answer, it was someone else who responded, "Of course! Colin can take you in."

Colin turned slowly around to see it came from none other than Roy. He was thankful later that Shane and Katie couldn't see his mouth opening and closing like a gasping fish out of water.

Katie was the only one to respond. "You can, Colin?" She asked out of courtesy. She already knew the answer.

"Sure he can." Said Roy happily, patting Colin on the back maybe a little too hard. "It's a family thing, helping out how we can. You would be surprised how much free lodging and food can really help change a person's fortunes around." Roy looked up at Colin just then, expectantly. It was strange to Colin, feeling so manipulated by Roy like that, but knowing how much free (or at least ridiculously cheap) lodging and food really *could* change someone's life, there really was only one answer to give. Even if he didn't want to.

Locking eyes and nodding his head at the older man, Colin accepted the challenge. "You know Roy, you're right." Turning to Shane, Colin extended his hand, "Shane, you're welcome to stay with me, but I have to warn you all I have is a couch and I need to be up by 3:30 for work."

Looking at Shane's face, you would have thought he won the lottery. "Really?! Oh, wow! That, that's… I really appreciate it. Thank you both so much." After shaking hands with all three of them Shane turned to help one of the fair-goers eyeing his stand. Colin was surprised the man didn't even flinch at the 3:30 morning wake-up call he threatened, but it was quickly overshadowed by pride. He had just been called one of the family.

Roy told Colin to make sure the "young lad" had a parking spot behind the café for his produce truck but then turned to Katie with a somewhat less if not downright disturbed, demeanor. "Katie, can I have a word with you?"

Katie and Roy walked away. From his point of view, Colin could see neither of them spoke until they were out of eyesight. Also, from his point of view, Colin could see it was a terrible time for her to leave because they were getting quite a line forming at the stand.

"Excuse me, Colin," came Mrs. Minton from the front of the café line. "If you don't mind, I'll be taking one of those cinnamon rolls now. Or do I have to go somewhere else to get some decent service?"

"Empty threats, Minton. You know as well as I that there isn't any other place to get cinnamon rolls like these." Chuckling as he took her money, Mrs. Minton whispered something for only his ears to hear, taking all the myth out of the situation. "It looks like you're going to play host for the week, but you and I need to have a little talk once this fair is done." With no explanation, Mrs. Minton turned, leaving Colin with his line of customers, but before he

could attend to any of them, he whispered to himself,
"What is it with these townspeople and their cryptic
messages."

CHAPTER 25

Katie was not seen for the rest of the night, and since he was playing host to a man he didn't even particularly like, Colin couldn't just leave and go find her.

Even though the fair was still in full swing, the men called it quits at 7 pm and headed towards the apartment. Roy or Helen must have wanted to show their appreciation for Colin's help and had left dinner for the two of them, courtesy of the downstairs café. It didn't take long for either of them to eat, set up the couch, and then sit in a most awkward silence, unsure what to do next.

Shane was the first to speak.. "So…was Katie only going to work this evening, or do you think something happened?" Seeing this was asked more out of concern than personal interest, Colin let out a deep sigh he didn't even know he had and decided that, if Shane was going to be spending a whole week with Colin, the best thing he could do is tell the most truth he was able to.

"You know, I'm not really sure. It isn't like Kate to get pulled aside by Roy and not come back. Something must have happened."

"I hope everything's fine. Who was that man?" The concern and curiosity was evident.

"Oh, Roy? He's Kate's father." Everyone must have forgotten to mention that little detail. No wonder Shane was a little shaken over Katie's disappearance.

Shane's brows knit together as he said, "Well if my father pulled me aside like that and I didn't appear again all day, that means something bad must have happened. Do you think someone is hurt?"

Injuries were not exactly uncommon in the Brigham family. Just last week Katie was distracted and burned her wrist on a hot oven. Thankfully she healed. Colin's burn the day after? It was still stinging. Shaking his head, Colin said, "No, if someone was really hurt, I would have heard about it."

With that, the two of them sat for a few minutes in the living room, Shane on his temporary bed and Colin on the stuffed chair.

Shane looked around the small apartment, trying to find something to distract him or talk about. When he could find nothing, he looked back at Colin and said, "So, you and Katie. ..Or is it Kate?"

"It's really Kathleen. Everyone calls her Katie, but she's Kate to me." Colin couldn't remember when he started to change her name, all he knew was that she was and would forever be Kate to him.

"Huh," Shane said with a contemplative nod before continuing, "So, you and Katie. Are you…?"

"Oh god, this is happening now?" were Colin's screaming thoughts. If this was how the first night was going to go, Colin didn't know how he would get through the entire week with this man.

Interpreting his slightly reddened face wrongly, Shane poked, "Well?"

"Well," Colin tried to think of a tactful way of explaining and failed, "that's sort of hard to explain."

Shane chuckled. "What's hard? You're either seeing each other or not."

Instead of looking out the window where all the fun and excitement was still happening, Colin turned towards the door; the way to the café, and mumbled, "You'd be surprised."

They sat in silence for a little while before realization dawned on Shane's face and he asked, a little too enthusiastically, "Oh, you're like, in the friend zone, aren't you?"

The friend zone? Hearing that phrase made Colin think back to dopey high school boys tripping over girls who were out of their league. Or a poor soul, falling for a girl who toyed with his heart and manipulated him into giving into her demands, never reciprocating physical affection before pushing him away when a better victim came along. That was offensive, and worse, made Colin think Shane viewed him as a wuss.

Colin responded roughly, "No, I'm not in the friend zone!"

Unconvinced, but willing to leave the man his dignity, Shane challenged, "Then what is it?"

In life, the truth is the best answer. But when you can't give the whole truth, sticking to it as closely as possible is the next best thing. Especially when you want to keep the facts straight but lead the other astray.

Giving a big sigh, Colin worked out a reasonable answer. "Kate used to be engaged to a family member of mine who is now dead. I love her, and if things were different, I would definitely pursue a relationship, but they're not. That's just the way it is. But, I'll take what I can get and be happy with it."

The other man seemed to deflate a little. "I'm sorry man, that sucks. Was it your brother?"

With as solomn a face as he could manage, Colin replied, "He was closer than a brother. More of a father figure, really."

Shaking his head, Shane laid down on his makeshift bed and let out a sigh of his own. "Well, you're doing right by him. I can respect someone with your integrity."

Colin was beginning to like this guy.

"So…do you mind if I ask her out?"

Never mind.

"Well, yes I kind of do. But it's not like I can stop you, can I?"

A knock at the door interrupted Shane's reply. Charlie didn't wait for an invitation but let himself in, appearantly angry. "Seriously dude, do you never check your phone? Oh," Charlie finally noticed Shane on the couch, "Hey I'm Charlie, Katie's brother." Turning back to Colin he continued with a little more caution, "Katie had an unexpected *incident* and couldn't make it back to the booth today. She's been trying to call you all afternoon and when she couldn't, she sent me to come find you. Thanks a lot for that."

Colin dug through his back pocket, and all three of them saw it was dead. Charlie's anger understandably resurfaced.

"Are you kidding me?! I'm missing out on a hot date with a leggy blonde over a freakin' dead battery?! You owe me, Colin."

Shane had sat up again and was watching the interaction between Charlie and Colin before interrupting and asking, "Um, sorry, but, is everything all right with Katie?"

Colin was wondering this too but didn't quite know how to ask Charlie and get an honest answer. Colin also was distracted by Charlie's comment about a leggy blonde. Was it a joke, or did this bad boy Brigham have crazy charisma with out-of-town ladies?

"Yeah, no worries. Just an order mix-up that took a while to untangle. Nothing but a migraine and copious amounts of margarine to deal with."

Charlie lied so convincingly, but Colin knew it was a lie. The answer seemed to put the younger man at ease though, and he settled himself back down on the couch. Walking Charlie to the door, Colin whispered, "What really happened?"

In an equally quiet whisper, Charlie answered, "She's a bit out of sorts. Roy needed her help at the store moving some things in the back and a box fell on her. She took a hit to the face and it left a good cut on her forehead." When Colin's eyebrows raised, Charlie held up a hand as a warning not to make a scene in front of Shane. Still keeping his voice down, Charlie said, "It's nothing serious, just noticeable… especially when it disappears tomorrow. So, she's held up at home until then."

That wasn't the best news, but compared to what it could have been? Katie would take a boring day at home over being discovered.

Charlie was nearly out the door before turning to say, "One more thing. She said to stop trying to make the coffee. Good night!" and with that, the man was gone.

CHAPTER 26

Colin's alarm jerked him awake. Covered with a fine layer of sweat, he hurried out of bed to find his couch was indeed occupied by another man who proclaimed at least physical attraction for his Kate. His Kate? Where did that come from? Still trying to process how he felt about that, Colin quickly readied himself for the day and was in the kitchen making mini cinnamon chip rolls before 4 am even came.

Around 4:45, Shane followed his nose downstairs to a most aromatic kitchen. Colin knew he would, so he memorized the recipe to keep Katie's precious recipe book from being vulnerable to snooping eyes.

"Wow, that smells good. Trade you some produce for a roll."

It didn't take Colin long to agree. They were always needing produce or fruit for one thing or another, and Colin saw Shane's produce stand yesterday. His goods were top-notch. Returning from his truck minutes later, Shane brought in a few onions, leeks, and potatoes, as well as some berries and Honeycrisp apples. "Will this do?"

"Shoot, for that, consider yourself set for the whole week." Throwing a roll to Shane, the two sealed their deal.

"Great!" Shane said with a mouth full of warm cinnamon bread. He looked around the kitchen a little before gesturing towards the coffee maker, "Mind if I start some coffee?"

Katie was the only person able to make a decent pot of the kitchen's ancient coffee maker, and Colin was going to tell Shane to wait for Katie, but he was too late. No sooner had the first drips begun to fall when a flurry burst through the door. "I'm so sorry, Colin. It shouldn't take this long to get ready, but I'm out of sorts this morning, and-" Seeing it wasn't just Colin in the kitchen, Katie nervously laughed and started pulling at her again short, dark hair and foreign clothes. Wearing black, fitted Bermuda shorts to accent her hair, Katie expertly paired them with a flowy, cream, and floral top. But what Colin liked most about this getup was seeing her tie it all together with her signature carnation red lipstick. He was surprised how one day without it made him miss seeing it on her so much.

Both men greeted her at the same time.

"Good morning, Kate." "Wow, you look great."

Blushing a little, Katie answered, "Good morning, gentlemen." Then her smile shifted into a more reprimanding smirk. "Who made the coffee?"

Colin's response was a little too quick and full of that tattle-tale taunt, "Shane did!" A bit confused, Shane turned to Katie. "Oh, I'm sorry, I wasn't told not to. Are you upset about it?"

Katie put down her things and grabbed a hair net before answering, "Well, it's not so much that you made it, but whether you made it *well*." Pouring a cup and taking a tentative sip, unspoiled, Katie can't help the smirk that turns up the right corner of her mouth. "If you can make a pot like this, you guys can go ahead and start your caffeine fix without me."

Shane beamed from the praise and it ignited a flame of envy inside Colin. He was still banned from even touching the coffee pot without her around. Seeing how uncomfortable he was, Katie decided to put Colin out of his misery.

"Thank you, Shane, for the lovely coffee, but would you please excuse us while Colin and I continue getting ready for the day? Since you are not an employee, I really don't feel comfortable having you in the kitchen while we are working."

"Oh, sure thing! I'll be out of your hair in just a second." Grabbing a cup of joe to go, Shane also grabbed another cinnamon roll and headed upstairs to shower.

Once he was gone, Katie let out a deep breath and frantically searched the kitchen countertops. "Where is it?" Knowing what she was talking about, Colin pulled out her precious book from the center island and held it up to alleviate her panic. "Don't worry Kate, I would never let anyone take these from you. I even memorized a few recipes so it wouldn't be out."

"You did that for me?" Colin could see the tenderness in her eyes and the great relief of having her book safe. It made Colin's insides heat and his stomach do a little flip.

"Well yeah. I know how much they mean to you." Colin said, not looking Katie in the eye.

Trying to get back to work full-steam, but losing to his curiosity, Colin asked, "So, what happened this morning that made you so upset?"

Katie stopped stirring the muffin batter she was working on and said, seriously, "Hopefully nothing happened yesterday. Mom and Dad got the weirdest letter from a realtor's office. It gave them a date for a home inspector to look over the house before it was sold."

Shaking her head, Katie scoffed at the idea before continuing with the muffin batter. "But that's crazy, my father would never sell it! I mean, how could he? Hopefully, it's just a prank. Either way, The Minton is on the hunt, and will likely uncover some scam. Honestly, what do people think of these days?"

This sounded more serious than her nonchalant attitude warranted, but, as she said, this was most likely a bored teenage prank or a scam to steal small-town properties. Pushing this aside, he got to the question he really wanted to ask.

"And….what about the cut on your face? Were you all right?"

Katie was already filling the muffin tins with expert symmetry. She started of with a calm reply, but her voice had a bit of a bite to it by the time she was finished. "Oh, yeah. That was only a minor accident. Mom was a bit more worried over it all than the rest of us, so I humored her and stayed in my apartment. But what's the deal with you not answering my calls?!"

Colin shrugged apologetically and said, "Dead phone."

"Oh. Okay then." His lack of emotion and simple answer caught Katie's attention. The two of them were very efficient worker, and when Katie though back to the time before she had a helper in the kitchen, she was amazed she even got it all done. But this morning, there was barely anything left for Katie to do. Taking a closer look at her kitchen companion, Katie noticed Colin's eyes were a little more bloodshot than usual, and he was sloppy on his morning shave. "How long have you been working?"

"I've been here a little over an hour and a half, but I've been up since before two." Katie arched an eyebrow, hoping that was question enough. "Shane's a nice guy and all, but it was a little difficult being around him last night. And when I woke up early this morning, I couldn't fall back asleep, thinking about how to pull off the story I fed him last night about you."

"Oh really? Wait, what story?" She couldn't help laughing a little in anticipation. It wasn't easy coming up with excuses or back stories, and she was curious to see what Colin came up with.

"The story where you had friend-zoned me after my brother Bill died."

Wide-eyed, Katie whispered, "No, you didn't."

Flustered, Colin said, "Oh, I did! What else was I supposed to say?"

Closing her gaping mouth, Katie said, "I don't know, but not that! Wouldn't it have made more sense to say we were a couple?"

Colin all but yelled, "I had that! I came this close to calling you mine, but I wasn't sure what you would think about that. Plus, I wouldn't know how to pull off a believable relationship without…you know." Colin gestured between the two of them before groaning running his hands over his face.

Katie did know, and she couldn't keep the laugh that came out at the thought of it. But what Colin didn't know was that the laugh was to cover up the hurt he would have seen in her eyes if his face wasn't covered. Taking her mirth the wrong way, Colin slowly lowered his hands and said, "It's not funny, Kate."

"Really, you considered us a couple?"

"Yeah, but I sure as hell can't now!"

Seeing he was upset over this whole ordeal, Katie decided to defuse the bomb about to explode. As gently as she could, Katie said, "It's true, saying that would have made things more complicated. Either way, I would have preferred you not bringing Bill up."

Colin's scoff told her he didn't like it any more than she did. "He thinks our *accurately* perceived platonic relationship means you're available, and trust me, that guy won't be one to give up easily."

"And if I don't give him reason to give up?"

Now it was Colin's time to gape-stare. "Why would you say that?"

"Well… you know it's not exactly easy having no one to…be with. To care about *that way*. Even if it is temporary." Katie could feel her face warm at the very though. Seeing it, Colin flipped out.

"Whoa, stop right there. I don't want to talk about this. I *really* don't want to talk about this. And we don't have the time. And he's right upstairs. And--" Katie thankfully interrupted him.

"Colin, *Colin*! Don't worry, I'm not being serious. At least not with macho-man Shane."

Katie couldn't help but laugh at Colin's face. It was comically mad and joyful at the same time, and Katie realized she took too much pleasure out of his reaction.

"Don't worry about him, Colin. I'll let him down gently."

The Sweets Shop and Katie's Café were becoming the most popular stop on the food strip. With a near-constant line of customers, Katie had no time to talk with Shane, and it wasn't going to happen during their lunch break either. There was one last secret Katie had about her town, one she never planned on sharing, until today.

CHAPTER 27

Katie didn't answer any of Colin's questions as they walked down Gunther Street. In fact, she didn't say anything at all. They moved away from the happy screams and the smell of deep-fried food, the street eerily empty, and once they rounded the corner between the bank and Living Color, everything and everyone seemed to fade and die away.

Colin knew of the river that oozed through the countryside. He saw it upon his arrival to town, but since Michigan is known for many things, mosquitos being one of them, he usually stayed away. He also had no real reason to be near the river, seeing as it marked the northern town boundary where it crossed under Gunther Road. As far as Colin knew, there was no way to get to that river.

Katie finally broke her silence after they stepped off the paved path and onto a hidden dirt one. "I come here most summer evenings to be alone. I like watching the water and letting my thoughts wander. And then, on particularly hot days, I even get in the water a little. It's freezing, but it's one of the few things I loved so much from my childhood that I can still do."

"How can that be," Colin asked, "I thought the river was the town boundary."

Colin couldn't see her, but he could hear the faint smile in her voice as they continued walking. "On the north side of Gunther Rd, yes. But do you see those red posts over there, on the far side of the bank?"

Colin would have never noticed them unless pointed out. There, posted every twenty yards or so, were old, wooden posts; their red paint so weathered and peeled from time, it was amazing Colin could even tell they were originally red.

"Some of our town boundaries are obvious, like the river north of Gunther Road, and the highway. But even before the fire, posts were erected to distinguish town lines. It could have been because of something important like who had voting rights or as petty as determining who got city utility benefits or not, who knows. I'm not surprised you haven't seen any, since most people have removed them from their property, but no one technically owns this land, so here, where the boundary isn't as obvious, are the remaining posts."

The path they were on was rough and well hidden by overgrown plants that Colin didn't necessarily wish to push aside. It looked as though it was only worn by Katie and a select few who, over the years, had discovered it. Sloping downward, they soon emerged into a small clearing along the bank and Colin was surprised that this place was but a few minutes away from the everyday of Vernon.

There was a clearing, and amid it sat an old metal park bench facing the water. Along the edge of the clearing were daylilies, lilacs, and a whole host of flowers Colin was unqualified to identify, but that didn't keep him from admiring them. It was private and beautiful, and it allowed the two to just sit there for some time, enjoying the peace and each other's company.

Spying another marker across the river, closer this time, Colin noticed that the bench they sat on looked older than the town boundary posts. Colin voiced as much.

"Oh, no, they aren't original. Back in the 80's, there was a bit of a scare. Charlie and Jack were out messing around with some of their toys. I think it was a go-kart or something. Anyway, they didn't see the boundary marker until they were right up on it. They jerked the wheel so hard they flipped. After that, Roy paid to have any of them not on private property redone. Katie looked at the red marker and sighed. "Too bad he didn't think of how quickly red gets weather-worn. I told him he should have chosen a hardier color."

They sat in continued silence for a long time before Colin ased, "Kate, can I ask you an awkward question?"

Katie couldn't help but smirk as she asked, "Funny awkward, like that time you asked if I could walk through walls, or seriously awkward like that time you asked if someone has ever tried to re-kill me?" She already knew the answer before he said anything,

"More like the second one."

"Wow, you really know how to spoil a good moment."

Katie let out a sigh, hoping they could have at least eaten something or gotten through the busy afternoon before getting into the heavy stuff. "I knew something was bothering you. What's on your mind?"

"It's about…other guys."

Katie couldn't help it. She laughed. A lot. And not her sing-song tinkle, but a real guttural, bringing tears to your eyes kind of laugh.

Colin, a bit embarrassed now, could have kicked himself for opening his mouth. "Forget it, never mind."

"No, oh no, Colin I'm sorry. I was expecting something like this, especially with Shane around, but it still caught me completely by surprise."

Colin waited for Katie to compose herself before charging on. "So, have you been with Anyone since my dad?"

That was a tough question for her to answer. "Well, I mean, there's been a few guys but… well it's not like I can have anything serious or long-term with anyone. It's like Jack's problem with Lisa. Sooner or later, he would figure out I'm not getting any older, or there would be an accident and I'll wake up in the morning without a scratch on me."

"Yeah, but what if he's okay with you being, you know, dead, and wants a future anyway?"

Meeting this question with a doubting look, she got straight to the heart of the problem. "Well, then there's the whole… necrophilia thing. I mean, think about it. I *am* dead, and he would be willing, you know, *to be* with a dead person. None of the guys I've been with over the years knew that part about me and for a *really good* reason. I couldn't purposefully traumatize someone like that."

Knowing Katie like he did, he knew she was telling the truth. She wouldn't willingly hurt someone, hurt Bill, like that. Thinking about his father, it was hard for Colin to admit that not coming back to town after all, leaving Katie heartbroken for years, might have actually been the best thing that could have happened to Bill. And the heartbreak Katie had over his father not coming back would have been nothing compared to him coming back and choosing to leave her again.

With a bit of cheekiness still left in her, Katie interrupted Colin's thoughts and asked, "So, have you ever thought about us? You and I…?"

Colin cleared his throat before tackling that question. "Um, there's been a time or two. You looking like a completely different person doesn't help any, by the way. But you're right. You know, about the whole… necrophilia thing." Colin felt so awkward saying that last part out loud, it barely came out as a whisper.

Katie laughed her second deep, belly laugh that afternoon. It seemed she was laughing more often than not these days, and he was hoping this new side of her would become the norm.

Colin began to feel like her laugh was lasting a bit longer than necessary, and his feeling of embarrassment was turning to defensiveness. "Okay, you can stop now. Yes, okay, I have found, and still find you to be…a very attractive woman. Inside and out. I just don't think I should be having those therapy-inducing thoughts about you."

Kate's laughter died fast with that last bit. Colin could see that what he said hurt her, but the colored contacts kept him from seeing how deep that cut went. Wanting to be as honest as he could with this woman, but also knowing there was a definite physical boundary that was uncrossable, Colin silently promised himself, no matter what, he would not lose this woman. He wouldn't become his father.

"Come here." Pulling Katie off of the bench with him, Colin stood and wrapped his arms around her in the most fierce, compassionate embrace he could give. After a few seconds, he fully opened his heart to this woman in his arms. "You know, we can't be together, and that sucks. It really, really sucks. And you have a past with my father, which is also weird. I will get older every day, and you won't, and that will be hard for both of us. But the hardest part for me, right now, is knowing we'll never have anything physical between us. Nothing more than what we have right now. And like I said, that really sucks."

His blurting seemed to be getting nowhere fast, and he was pretty sure Katie had already thought about and processed all of this. Not wanting to make things worse, but also not wanting to end on such a sour note, Colin held Katie back enough to look into her face and confessed, "But you know, despite all of that, I can't help falling for you anyway."

That comment shouldn't have made Katie perk up as much as she did, but it couldn't be helped. When Colin saw it, he wasn't sure if he felt proud or guilty. Making sure she didn't assume too much, Colin had to fix this. "Well, I mean, let's be honest. Physical boundaries are good to have in complicated relationships, and this is no exception, right? Guys and girls simply can't be friends, but that doesn't mean they have to be animals. Or am I misquoting a self-help book out there somewhere?"

The laugh he had hoped to get from her came out half-hearted and a bit strangled. Something told Colin that neither of them would get what they'd hoped out of today's adventure.

They would have stayed in that clearing longer, staring at the calm river and listening to the faraway fair cries, had it not been for the alarm Katie set on her phone, signaling the end of their lunch break. Getting up and heading out, Colin had one more thing to say, "Thank you for bringing me here Kate. No matter what I said earlier, I do think of you as mine."

Katie couldn't help but look down and blush. It was adorable, and Colin wished he could have seen it head-on. "And as weird as it is, you're mine too." Looking up at him after her confession, the two continued making their way back to their booth, knowing they would have a love--no matter how unconventional--to last their lifetimes.

CHAPTER 28

Days usually pass by quickly for those in small towns; especially those with repetitive schedules. But the last day of the fair came all too quickly. Although he had professed growing feelings for her, Katie and Colin continued working side by side as before. In fact, now that their feelings were shared, as well as why they couldn't hope for more, work became even more enjoyable. All week, the only unpleasantness in his day came in the threat of a very attractive, hard-working farmer in the booth next to them.

Shane spent the better half of every evening asking about Katie. Colin had to remind himself that it wasn't the young man's fault for being so hung up on her, and with the lies Colin fed him, it was only right for Colin to answer the poor man as honestly as possible.

Sometimes, the questions made Colin grit his teeth.

"So, have you ever tried to Kiss Katie?"

"No."

"Would you go after her if Bill could somehow give you his blessing?"

"No."

Foolish, unknowing man.

Other times, the questions were quite comical.

"How old is Katie?"

"87. She looks good for her age, doesn't she?"

"C'mon, I'm serious."

Jack and Charlie never let more than a slight chuckle slip their lips when they passed by the bakery stand. It wasn't hard to see that Shane had an eye for Katie and Colin was playing defense. Colin assumed they got some sick pleasure out of the predicament Roy and Katie put him in, but no matter what, he still put on an air of politeness the whole week. That was until Shane decided to change things.

Colin should have known something was up. Shane was a little off all day, and although Colin appreciated the quiet, it made him feel uncomfortable. Then, as Katie and Colin began packing up their stand, Shane asked for a moment of Katie's time and became uncharacteristically fidgety while she put the last of the unsold goods in storage containers.

Katie knew what was about to happen, and she didn't know if she was silently elated, praying for him to ask her out, or praying for him to say he would never come around again. Both sounded tempting to hear, yet only one was fated to happen in the end.

"So, Katie, I know you and Colin turn in early, well not together, I know that, but, um…"

Colin tried not to let a smirk show. He could hear the terror in Shane's voice from where he stood a few yards off. If only the poor fool knew how hopeless his bravery would be in the end. "I hope, I was wondering, well…" For such a confident and smooth person, Colin couldn't help but feel a twinge of pity, as well as delight, while eavesdropping. "Can I at least spend the last evening with you? If you need to turn in early, I understand, but I'd kick myself forever if I didn't try."

Oh, he was good. Taking a quick glance at Katie, Colin instantly knew she wanted to say yes, but wasn't going to. Was it for her sake or his that she was hesitant? Either way, what a great woman.

It should have all ended then and there. Shane would spend one more night with Colin, moping and wondering "why?", and Colin would go back to life as normal with Katie by his side. All would be right in the world again. However, none of them knew the Charlie and Jack were within earshot to witness Shane's proposal.

Nudging Charlie, Jack quickly whispered a plan and put it into action quicker than Katie could turn the man down.

Jack and Charlie yelled in succession. "Hey, Colin! There you are. Are you coming?"

"Yeah, we've been waiting twenty minutes for you."

Confused, both Colin and Katie answered at the same time.

"Uh, you have?"

"What are you talking about?"

Jack kept it up, ending with a sly wink, "Yeah, you said you would go out with us guys tonight. It's supposed to be pretty lively at the square and I'm sure we can find a woman or two who would look mighty pretty hanging on your arm."

"You don't mind, do you, Katie? Us taking Colin here out for a night?" Charlie couldn't keep the mischievous twinkle out of his eye.

Seeing right through their plan, and pinning them with her own stare, she was forced to go along with it anyway for the sake of not making a scene. And deep down, she knew they were only doing it for her welfare. "Well, I can't really stop him, can I?" If her look wasn't sharp enough, her accusatory tone told the three of them very well how displeased she was with their interference in her affairs, despite their good intentions. Now it was Colin's turn to be hurt. She really wanted him to go out with someone else too?

Colin tried his best to convey his dislike of it all, but the more he looked around the more he noticed people glancing in their direction, and ended up stating, "Don't worry Katie, you and Shane will have a great last hurrah tonight and me and the guys will too." Hearing Colin clearly, Shane beamed while finishing up tearing down his food stand while Colin and Katie did the rest of their work in silence. Though it was awkward, the work ended all too soon, and the two groups went their separate ways. The Brigham Brothers were pros, knowing which women to talk to. The brothers were not shallow on appearances but still ended up engaging with some spectacular female specimens.

A few drinks were had. The brothers were fairly touchy, but Colin was relieved to see them not go beyond what could still be publicly displayed. Colin, on the other hand, tried to engage with the dates Jack and Charlie kept introducing him to, but the whole evening was spent thinking about Katie. His dates didn't stay around for long because of it, and that was all right with him. If they spent the whole time thinking about someone they loved being on another date, he wouldn't want to be around them either. And thinking, he did. Could Shane be expected to be a gentleman? Colin heard of people's true colors being hidden for much longer than five days. Could Kate be in danger, going out with him?

Apologizing to the overzealous woman vying for his attention, Colin excused himself despite the looks of disbelief he got from the brothers. Making his way through the crowds and noise, Colin allowed his mind to wander into some dark places. Finding his way home sooner than anticipated, Colin was surprised to see a down-hearted Shane waiting for him at the parking lot door.

"Hey" both of them greeted at the same time.

A heavy silence fell between them as Colin unlocked the door and the two men silently made their way upstairs.

In the least awkward way he could, Colin decided to break the tension. "So, how was your evening?"

"I don't get it," Shane said quickly. His voice was breathy and his eyes were distant. Although this did not exactly answer Colin's question, the wait for clarification didn't take long.

Shaking his head, Shane began to share his woe. "I thought it was going great. We went to the lawn games and people-watched at the pavilion. She asked a lot of questions, and I thought we were both having a good time. Then we were heading to get a drink and ran into some of her friends; the candy lady next to you guys and her husband."

Shane stopped for a little, allowing his mind to go back and see it all again. Colin shifted in his seat a little, bringing Shane back to the present, and he continued, "Anyway, after talking with them for a few minutes I suggested a tour of the actual town, since I have only really seen the fair and up to the grocery store next door, and she just….stopped."

Colin arched his eyebrow. "She stopped?"

"Yeah! She said I was great, and the evening was wonderful, but I should know now that nothing would ever happen between us. It was so…so…" Shane looked around the room as if trying to find the right word.

Colin suggested, "Devastating?"

"Mechanical. Like she's said it a hundred times before."

"Oh." He may have been right about that.

Shane's forlorn look shifted to one of confused irritation before saying, "And when I asked why, she made up some stupid excuse about her not going to be the same person tomorrow, or something like that."

How Kate-like, thought Colin, telling the truth but being able to lie at the same time. Her life demanded that, often. "I know this won't mean much coming from me, but it's harder for her than you think and you're better off."

Colin thought that sounded stupid, even to his own ears, and Shane's look back confirmed it. Wanting to make things better for the poor man but knowing there was nothing he could do or say, Colin instead thought about Kate and what was happening on her end.

Colin asked hesitantly, "It's your last night and all, but do you think I can go check on her? The way you're describing things doesn't sound like Kate."

"Why Kate?" snapped Shane, "Why don't you call her Katie like everyone else?"

Colin did his best to excuse Shane's retort. This man put himself out there, and Katie is a truly amazing woman. Even after being assured night and day, there was nothing but a past connection between the two of them, everyone could see there was *something* special between these two. Especially Shane.

Colin shrugged and murmured, "I don't know why. She's just my Kate."

Oops. The "my" part slipped out and slapped Shane in the face. Nodding in defeat, Shane slinks down on the couch for his last stay. "Yeah man, you can go. I'll be up and out of your hair early tomorrow. And thanks. I know it was hard not giving me crap over my feelings for Katie and letting me stay."

Colin wasn't used to being thanked for actions grudgingly done, but in the end, it was nice having the company and he realized he would let Shane stay again if given the chance.

"Night, Shane. It wasn't that bad having you, really. And if you're ever in town again, let me know."

With that, Colin slid out into the evening, leaving a dejected and oddly welcomed Shane to the comfort of the empty apartment. Time would tell if this was the last time Shane would occupy this space.

Colin knew it was wrong to leave Shane rejected and alone, especially on his last night, but knowing something really bad must have happened to Katie for her to act that way overrode his conscience and pushed him onward. Katie meant more to Colin than being a good host anyway.

The Brigham's residence played host to the fair, it being practically on their front lawn every year. This made it difficult to get to when not in a festive mood, taking a back road and only coming into the light when required. Checking the front door first, Colin was relieved to find it unlocked.

He didn't quite know what to expect. The last time he was in this building, Dually died. The memory enveloped him, flushing out all other sensations. The sights, sounds, and smells of the fair all faded away and he was back to that night. Colin gave the pain some time. At least, that was everyone's advice, but he didn't give it very long. Pushing down the unwanted feelings, Colin navigated the hall until he stood at Katie's front door.

Colin should have known better than to knock without knowing what he was getting into first, but, as with most mistakes, hindsight is 20/20. His second knock was met with heavy steps and an exasperated sigh before the door flew open. Katie must have been expecting someone else because as soon as her eyes met his, the anger gave way to something else. If he could describe it, he would have called her guarded.

Not wanting him to come inside, but also not wanting to turn him away, Katie stood in the doorway teetering between the two options. Colin cleared his throat quietly before asking, "Can I come in? Just to talk, I promise." That last bit was tacked on at the end. He didn't know why he even said it. What else would they do?

Katie, as tired emotionally as she looked physically, nodded, crossed her arms, and silently moved to the side, granting Colin access. It wasn't long ago since he had last been there, but he also took no notice of the place that eventful night. In fact, until recently, he didn't even wonder what her housing unit looked like, but her choice of decoration perfectly personified who she was.

Like its owner, the small living space had an air of elegance. The furniture and decorations were minimalist, with random splashes of color in the form of a peacock blue or fiesta orange picture frame or bright red teapot peaking around the corner from the kitchen. Without being able to put his finger on it, the small space also gave off the feeling of adventure.

Taking a closer look, Colin noticed there were no people in the colorful frames littering the walls, but they were instead all of landscapes and architecture. The places were striking, bold, majestic, and melancholy. He didn't need to ask to know each frame held a place where she longed to be. But the pictures would have to wait.

"This place suits you," Colin said, turning around and taking his settings in.

"It should. I've had decades to decorate it." This line came out flat and lifeless but sent a deafening warning to Colin. *"What happened to make you so closed off? Did Shane do something to hurt you? Are you mad at me or the world? Will you just talk to me?"* All those thoughts rushed through his mind, one on top of the other, causing his anxiety to increase every second the strained silence went on.

Colin didn't do well with anxiety and desperately needed to put his suspicions to rest. Shifting from one foot to the other, Colin wasn't sure he would say things the right way, but he had to try. "Kate, what happened tonight? Did Shane try to…?"

Seeing where he was going with this slapped just enough life into Katie to see things from his point of view. Untangling herself from her arms, she waved his suspicions away. "No Colin, nothing like that" Then, with no grace or poise, Katie trudged to the couch, flopping down in a way only someone sporting oversized sweatpants and a hoodie could, and let out another exasperated sigh.

Where anxiety was, frustration replaced it. But it wasn't Colin who let his feelings be known first. "What are you doing here?" Taken aback by the snippy question, Colin's laugh had a hint of sarcasm in it.

"C'mon Kate, the guy is staying with me. No thanks to you."

Tears she didn't even know she had charged to the frontline. Pulling her knees up to her chest, and plopping her head on them, Katie pulled her hoodie hood overhead for an added layer of protection. She was a fortress determined to remain unscathed from the internal battle raging on.

Muffling something unintelligible, Colin asked her to repeat it. Lifting her head oh so slightly to oblige, Katie asked, "What did Shane say?"

With as little emotion as he could, Colin said, "That you were a confusing robot."

Fully lifting her head with the most puzzled look, Colin could tell some tears had escaped, leaving her eyes red and irritated from their contact. Colin continued gently, "I'm kidding, sort of. He said things were great, then all of a sudden you didn't make any sense and mechanically excused yourself for the night."

While he was saying all of this, Katie removed her colored contacts and haphazardly let them fall on the floor. It was as if she were throwing away the imaginary woman she had become. As unsettling as it was for Colin to see her this way, it was so good to see her blue eyes again.

Katie wiped her hand on her pant leg and sniffed. After she had enveloped her body in her arms again, her chin back to resting on her knees, she said, "That's pretty accurate. I had a really good time with Shane." That wasn't what Colin expected or wanted to hear, but it was better than the alternative thoughts he had earlier, and he was willing to carry the wound to his pride if it meant Katie was safe. But that didn't explain why she was being so cryptic. Colin nodded his head, encouraging her to go on, but when she didn't he let out an "and then…?" as he took a seat next to her on the couch.

Screwing up her face a little, Katie said, "I had a great time, actually. After all, this was my last night being her." Katie indicated with a wave of her hand the contacts on the floor and her modern hair that would revert back to normal after tonight.

Settling back down, Katie stared straight ahead and said, "Oh, I hate that I played him. He's such a sweet guy." Colin's pride continued to get punched, but he continued to nod in agreement until Katie said, "And he's really good-looking. I mean, wow."

Colin stopped acting like a bobble head and brushed that last statement aside. He already agreed Shane was a good guy; there was no need to rub salt in the wound.

Katie settled back down, tilting her head in Colin's direction so her left cheek was now on her knees. She looked at Colin for a few seconds, before saying miserably, "The whole time I had to keep the conversation on him. We talked about his family and all the plans he has for the future. But no matter how hard I tried to direct the conversation, he kept turning it on me. I had nothing to say to him, Colin. Nothing. No dreams, no wishes, no changeable future."

Katie squeezed her eyes closed, the pain of seeing an endless future with no change, no dreams of her own, haunted her. But Colin's gut knew there was more to this.

They had somewhat been down this Groundhog's-Day road before with his ceaseless questioning, and even though the lack of a future bothered Katie, it had never bother her *this* much.

After a few gasping sobs that feebly attempted to hold her emotions in, Katie sprang onto her knees on the couch in a way that frightened Colin. Shock pinned him to his seat as a string of sentences came out so fast it was as though they were escaping on their own accord and the briefest pause would cut them off forever.

"We were walking the fairway and decided to get a drink in the adults-only section and ran into Marcy on the way. We asked if she and her husband wanted to join us, and she said she couldn't. I didn't know why until Steve came behind her and put his arms on her stomach, and…" she paused, and the words were cut off.

Katie's fists balled up next to her temples, and all she could do was shake her head to rid her mind of the screams from her internal war. "Colin, I'm never going to have a family of my own."

Turning from him, Katie resumed her turtle-like posture and let some of the pain escape with her sobs.

So that was it, then. Marcy was pregnant. What should have been a blessed moment between lifelong (on Marcy's side) friends turned into a frayed rope bridge with Katie's heart in the middle. Any more weight would snap the rope, and Katie's heart was sure to fall.

Katie's voice was barely audible through the sobs and layers of clothing, but Colin made out the words, "I'm really happy for her, but I'm also heartbroken."

Colin drew her close to him on the couch and let her have a full vent of her tears. Katie always wanted to go out and live. Colin didn't realize until now having children and a family of her own was part of that unachievable wish too. He, himself, didn't share those same dreams, but it didn't mean he couldn't feel her pain.

"I'm sorry Kate." There really wasn't any more to say. As if on cue, she began to cry in earnest all over again.

It took her some time to calm down, but once the tears slowed, Katie dropped her harms to her side and rested her back against the couch, head towards the ceiling and eyes closed.

Breathing heavy, Katie said, "I couldn't let the date go on after that."

Colin missed having her in his arms, but he was glad to see her control her emotions. Taking a risk, he said, "Makes sense. No one would blame you for calling it a night."

With her eyes still shut, Katie said in an exhausted voice, "I try so hard, So Hard, to be appreciative of what I have. To help others, be there for them. But it hurts so much sometimes. It hurts not having a husband or a family of my own. To be stuck in this town. To have a date with a great man who won't even recognize me in the morning. It hurts, and right now I wish it would stop."

That turned Colin's blood cold. What did she mean by that? *Stop, stop*, or just subside? Shocked, Colin asked, "What do you mean, Katie? You wouldn't try to leave town, would you?"

Finally opening her eyes, Katie asked in a muted tone, "Well, why not."

Rising from the couch in disbelief, Colin shook his head. She was hurt, but was she also blind? Fury boiled up inside of him in a way he hadn't felt in a long time. It was familiar, though, and familiar things are easiest to fall back on, and she was about to know *everything* he felt now. It didn't even take long until he was yelling at her shocked and trembling form on the couch.

"Why not? Why not! Me, that's why not! What, we can't be together, so I'm not good enough to stick around for, is that it?"

"Oh Colin, no I--."

"I can't date you, marry you, or even think about touching you, so this (indicating the connection between the two of them) isn't good enough?"

"Please, I didn't-"

"Didn't what, Kate? Didn't what!? Didn't know you completely changed my life and I'd be damned without you in it?"

Just as upset and defensive, Katie popped up from the couch to join in, shouting. "You only like this." She indicated her temporary appearance.

It wasn't that she was right, and she wasn't exactly wrong either, but the anger began to drain away from him.

Nothing would get through to her tonight, and he knew it. It was best to give up and try again later. "Kate, you're not listening." Colin turned and made his way to the door, and surprisingly Katie showed no signs of wanting to stop him. This cut Colin deep. Giving up, Colin said, "I'll see you in the morning, okay? And next time, think twice before you say anything stupid like that."

Shane was asleep when a still-fuming Colin made it home. That was probably for the best; he wasn't prepared to share anything about his visit anyway.

Making good on his word, the younger man was gone by the time Colin's alarm went off the next morning. That young man would never know how much of an impact he would be leaving behind. Feeling more alone than he had since the first night Dually was gone, Colin was not ready to go downstairs for work. But he knew he had to face Katie sooner than later.

CHAPTER 30

Katie would have arrived to work with the worst of puffy eyes if not for her blessed curse. Not sleeping a wink, she stayed up thinking about what Colin had said. Could she really mean that much to him in only three months?

Colin was sitting at the kitchen island, waiting for her. The smell of coffee hung in the air, giving comfort like a cozy blanket. Shane had taught Colin how to make the warm morning addiction, and the two of them would always be grateful for this reminder of their fair friend.

Standing in front of him, Katie was in every way herself again. Until then, Colin didn't realize how much he missed her chestnut brown hair that bounced with each step, her blue starburst eyes, or her carnation red lipstick. But beyond her physical appearance, he didn't realize until now how much he simply missed Katie, free from any chain of deception. He could see in her every fiber the weight taken off her shoulders.

"Good morning." Even her voice sounded more Kate-like.

"Hey. I thought you would want a cup of coffee when you came in." Indicating to the cup that was already poured and waiting in front of him, he resisted speaking again until the first sip was taken. "Kate, I think we need to talk. And I know work isn't exactly the ideal place to do it, but knowing your baking skills and my amazing dishwashing skills, I thought we could try and figure this out."

Without another word, Katie sidestepped the island and gave Colin an unexpected hug. Like most men, Colin was unsure exactly where to put his hands, causing him to just sit there and let her do all the touching. She held him for a few seconds before saying in a quiet voice, "Thank you, Colin. I'm sorry about last night. I was being selfish, and let the hurt get to me. I promise I will never talk about leaving again."

Pulling away from him, Katie gave a smile that communicated all the gratitude she felt towards this man. He had stayed, for *her*, and even more so, he practically said he would never leave.

"Okay then, I guess that whole confusing, awkward conversation was avoided," said Colin hopefully.

"Oh, no. We still have *a lot* to talk about," said Katie with a small laugh, "But it's not like we don't have the time for that later."

CHAPTER 31

The hot and humid August melted into September, where vibrant colors bled into October's cold.

The weeks blew by nearly as fast as the wind, bringing to Colin's mind questions of how the Brighams, living every day practically the same, year after year, could change their perception of time. He made sure to add the question to his Saturday night's Q&A.

Saturday game night had been a tradition with the Brighams for many years now, but it was only after the fair, and because of how Colin handled the Shane incident, that Colin was allowed to join them. Thinking there would be the traditional Monopoly, Life, or Poker game, he was sorely wrong, for he never knew what game to expect next. The Brighams made it a competition of sorts to find not only the most unique games they could but also one they all enjoyed playing. The latter of the two was the most challenging since they all had different game preferences. Katie and Roy were board gamers, whereas Charlie and Jack preferred live-action role-playing, and Helen was a surprisingly cutthroat poker player and strategist.

Every week was someone else's turn to find, bring, and teach a game to the family. Everything from North America's Pictionary to Germany's *Mensch argere dich nicht* had been played over the years.

Everybody was in Jack's dining room since it was his week to host. While he was setting up the South Asian game Carrom, Colin decided to casually slip his question in the least prying way he could.

"Man, it feels like only a month ago I arrived in town and here it's already the beginning of October. I can only imagine how fast time must fly for you guys."

Charlie groaned. "Ah man, now we'll never get to the game." Colin was beginning to think Charlie regretted his presence at the family table. He would find out later it was just Charlie's competitive side that made him anxious to learn and dominate their Saturday pastime.

Helen looked up from the game's rule book in her hands and looked as if she were truly stumped by Colin's question. She loved strategy games and was putting all her effort into figuring out how to beat, or at least keep up with, Charlie who had won the previous three games. She was the first to speak.

"Well Colin, that is yet one more phenomenon to our existence. At least for me, I experience time the same today as I did when I really was 52." After a few long seconds, Katie spoke up too. "You know what, I don't think I've ever thought of it before, but I guess I experience time the same way too. I know it was speeding up before when I was getting older, but I can't say it's passing any faster now than it was back in 67."

Colin was not sure if he was satisfied with that answer to his question or not. But the game being set up looked really interesting, so he chose not to pry further.

Charlie won the game, much to Helen's disappointment, and was therefore challenged with the task to find next week's game in her stead. Knowing how much cleaning he had to do to get his place ready in a week made this a bittersweet victory indeed.

The family never answered his question, but Colin would simply use lunch after church the next day to ask again. Colin bid the family a quick farewell and went to retrieve his coat from the front lobby. He didn't know Katie followed him so was a bit startled when she suddenly started talking, giving the literal haunted house an even creepier vibe. "You begin to forget, being stuck for so long."

"Geez, Kate!" Colin jumped at her disembodied voice.

The smirk she gave him after that didn't help to slow his heart rate any. "Huh?"

"You begin to forget how things were before. Like how fast time goes by, reasons behind petty arguments, or, like you asked last week, if food tastes the same or if our taste buds have become bored and dulled."

"So, you know I'm using game night as a Q&A session?" He wasn't as covert with the questions as he thought.

Katie's laugh could be heard in nearly all the apartments. "Well yes, dummy. Our reasoning abilities haven't dimmed. We know you've been slipping us your most pressing questions every week for a while now."

Colin was a little embarrassed to hear that. He muttered, "Sorry, Kate. I didn't think you would all want me to make a big deal out of it. Bree said people don't speak about you guys and I thought it was because you guys were the ones who didn't want to talk."

He didn't mean to be so honestly blunt, and her eyes gave away the moment he struck a nerve. It was amazing how quickly they could turn so cold. Agitated, Katie said, "No, that's not it at all. It's because people started getting bored with the idea that we were dead, or at least comfortable, or something like that."

If he hadn't seen how steely her gaze became, he would have said, "You don't know the half of it", but she did know. Gossip in small towns goes away as soon as the next scandal pops up, and even a secret this big ran its course a *long* time ago.

More to herself than to Colin, Katie said, "People stopped asking questions and we began to forget." Getting slightly choked up over her realization, Katie pleadingly looked into Colin's eyes as if she could find some shelter from her emotional storm in them. "I don't want to forget, Colin. I really don't want to forget."

"It's okay, Katie. I won't let you." They stood there in the quiet, waving to the brothers headed to their own apartments. Once they were alone again, Colin asked, "So, does this mean I can ask as many questions as I want? Even more than I already do at the café?"

With a hint of a smile in her voice, Katie said, "If they're anything like the ones you ask at the café, no. If they're good questions like the ones you ask at game night, yes."

Colin soon covered every topic imaginable. They could still dream. Though their taste buds had not lost their sharpness, food preferences changed depending on how often they indulged in their current favorite foods. Pain tolerance doesn't get better (Katie tried to get a tattoo once from a traveling artist, but was glad she couldn't keep it and didn't have to finish it once she started and gave up). If any of them ever sustained a life-threatening injury it would go away the next day, but no one had ever 'died' again, so there was no way to tell how far the healing powers of the house went. They could retain new information but apparently would start to forget things from the past. And for big city events, like the town fair, they always wore disguises and had false identities so no one would recognize them. This was becoming more and more important with the growing popularity of social media.

All that, he learned in a few weeks. Then, one day, Katie snaped. "Oh my goodness Colin, will you please give it a rest!?" Katie regretted her invitation to Colin's prying questions. She knew he meant well, but it was starting to put a strain on their relationship. Not to mention, slow them down at work.

"I can't concentrate when I'm thinking," she said, "I mean, I can't think when I'm trying to think about what you want me to think about."

With a straight face, Colin replied, "That has to be the most unintelligent thing you've ever said."

Agitated, Katie said, "See! Now shut up and help me. I'm already behind on these cinnamon rolls."

CHAPTER 32

The year's end quickly came and went, and with it some very famous holidays. The kind of holidays kids cherished, and spent with their families. The ones teenagers looked forward to because it meant getting out of school. The ones with traditions adults wished to pass down to their children. The ones that leave the broken, like Colin and a handful of dead people, behind. But this year was different.

It turns out, a town with literal ghost residents loves to go all out for Halloween, despite the high number of religious converts. Thanksgiving tastes amazing when the main cooks have had decades to perfect their culinary skills. Christmas wasn't colorful at the Brigham house, since no one was brave enough to decorate the place in flammable tinsel and tons of lightbulbs and candles, but the café was breathtaking. If the town ever gave out awards for decorations, they would win it, hands down. And the gifts? No one would beat the Brighams in generosity or personalization. New Years wasn't a big deal to any of them. What's another year when you've lived so many? And besides, the café and supermarket were planning on being open the next day and everyone needed their rest. Valentine's Day saw much too much pink, and the café was swamped with personal orders, some of which Colin was capable of tackling on his own.

Winter's frozen grip began to loosen mid-March, and the first of the robins were out. There was something about that bird that stirred anticipation for spring in the people of Vernon and urged them to look for other signs of new life and growth.

The staircase between Colin's apartment and the café was not temperature-controlled. At one point in January, he tied in a heating unit from the café's electrical system to the stairwell. His drywall patching skills needed some improvement, but after the initial shock of feeling how cold the stairs could get, Katie let Colin off the hook fairly easily. She simply asked that he put it on a timer so it didn't run all night, and the next time he tried to tackle a home improvement job, ask someone who's done it before to oversee it.

With the arrival of the robins, the heater went away. This didn't mean the mornings weren't still cold, just not frigid. Even though the sun didn't break the horizon until hours after he woke up, and he still had to go down the freezing staircase every morning, Colin was happy with his early shift at the cafe. It made the warm kitchen with hot coffee and good company more appreciated. So, when he entered his haven to find it cold, dark,, and empty, an ice shard cut through his chest more violently than any winter storm he had so far endured.

"Kate" was the only word that would escape. Colin now understood Kate's panic the first time he was late for work all that time ago. The fear that something was wrong and not knowing what happened to one you care for.

So much was his confusion he nearly missed the rapping coming from the front door. Colin dashed through the kitchen's double doors, knocking over two chairs in his haste, and unbolted the glass door to a partially frozen Mrs. Minton.

She didn't even bother to explain. With a "Mr. Warrington, come", Colin ran to grab his coat and they were off, bracing themselves against the cold morning wind. So familiar was their route that Colin could have walked to their destination blindfolded. They were hurrying to the Brigham residence.

The two of them were still three houses away when Colin saw it. One of those large advertisement boards that took up much of the front yard was erected overnight. The Goliath shouted his message loud and clear with big bold letters.

Coming Soon, Fall 2013

A modern fourplex townhouse-style building on the front silently mocked the house's impending doom. The Brigham house was going to be torn down.

Colin would have stopped and gawked if it were not for Mrs. Minton urging him on. How similar this all felt, as a flashback to last year's eviction notice danced in his head.

Knowing there would be answers once inside, the two rushed up the front steps and burst through the main doors. Inside the main foyer were all five family members. Roy was holding a distraught Helen on the couch, trying vainly to hush her cries. The boys looked as though they would punch through the nearest wall if remodeling were

202

not tabooed. Katie was frantically pacing back and forth, chewing on her left thumb as was her customary reaction to stress. If the thing didn't grow back every night, he imagined she would never have a thumbnail.

"Sit down everyone, please, and I'll tell you what I know." Mrs. Minton was always one for manners. Even in this crazy situation, she dared not deviate from them.

Once the six of them settled in some way, Mrs. Minton stood in front of the group and said in her usual business voice, "As you are all aware, Kate informed me this morning about the sign erected in your front yard last night. I am burdened to say that, since the building has been declared vacant since 1967 in all town records, a property investment agency sidestepped our offices and officially bought the property last month. They have also sidestepped us regarding building permits and property rezoning, filing it under a non-profit organization that only needs state approval."

"Who is the new owner?" No one ever interrupted Mr. Minton, but Colin simply had to know.

Seeing the desperation in all their eyes, Mrs. Minton's manner softened and as she spoke, it was more like a friend than a politician. "It's called Renewed Living. Some sort of charity that takes abandoned buildings and turns them into affordable luxury apartments."

There was a scoff. "Renewed Living? Isn't that a bit of an oxymoron, with what it will do to us?" This time it was Jack who spitefully interrupted.

Trying to regain control of the room, Mrs. Minton stated, "I'm only telling you what I learned in the last thirty minutes. And, given the hour, it's surprising I learned anything at all."

Katie, more level-headed, asked the question that was burdening them most. "How long do we have? The sign only says Fall." All eyes turned to Mrs. Minton then. Even Helen became silent, waiting with bated breath for an answer.

With a frown, Mrs. Minton shook her head and said, "I don't know. All I could find out was, by the end of summer, this place will be demolished and four townhouses will stand in its place by fall."

"They can't do that! It can't be true!" Helen began to cry all the more earnestly into her husband's chest.

With resolve, Mrs. Minton said over the group's cries of disbelief, "As of right now, it is true. But Mr. Warrington and I will do everything we can, starting now, to make sure it won't follow through."

This surprised everyone, especially Colin. Even Katie stopped biting her nails. But one look at all of them, his family, and there was no one who could stop him from fighting for them.

"You're damn right I will."

He sounded much more confident than he was, for Colin knew nothing about real estate law or construction.

"What can we do?" Charlie, being a natural leader like his father, couldn't stand the thought of sitting and not doing anything.

Mrs. Minton didn't miss a beat. "You will have to continue life as normal for right now, so as not to raise suspicion. But first, you and your brother might want to take down that monstrosity (she inclined her head towards the sign) so as not to alarm the town. I only hope no one else has seen it."

But someone had, and like wildfire, the whole town was consumed with the news. This kept Katie's café, Roy's, and Brigham Brothers busier than usual, for everyone wanted in on the gossip. Poor Mrs. Minton was so busy putting out rumors that kept sparking up that a town meeting had to be called before the end of the week.

"May I have your attention please!" she called from the podium of the south church, which served as city hall. "By now, we all know the Brigham residence has been purchased with development plans to tear down and rebuild another housing unit. We also know this threatens our beloved Brigham family's existence. However, I did not call you all here tonight to tell you what you already know. I called you here for help.

"First, keeping the Brigham secret is still the primary duty of this town, and gallivanting through the streets, talking so openly, will *not* be tolerated. So please, limit public conversation regarding the matter at hand."

There were a few hushed responses to this request, but no one seemed to object.

"Second, I request any help in going over construction codes and laws. If there are any t's not crossed or i's not dotted, we need to find them. They may just help halt construction."

There was even less side-conversation regarding this.

"And the third reason I have called you here tonight," Mrs. Minton hesitated for just a second. It was so unlike her to be unsure of herself that everyone sat in attention, ears prickling to hear what she had to say. When she did find her voice, it took on a softer tone, as if she herself couldn't believe what was about to be said. "If we cannot find any legal way to stop them, we have been asked by the family not to indulge in any illegal actions such as vandalism, violence, or anything else outside of the law. A peaceful protest may take place, but noone else need be harmed."

In case they can't stop the demolition. That bit wasn't said, but Colin heard the message loud and clear. Everyone did. Colin had thoughts about the "what ifs", but to hear the toughest woman in town voice them somehow hit like a sucker punch to the gut. They just *had* to stop the force behind Renewed Living.

The town meeting was dismissed shortly after Mrs. Minton made her requests, and for the second time in over 50 years Roy's, Katie's Café, and the Brigham Brothers were all closed for the rest of the afternoon and the following day.

After much talk, it was decided that, just in case, the family would put their affairs in order. They had prospered over the years, their situation being as it was, and at least there was some form of warning of things to come, unlike the others who had gone before them.

Jack and Charlie, like Colin, felt this to be a betrayal, a white flag of sorts, showing they had given up. But, once put into perspective, the brothers consented and began taking inventory of their possessions that afternoon.

"It's not a sign of giving up," Katie told them, "It's a way to guarantee those we care about get what we wish to leave them. Like Michael at the fire department getting your '68 Chevelle, Jack. The one he helped build with you for his high school shop project. Or Karen, at the police department. She is going to need a little nest egg for retirement since Terry died and her funds were drained from his medical costs. If we're going out, we can at least take care of others in our absence."

Striking the hero chord, the guys put more effort behind their wills, but it still felt like defeat.

The community put on an air of normality after the town meeting was held. The café regulars still showed up every morning. Coffee and confections were still sold. Family Saturday game night was still played. But even with the days ticking by just the same, there was still a heaviness in the air, for now it was the end of April, and Mrs. Minton still could not find a way to stop the demolition.

CHAPTER 33

Mrs. Minton sat in her office and grumbled, "Whoever did this sure knew their way around the law. The only thing I could find was that Renewed Living is owned by G&H Realty, one of those big conglomerates. And they are so large that, even if I could go through every employee, past and present, I'm sure to find multiple people connected to Vernon in some way, but no one significant enough to make any changes."

Tired of afternoon after afternoon looking through records and researching laws, Colin wiped his face with his hands in exasperation and sighed. "I feel like we're going about this all wrong. Could it be bigger than some random employee? What does G&H stand for?"

"Greene and Holt. They're based in Detroit." It was found on one of the letters on top of the stack on her desk. She had gotten to work immediately when the sign appeared, and her office was quickly filling with paperwork from the Renewed Living charity.

"And do they have any connection with Vernon? Do they have anything against the Brigham?" asked Colin.

"There was a family who lived here with the name Holt, but the father died of an unfortunate drinking problem, and the other two I can't see ever owning such a successful company. No, I don't see how anyone at Greene and Holt would be personally involved with Vernon."

"But if they were, shouldn't we--"

"Mr. Warrington, everybody loves the Brighams. And if they didn't…" Mrs. Minton didn't bother finishing that sentence. If anyone had a grievance against the Brigham family, she would be the last person they would tell.

"Then we need to go straight to G&H to see if they'll stop the charity from going through with their plans." Colin said with resolve. "After all, would a company want to spend a ton of money on a project when the whole town they are trying to improve is in opposition?"

Mrs. Minton looked at Colin with tired eyes, and said in a dull voice, "I thought of that myself and already sent a letter. If they want a signed petition, I said I could get no less than 80% of the town's residents of legal age to sign against their development plans." Mrs. Minton sounded like she was about to say more, but stopped there. After giving her some time, Colin asked, "And what did they say?"

"I'll let you know as soon as I hear back."

Most evenings began the same. Colin would come to the town government offices. And each one of those ended the same, going home without anything changing. To add insult to injury, no one else thought themselves adequate for the job, leaving Colin and Mrs. Minton to sift through the legal documents Renewed Living graciously sent. The papers took up nearly all the spare room in Mrs. Minton's office. Even with so much paperwork, they had gone over every sentence multiple times, trying desperately to find something the corporation missed, yet still found nothing. Now and then there was some hope, only to be quickly dashed. Like Mrs. Minton said, Renewed Living sure knew what they were doing.

It was another late night for the two of them. Colin fell back into his chair in frustration and blurted, not for the first time, "If only there was a personal name on record as to who bought the property, instead of a business name. Then we could go to them directly."

"And do what, Mr. Warrington?" Mrs. Minton countered. "Tell them ghost stories or threaten them?" Mrs. Minton replied with the least amount of amusement possible.

"Touché."

It was now near the end of April, and there was absolutely nothing they could find to deter, postpone, or get across to the company that they didn't need, nor want, the affordable, luxury fourplex in their little town.

"As much as I appreciate your willingness to help, there really isn't much more for us to do right now. At least, not until G&H gets back to me. Why don't we call it a night?" That was as nice of a goodnight that Mrs. Minton would give him. After stretching, Colin collected his things and turned to go, but only made it to the door before Mrs. Minton called out, "And, Colin? There's no need to come in tomorrow. I'll let you know if I need further assistance, but until then…best go about your business."

Colin wanted to feel offended for being pushed aside, but instead, he was only left feeling ashamed. Her ending sentence told him there was nothing more they could do, so why did he feel a slight tinge of relief? He was failing his family. He was *losing* his family. Shouldn't that spark any other emotion besides relief? It was now six weeks last Tuesday since the sign appeared, and they were no closer to permanently removing it now as they were then, and they may never be.

Taking the long detour to the Brigham residence before going home became habitual after the second week.

"Any news?" This was his frequent greeting by Helen. Surely, she didn't believe he needed prompting to release any news, but it still hurt slightly to be asked, knowing there was nothing good to relay. It also hurt knowing she was going through much worse, emotionally, than the rest, and because of that, Colin was able to swallow his feelings for her sake. After all, not only was her existence on the line, but this loving woman would lose her husband and her remaining children if no answers were to be found.

Giving her his best fake smile, Colin said, "No, not yet. Mrs. Minton was able to locate the owners of Renewed Living, though. Some big-shot company called G&H Realty. She is also waiting for a response to a letter she wrote the other day. Until then, there really isn't much for me to do."

"I hate this waiting game." Katie should have been asleep by now. Colin should have been too. . Staying up late to help Mrs. Minton was taking a physical toll on them both that even extra strong coffee was unable to cure. Yet there Katie stood, waiting with her mother, like she did most nights, just to hear nothing new.

Colin tried his best to give these women at least some good news. "If they don't answer by the week's end, Minton and I will go to G&H ourselves. I'll get them to stop construction no matter what." He could only imagine how Mrs. Minton would feel about this impromptu trip. "But we still don't have a demolition date, right? The weekend could be too late." Helen was worrying again. Known to be a pillar of strength, it was hard for everyone to see Helen start to crumble. Now a new crack appeared on almost a daily basis and all were waiting with baited breath for her to dissolve entirely.

Colin shook his head and reassured her, not for the first time, "No Helen, Minton has access to their state filings. They need to give the city at least a two-week public announcement and so far, all has been silent. If they attempt to violate that law, we can legally stop them, for good. So maybe it's best that the week's end *is* too late."

This brought a little reassurance back into her eyes, but it was evident that the poor woman didn't have the strength to hold on to hope. Colin, like many others, feared what lengths she would go to be rid of the stress.

"Hey, what are you guys still doing up?" Charlie and Jack just entered the main house, trying to be quiet so as to not wake anyone. No one bothered answering that question; Colin was there, so Jack and Charlie already knew why they were still up.

"I have something for you, mom." This time, it was Jack who spoke. He handed a stack of papers to Helen and she looked over them slowly. "It's a signed petition of nearly everybody in town, mom. They don't want us to leave any more than we want to go. We just tried dropping it off at Mrs. Minton's, but she wasn't in her office."

Tears sprang to the woman's eyes once again, but at least these weren't the result of stress or sorrow. "Thank you, boys. I'll keep them safe and take this to her first thing in the morning." With no more fanfare, Helen rose from the sitting room couch and headed towards her apartment.

"That was really great, guys." Katie's pride in her brothers could be seen in her tired eyes. They were still trying to put their affairs in order, as well as scratch off a few more things on their bucket lists, but the rest of the family didn't know they were secretly getting signatures from everyone in town petitioning for the construction project.

"Oh, that's not all." Charlie's mischievous smile was a sight for sore eyes. "We're going to throw our May Day festival as always."

"It's mom's favorite community celebration," Jack added, "and everyone agreed to get it set up in time to surprise her. Of course, we can't take her out of town to make it a real surprise, but everything will go up tomorrow."

Everything went according to plan, and the town had never had a better May Day. For the first time in a long time, it didn't feel like life was going to fall apart, and there were no tears to be seen. The whole time was bursting with color and life. It may not have been Colin's favorite community festival, but he could put it in his top five.

CHAPTER 34

May 3, 2013. It started like every other day. Colin and Katie laughed over a stupid joke while making cinnamon rolls. Coffee fumes were strong in the air. The weather, now given way to a pleasant spring, meant all the windows were cracked for the first time that year. The heat of the kitchen was allowed to escape and a refreshing breeze took its place. All was right in their little world.

The morning regulars came and went, the gas station deliveries were sent out. Bree was sitting in a corner with her husband enjoying each other's company during the lull between breakfast and lunch, and Mrs. Minton was strolling through the door like she always did around this hour. But no treat was to be had.

"Katie, please ask Bree to take over for now, you and Mr. Warrington need to come with me."

No, it can't be.

They didn't move from their spot. They couldn't.

"Please Katie, let us not draw too much attention. You two head out the back, then around to my office, and I will speak with Bree and Justin."

Stepping out the back didn't soften the blow they just received. Walking through the kitchen, Katie's head swiveled non-stop, absorbing the all too familiar sights and smells that had been her life for over half a century. Now that she is finally content, finally happy, will she be forced to leave all this behind? Her home? Her café? Her Colin?

There was no way for her to know that Colin was thinking along the same lines. He said goodbye to the only person he loved not too long ago, and to Dually just last year. How can he go through something like that again and with so little time spent together?

Taking her hand in his, the two made their way outside the café, and Colin's shock made way for anger. "I can't fail you, Kate. I promised I wouldn't fail you!" Katie's continued silence didn't condemn nor acquit him.

Mrs. Minton beat them to her office. Her poker face set ever so well; it was hard to see she was just as somber as the two individuals slumped on the chairs in front of her desk.

Her hesitation was the only tell-tale sign of the bad news to come. "The letter came back this morning. I thought it was best to tell you first. The demolition will continue as scheduled, and the date has been set for May 15."

"But that's only twelve days away!"

"I know Mr. Warrington, and we leave for Detroit as soon as we are done here, with the city petition signed on May Day. If it's a court battle they want, it's a battle they'll get."

"Mrs. Minton, please don't make Colin go unless he has to." Katie's voice was small, but it carried a lot of weight.

"What?" Both turned to Katie, shocked by this. Colin couldn't believe it. Did she really just ask him not to go? Not to fight?

An explanation was in order, but shame was the reason behind her lowered face. "Everything is being taken away." The catch in Katie's voice didn't give her the understanding look she was hoping for, but what did that matter now? "You don't understand, either of you. Knowing the end is certain, knowing you're *going* to die, and just waiting for it, is harder than it actually happening. If I have less than two weeks to live," *Ha*! She bitterly thought to herself. *A whole lifetime has gone by, and I haven't lived a day of it. Not really.* "I mean, only two weeks to be here, I want you here with me." This last part was directed towards Colin, pleading tears coming to her eyes.

"But Kate…" "Yes, of course." Mrs. Minton's interruption was just as sudden as Katie's request to keep Colin in town. Turning to Colin, Mrs. Minton hoped he would understand, but he was still young enough to think death was something you could fight against. A major charity corporation could be stopped, sure. But what then? What about next time? What about when he was gone as well?

Colin wasn't quite sure why he felt caged by this; tethered to fate instead of free to change it. It didn't sit well with him, and he was ready to have the rest of the day to himself, even contemplating a trip outside of town. But he knew he would never do that, not to his Kate.

"I'll stay, but I'm still going to fight however way I can," he said to Katie. "Say the word and I will be out there, by your side," he directed at Mrs. Minton. He was up and out of his chair before either woman saw his words as a salutation, but Mrs. Minton did get the last word in before he was out the door.

"I hope my government debate skills are good enough that it doesn't come to that, Colin, but if I need you, I will call." All self-boasting aside, she fixed Colin with a stare that meant nothing short of a threat, "Take care of them for me." And with that, Colin took his leave; ready for this day to already be over with.

CHAPTER 35

Still in her office, Katie watched as Mrs. Minton busied herself, gathering papers from her desk and charts from filing cabinets. "Since it is just me going on this endeavor, communication will be kept to a minimum. But don't get too concerned if I call, I'll be reporting whether good news or bad. With it being a Friday, I plan on getting in touch with a judge I know up there over the weekend. Perhaps he will be willing to hear our side, nix the ghost part."

"You're too good to us, Minton." Katie's words stopped the woman's frantic movements.

"No dear, you are too good to us. That makes you worth fighting for."

"Have you told the others yet?" Katie's question could have been answered with a quick walk across the street, but if they weren't, she wasn't going to be the one to tell them.

"No, I'm afraid I haven't. It's a coward's way, but I figured breaking it to the two of you first would be the easiest. And seeing how Colin took it, I've been trying to figure out how to tell the rest and each scenario I play through my mind is worse than the last."

"Don't worry. Go and get packed, I'll tell them." Colin was back. Both women gave a little start, not hearing or seeing him enter the building. Seeing him in a new light, Mrs. Minton nodded in appreciation, or at least in relief.

"Thank you, Mr. Warrington. I would rather not give this particular news." With no ceremony, she ushered them out the door and closed her office, leaving the two of them the painful task no one wanted.

No one could prepare for the events that transpired next.

Katie thought it best to go to her father alone and let him break the news to Helen. However, poor Helen was in the office when they arrived and knew right away something was wrong. Expecting her to be inconsolable as in the past, everyone was astonished the tears were finally over. Passing off her duties at the store, she decided to go to every member of the community and show them in some way, whether through a gift, story, or shared experience, just how much each and every one of them meant to her.

Roy resolved to make the final tweaks to his business affairs, promoting his most valued employee, and training him to take over the place once they were gone. With the way the older Brighams responded, Colin was glad Mrs. Minton was not in town. It did not show much faith in her ability to stop their impending doom. Knowing they still hoped for the best outcome, it was still good to see them prepare beyond a written will, just in case. But what else would he expect from a Brigham?

Just as baffled by the older Brighams' response to the news were the brothers' responses. Jack and Charlie were always a bit foolhardy, but now they seemed to become downright crazy and reckless. Breaking out all the "toys" they built over time, the two of them would go on daredevil drives through streets they personally blocked-off, playing chicken with the town line. After being chastised for their conduct, they were asked to relinquish most of their physical possessions, but in a unique, Brigham way.

Wills were only finalized after death, so with a quick re-writing, the Brigham Brothers' possessions were to be given out in different ways. Shooting games, drinking games, see who would get the craziest tattoo…They came up with some unprecedented ways to win a Brigham prize.

They were still fair in their giving away, though. Knowing all twelve people who made up the police force and fire department, the brothers arranged it so to be sure everyone won at least one thing to remember them by.

Katie had not changed things in any way. Her schedule, her bakery, everything stayed the same. Whether this showed the most faith or the most doubt was debatable.

CHAPTER 36

The two-week demolition notice was half-way over.

It was not until this last week that Colin knew about the graves. He was unsure why it had taken the Brighams over a year to divulge. True, they were a form of lie, and they were a personal reminder of what they had lost, but now that he was aware of something kept hidden, he began to question what else Katie and the family could be keeping from him.

They all technically had one, having "died" and keeping the house fire story and deaths on record to protect them.

Colin and Katie, while on a rare walk during their lunch break on the north side of town, had seen Jack standing next to Nora's headstone. Not knowing if she was in there or not, neither of them really wanted to know the answer. But they still wondered what it was like, and what to expect. Jack was the closest to Nora before she disappeared. Would they be close once again in some sort of afterlife?

Pain etched Jack's face. How often he had mourned his wife, son, and sister Nora. A bit of him was thankful she didn't have to go through what they were going through now, but he was also mad at the way they lost her presence so long ago.

Not wishing to disturb him, the two backed away without his noticing. His grief was his alone today, and if he needed someone to share that burden, he would at least let Charlie know.

It was Thursday, May 9th. By all other standards, it was a perfect day. If only time would slow down for them.

Colin could see the melancholy in everything Katie did. Her hands moved a little slower, her eyes blinking a little longer, a sigh punctuating her breath. Thinking it was due to seeing her brother so vulnerable and full of questioning remorse, Colin tried to reassure her. "He'll be all right, Kate."

It was some time before Katie replied, "It's not him I'm thinking about."

Pushing the weekly order sheet aside, she took her time forming the questions she wanted him to answer the most.

"What will you do? When I'm gone?"

Without even needing to think about it, Colin answered, "You're not leaving, I won't let you." He refused to think of the alternative. Never would he allow her to go.

Not letting her push the questions away, Katie said, "But *if* I do, what will you do?"

What a way to put him on the spot. It was not that he hadn't thought about that question himself, but he had shoved it into the back of his mind so many times that now forcing it to the forefront felt overwhelming.

But there was no time to put off the inevitable. Mrs. Minton had phoned the other day saying her judge friend would not take the case, and by all legal standards, the charity had the right to do what they want with the property.

With the heaviest of sighs, Colin leaned on the island and rubbed his face with his hands. "I don't know. I don't know what to do, Kate." After what felt like an eternity, Colin lifted his eyes to meet hers. "I don't want to leave Vernon, but…" But what? Could he brave the pain? Overlook the daily reminder of what he had lost? See the world take shape into something new, something void of Kate? "I'm no better than my father. I understand why he couldn't stay, why he never came back, and all I want to do is follow in his steps."

There it was, out there for her to hear. After she was gone, there would not, could not, be a Vernon for Colin anymore. "I'm doing everything I can, stealing myself from the possible pain. I mean, you were supposed to be here forever. To be my Kate, and now…how can you leave and I not?"

As usual, her eyes were the only tell-tale sign of the heartbreak within. But the pain would have to wait. She had business to get down to. "Does that mean you don't want the café?"

The café? Did she really mean that? How could she ask him to take on such a thing?!

"I didn't want to talk about what will happen if things worked out…but…I want you to have the café and that requires me showing you the business side of things."

Colin's response was not what Katie had expected.

"How could you do that to me?"

Excitement, confusion, sorrow. Those seemed to be proper reactions to hearing you were inheriting a successful and well-loved café, not this…was it anger?

"No, Kate! This doesn't feel right. I'm not sure if…if I could do that, not without you."

Opening her mouth to interject, Colin cut her off before she could say a word.

"I know you're not trying to hurt me, but damn, Kate. I just don't think things can be like, well, like this anymore." Colin used hand gestures to indicate everything. "All of this? There will be no normal for me to go back to, at least not for a while, and certainly not here."

On the verge of tears; Katie nearly shouted what she had been trying to say this whole time. "But, but that's all I have to give you! You have to take it; I don't have anything else!" Dissolving into a puddle of tears, Colin quickly skirted the island, trying to scoop her up, but she kept pushing him away in her hurt, slipping like water through his hands.

After the third attempt to hold her, Colin was getting a little fed up with her worshiping her own misery. "Oh, come on, Kate! That's not at all true, and you know it. You gave me something I could never lose. You taught me to have a thirst for living. How to see the world in wonder, even if we can't experience it the same as most people.

"You taught me how to cherish someone more fully and completely than I ever thought possible. So much so that I will die when you leave. If given the choice, I would gladly give up myself to save you and your family. I can't imagine my life without you in it, and I regret all the years you were waiting here, and I didn't come sooner.

"You gave me everything, and I love you."

Never saying those words before, he was unashamed to let them out now. He loved her, with every fiber of his being, he loved her. And she needed to know.

"I don't need a café to remember you by. And I don't need some token of appreciation to know you love me too."

Crying now, Katie threw her arms around Colin. She would never have him fully, in the physical sense, but Katie knew she loved Colin more than any other before him. Even Bill. If only circumstances could be different, both would be willing to hold the other for eternity.

There was no way of knowing how much time passed before they let each other go. But it didn't take long for Katie to break the silence once they did. "If you won't take the café, then can you do something else for me?"

Not sure if he could deny her anything else, but still not wanting to make a promise he couldn't keep, Colin asked what it was, with as little rejection in his voice as he could manage.

CHAPTER 37

Pulling out a folder from the kitchen island, Katie opened it to reveal some of the pictures she had in her apartment. "I've thought about it and decided that if you don't want the café, then I want to be your sugar mama."

"Wait, what!?" Colin wasn't sure she knew exactly what that meant.

Not missing a beat, Katie went on. "Well, I couldn't think of a better way to put it. If you can't stay, then I want you to go. I want you to see, explore, and live life… for me. The town has been so tied down because of us, Colin, and I don't want the same fate for you. The more I think about it, the harder it is on me. We kept Vernon from expanding. We kept a lot of people from leaving and having their own lives. I mean, look at Minton! She spent her whole life here, keeping us hidden from the world, and she never got to see it either. And, being a business owner stuck in a small town for 50 years does wonders on one's bank account."

Colin took a small step back, not believing what she was saying. "Kate, stop. I can't do that."

"Sure you can! You're probably the only person I know who *can*. And, I already have a tentative list of where you should go."

Slightly affronted, Colin said, "Kate, stop. I'm not some pet or toy. You can't expect me to feel comfortable blowing your life savings just to have fun when you're gone."

Saying that out loud left a bitter taste in his mouth. He can't be expected to enjoy a life her second death made possible for him to have. He had to make her see reason. "That won't work. That won't kill the pain. First the café, now this? Do you have any idea how insulting it all is? That I can't go do these things for myself, so my dead, rich friend has to buy my way to make up for not being there?"

"Colin, I'm not trying to do that."

"Then what are you trying to do? Because it feels like you're grasping at straws now. I mean, you even planned where I should go? What I should do!?"

Katie was shocked and said in a voice that didn't even try to cover her anger, "*I'm* being insulting? You're the one who said you had to go, remember!? I wanted you to stay. I wanted to know you'll be taken care of, that the café won't be ruined, and that Bree and Justin would still have jobs. How am I the bad guy now?"

Colin couldn't say anything to this. She wasn't the bad guy, G&H were the bad guys. He needed to keep the right perspective on things.

After a brief pause, Katie continued, "So, if you can't stay, then I want to have a hand in helping you go. You have to let me give this to you."

"But why?!"

"Because you're the only one not trapped and you stayed with me anyway. I'm trapped, Colin. I've been trapped forever. Do you honestly think I want my best friend to leave, again, and see the world without me? Of course not. But at least I would have some consolation knowing you'll be able to go on without worry and take a part of me with you. I'm not putting a leash on you; I'm setting you free. And there is no one else I would rather do this for."

Colin glanced at the pictures again. He had seen them now countless times while over at Katie's apartment. She had even hand selected his favorite ones. Seeing them here, in a folder, knowing Katie wanted to send him to those places…what was he supposed to do about that? "Kate, I don't know if I can handle this all right now. Do you think I can have some time to think it over? Please?"

She nodded her head and closed the folder gently. "Fair enough."

Trying to see her side of things, Colin added, "And, *if* you want to show me some of the business side of the café, I'll be willing to go over it with you. But I just…I can't promise I'll stay."

All Katie could do was nod in agreement again. "If you don't think you'll be able to do it, I'll look into giving it to Bree or put it in Mrs. Minton's hands to sell to a capable entrepreneur."

The whirlwind of conversation ended as abruptly as it started, and the two of them finished their daily chores without much more conversation. Making their way towards Katie's place after work, the sign, still boasting in the front yard, was now nothing more than a display of where Jack and Charlie held a paintball aiming competition. Whoever successfully covered "Fall 2013" must have been declared the lucky winner.

Katie filled their time discussing places she wanted him to see first, with or without her vanishing. Apparently, she decided he would be going on all these adventures with or without her still around, but no sooner were they on the front steps when they heard it, the landline phone ringing. The conversation died on the spot. Only one person would be calling on that line, Mrs. Minton.

Bolting through the front door, Katie fumbled her first attempt to pick up, accidentally hanging up on the waiting party. After waiting a solid thirty seconds, the phone began to ring again, this time connecting with the woman on the other end.

Mrs. Minton's voice was stonier than usual. "Katie, they just won't back down. I've done everything I can do. I am so sorry, but I'm coming home."

Without any farewell, the line went dead.

CHAPTER 38

May 10th. There were only five days left until demolition day. Mrs. Minton had just returned the night before. Keeping her distance due to shame and fear, most of the morning had passed before bravery, duty, and her favorite muffin pulled her to the café. "I did everything I could. If there was any foul play on their part or illegal activity, Judge Hartford would have taken the case, but they are a law-abiding business whose sole purpose is to enrich small towns. If anything, *we* look like the bad guys."

Sighing deep into her coffee, with eyes a red that rivaled her carnation lipstick, Katie took a deep inhale before informing Mrs. Minton all that had happened in her absence.

Though they hoped and prayed she was able to win the residential battle, they had made peace with the situation and were ready, come what may. Well, not all of them.

Colin was still treading the hellish waters of indecision and the unknown.

A worn Mrs. Minton left the café with a list of to-dos on her mind. Only when she was unlocking the glass front door of her office building did she see Colin following her.

"Save your comments, Mr. Warrington, I have no strength to fight."

"We missed something; I know it."

Exasperated as she was, Mrs. Minton still had some fight in her. She just didn't want to waste it on Colin. Turning around to Colin, Mrs. Minton said in the most motherly voice Colin had ever heard, "No, we didn't. This is hard enough for all of us, but please, please just let us enjoy these last few days together."

"I can't! I saw them, Minton. I saw them give up, just like that," Colin snapped his fingers, "and I can't just sit by and do nothing!"

She could not argue with this. She was not there to witness it for herself. Whether this was a blessing or not, Mrs. Minton could not decide, but just the thought of seeing the Brighams give up was hard enough.

Hating to play devil's advocate, Mrs. Minton justified herself by sticking to the facts. "They didn't do anything wrong. On both sides."

Mrs. Minton finished unlocking the door and both Colin and Mrs. Minton walked into the stale room and heard her phone ring. He knew he shouldn't keep her from any more work. She had already sacrificed a great deal of time and other mayoral duties for their sake. Taking a silent seat nearest the window while she answered the call in her full business voice, he still wanted her to know he wasn't finished.

"City of Vernon, Mayor speaking." The blood visibly drained from her face, bringing Colin to his feet. Who was on the other line, and what could have frightened her so?

"But, you can't! I won't allow that…..The date was set for the 15th!"

The question was answered, and it was not good.

"I don't give a damn if the required days have been met, we've been trying to stop this process since the very beginning. You can't just go and push the date up."

"Damn it, when?" Colin couldn't help his interruption, and Mrs. Minton shooed it away like a pesky fly.

"Fine then, that's exactly what I will do."

Hanging up the phone, Mrs. Minton showed a near-feral side he hoped would never be   directed towards him. But that didn't keep him from being cheeky. "Still think there's no foul play?"

"Oh. shut up, Mr. Warrington, and get your things. They moved up the date to tomorrow."

"Tomorrow! Damn, we need to tell Kate!"

"There's no time!" The panic and internal rage could still be heard in Mrs. Minton's voice. Despite what Colin wanted to do, he knew he needed to listed to her. "The office of Greene and Holt is three hours away. If we don't get there ASAP, we might as well not fight at all."

Fight. Colin wanted to fight from the beginning. Never being one to shy away from that path, yet always being forced to run in the other direction because of his father, and now Katie, he knew today had to be different. Today, he had to stand up for her. For Vernon. For himself.

Running out of her office, Colin skirted the café. Not because he cared about disturbing the customers, but because Mrs. Minton was right. He couldn't tell Katie. Colin couldn't face hearing Katie tell beg him not to go. He had to fight, and if he lost, he would come back and hold her until she dissolved from his arms. But if he saw her before then, he knew he would never be able to leave. And he had to fight.

Upstairs, Colin grabbed his keys, a bottle of water (to both drink and keep him from making unnecessary bathroom stops), and hastily wrote a note he prayed would be good enough. Colin at least wanted to help Katie understand.

I'll Never Stop Fighting For You

Pulling his car around to the back of Mrs. Minton's office so Katie didn't see him, Colin hopped out just long enough to get the building address where he and Minton would meet. Colin was to go ahead while Mrs. Minton quickly warned Roy. It was not ideal, but they did need to know, and Roy would be the quickest to inform. Also, in case Greene or Holt were to leave the office for an early weekend, Colin would be there to follow one of them as legally as possible.

The drive was a blur of passing vehicles and despair. Renewed Living knew exactly what they were doing. The town didn't want the development, so a date was set. Then Mrs. Minton drove out there with a petition, and they pushed the date up. Some good Samaritans they turned out to be.

Greene and Holt. He hated those names.

Once he sped past the first highway patrol, Colin realized he still had to be smart. Thank goodness the cop was watching the oncoming traffic and paid no attention to Colin; this was no time to get a speeding ticket.

Calming himself some, Colin knew a game plan was in order. A second glance at the address and an aerial map printed for him told Colin they were no longer dealing with some small-town charity organization. Only big-time corporations could afford that downtown address.

CHAPTER 39

During the drive, something bugged Colin. How did Mrs. Minton plan on stopping Greene and Holt, even if she did get to speak with them in person? She was an upholder of the law, a government official, and completely worn from the last few days of driving and politics. Did she bring him along, expecting him to find a way to get them to change their minds? He hoped not.

Going above the speed limit as much as he thought he could legally get away with, Colin made it to the offices of G&H in record time. He expected Mrs. Minton to arrive shortly, especially when the drive alone took up three and a half hours of their precious time. But when twenty minutes passed and Mrs. Minton had yet to show, Colin was being drained of both patience and pocket change. Paid street parking across from G&H was not cheap, and there would be no way for him to pay for more if she didn't show up soon.

Still wracking his brain for a way to get Mrs. Minton and himself inside to meet one of the top executives, not to mention getting them to cease a project they were obviously invested in *and* not give away any ghostly details, Colin was jolted into reality when his window was tapped.

Wishing it was a vagabond, Colin was disappointed to see it was instead a security guard with the letters G&H

proudly printed across the top of his jacket. The only other marking on the dark jacket was the name Curry.

"Hey buddy, can I help you, or do you have an appointment with Greene and Holt?"

Colin rolled down his window and did his best to respectfully answer the young security officer who looked like he wasn't having the best of days. "Oh, um…yes and no. I'm waiting for--"

"I'm going to have to ask you to move your car then, sir. These spots are only for urgent business or appointments only."

"You make people with appointments and emergencies pay for parking?" That blub didn't do him any favors with the young security officer. The man in his late twenties might be a good 10-12 inches shorter than Colin, but he could still get Colin in trouble with the law. Colin tried his best to fix his blunder. "I mean, I have an appointment. I'm waiting for the rest of my party to arrive before meeting with Mr. Greene and Mr. Holt."

Mr. Curry raised an eyebrow at Colin's statement before saying, "Well, seeing as how Mr. Greene is actually a Mrs., and she's out of the office for the next two weeks, I can assume you're either lying or will only see Holt, which, again, requires you to move, since your full party isn't present."

Colin swore on the inside. He couldn't let this be how it ends. Putting all his pride aside, Colin said desperately, "Please, Mayor Minton from Vernon should be here in less than a half hour, and she specifically asked me to meet her here. I did lie about having an appointment, but this really is urgent business. They're tearing down a building of great public importance tomorrow, and we are trying everything we can to civilly halt the process. Also, I just put all my change in the meter. If I move, I'll have no way to park within a square mile of this place, let alone meet up with my mayor."

Though given an adequate reason for someone camping out in their car and watching the building, the security officer was still more than anxious to get this specific car away from the entrance of the prestigious Greene and Holt skyscraper.

Feeling none too pleased about having to say it out loud, Curry decided to be as discrete, yet still specific, as possible for his real reason in asking him to move.

"Sir, I can't have *this* car parked here."

Oh, he understood now. It wasn't that Colin was there, it was that he was staining the nice façade with his beat-up Pontiac Sunfire. Was anyone allowed to operate such a generous charity as Renewed Living and be this discriminative at the same time?

Knowing he couldn't let it show, Colin bitterly swallowed the fury that rose up like bile in his mouth. It didn't change the fact that he still needed to somehow get *into* the building. That required playing the political game.

In the most pleasant way possible, Colin said, "I understand, Mr. Curry. I wouldn't be sitting in front of your building in this specific car if there were any other options. But I am under orders of Mayor Minton from Vernon, and if I'm not present when she arrives, there will be hell for me to pay and I can't have that right now."

Well played.

Curry must be a good guy, for the internal struggle playing out on his face told Colin he had a chance of and staying put. That would have been a relief, since he really did use the rest of his pocket change on the parking meter. But Colin was still a Warrington, and the world outside of Vernon was still against him.

Mr. Curry closed his eyes in what Colin recognized immediately as defeat. "Look, there will be hell to pay for me too if I let you stay out front."

Ah cruel fate, why must she mock him so?

"But…there is a parking garage around the back for long-term parking and employees. Here, I have a code that can get you in. You've paid enough for a day's parking anyway."

Could Colin believe his ears? He was so used to being shoved away or strong-armed, that he could not believe a stranger, let alone a security guard, would be generous enough to throw him such a bone. Was this the power of good political skills? No wonder many in that field eventually became corrupt.

Mr. Curry wrote out the parking code on a piece of paper, but before handing it to Colin, he said, "The parking garage is under 24/7 surveillance, and if I see this piece of crap in there by the start of my next shift, it's getting towed straight to the salvage yard."

Thanking Officer Curry, Colin stored his lackluster automobile in the belly of the whale and surfaced again. Waiting in the outdoor seating area of a nearby café, Colin had to admit that it was more comfortable than his car and gave him a better vantage point than he previously had. However, this café lacked as much luster as his car, rekindling his desire to see this mission through. One hour and one cardboard-tasting muffin later, the anxiously awaited Mrs. Minton parked in the same spot Colin vacated. Time to get to work.

CHAPTER 40

Once Colin and Mrs. Minton entered the skyscraper owned by G&H Reality, Colin couldn't hold a grudge against Officer Curry. His car really didn't belong out front.

The inside of the building was even more elegant than the outside, making sure there was no question in mind whether this was an important building and the people inside it were worthy of just as much prestige. If the two of them weren't on such an important mission and with such a time crunch, they would have taken at least a second to enjoy it all.

A quick look at the building guide told them Mr. Holt's office was on the top floor, naturally. The elevator ride to the top was both empty and uneventful. If Mr. Holt having his office located on the top floor wasn't enough, the entire floor *was* his office; the elevators opened in front of the receptionist's desk and, what he assumed to be the monster's lair, behind her.

Marching up to the front desk, trailed by a worn, weary, and out-of-breath Mrs. Minton, Colin didn't bother with any pleasantries, protocols, or even basic manners, but instead placed both hands on the countertop in a do-not-mess-with-me way and said in no uncertain terms, "I need to speak with Mr. Holt right now. It's an emergency."

Mrs. Minton was appalled by her company's introduction and thought either the young receptionist was impeccably trained or completely oblivious to Colin's rude behavior because she didn't bat an eye at his approach. Neither of them could have known that her lackadaisical response was because she was used to it. The angry people marching in and demanding to speak with Mr. Holt must have hated the man as much as she did. But she needed the job and therefore wasn't allowed to let any of them pass.

With a smile that didn't reach her eyes, the young woman began her usual spiel. "I'm sorry sir, Mr. Holt only sees people by appointment. If you would like to give me your name, I can leave a message for him and—"

Colin slammed his hands down on the desk now, causing Mrs. Minton behind him to yelp. With anger bubbling up inside, Colin demanded, "No, you don't understand! We need to speak with him now. Right now. It's an emergency. He's trying to tear down my family's apartment."

Dropping her fake smile, the woman continued her stony speach. "Sir, we only demolish our own properties, and only if we cannot repair them. I'm sorry, but I need to ask you to sit down."

Mrs. Minton tugged on his arm then, and thinking she would play the political card, he allowed her to pull him aside, back towards the elevator they vacated. "Come on Colin, we can't get through this way." Colin couldn't believe his ears.

Pulling his arm out of hers, he turned back to the poor receptionist and practically growled, "Get Mr. Holt on the phone. Now!" It was said in the most threatening manner, yet she was still an unmovable force to be reckoned with.

Now seeing red, Colin decided to bypass the woman and make his way to the double mahogany doors himself.

Startled for the first time, the young woman called after him, "No, sir, you can't go in there!" Not bothering with the phone, the receptionist hit the panic button under her desk and got down on the floor.

"Like hell, I can't," bellowed Colin after her. Oblivious to what the woman had done, and not giving a lick as to why Mrs. Minton was staring at the wall instead of helping him, Colin began to pound on the locked doors. "Open up and come out, you snake! You don't know what you're doing to them!"

From the corner, he could hear Mrs. Minton's last cry for reason, her voice strong despite her head being turned away from the scene. "Colin, you must stop, right now. You don't know what you're doing!" But when he didn't make any effort to comply, she resorted to sitting in the waiting room chair furthest from the doors, separating her actions from his as much as possible.

As soon as two security guards came through the door, Colin knew exactly what the scared receptionist was doing. Of course, Mr. Holt would outfit his office with panic buttons and personal security. One look at them and Colin knew he couldn't take the brutes, but that didn't keep him from trying to pull his arms out of their grips. With their training, the two men had Colin on the floor before he even realized the giant mistake he was making in resisting.

Only after Colin was confined and a safe word was given did the double mahogany doors open. From them emerged a smug, pompous, oily snake of a man. He was in his mid-60s, yet with the physique of a much younger man. Colin was wrenched from the floor and soon the renowned Mr. Holt came to stand nearly eye to eye with the crazed Colin.

Mr. Clinton Holt surveyed Colin with dark, emotionless eyes, then regarded him as though he were a loathsome article of abused and discarded clothing; only worthy to be thrown out. But before he did that, with as much self-satisfaction as one can muster, Mr. Clinton Holt couldn't help but have the last word.

"Oh, but that's where you're wrong, Warrington. I know *exactly* what I'm doing to them." Then, with a look to his security personnel, a weak-kneed Colin was half-carried, half-dragged towards a private exit.

Colin's temporary paralysis left him when he was still a few feet from the exit. Clinton Holt knew exactly what he was doing. He knew he was destroying the Brigham family. He *knew* everything. Not being one to think ahead in the heat of the moment, Colin tried again to break free from the security personnel and charge towards Mr. Holt. The guards were even stronger than they looked, which was saying something, and they had him back on the floor before Colin had taken two steps.

"You bastard!" It was hard for Colin to say anything more than that with his face ground into the carpet. But it didn't keep him from hearing from hearing Mr. Holt approach.

"Language, Mr….Warrington, isn't it?" Colin could hear the snicker in his voice. "Yes, I see the resemblance. I knew Bill back in the day, and he was a regular pain in the ass too." Turning to his guards, Holt said, "Get him out of here, quietly."

Before he knew it Colin was on his feet once more, despising being treated like a yo-yo. A sucker punch to Colin's lower right side guaranteed Colin's silence until he was dragged into the elevator. What happened on the elevator ride from Mr. Holt's top-floor office to the basement, where the security vehicles were kept, was neither documented nor shared by Colin, but all three men were bleeding and battered by the time they reached the bottom floor. Of course, Colin carried the bulk of the beatings. Practically thrown into the back seat of a private security vehicle, Colin was sent off to a small cell in the Detroit 3rd district jail.

He was only in there for an hour before Mrs. Minton worked her political magic to come and see him, and it was only after she came to see him that he realized he had left her completely alone on that top floor in the most shocking manner. A little worse for wear, Colin was able to at least sit up in a chair while getting the glaring treatment from Mrs. Minton.

"Of all the idiotic things I have witnessed, and *trust* me I have seen quite a few things Mr. Warrington, that beat them all."

"And you didn't even see the ride down." He would have finished his chuckle if it didn't hurt so much.

"Colin, this is serious. I can't get you out. At least not until tomorrow morning."

All the pain in his side was masked by the sheer terror in his heart. "Tomorrow! Tomorrow will be too late. Minton, I can't stay here!"

"Don't you think I know that!" Mrs. Minton was on the verge of tears. She groaned, "I've tried everything. You're just lucky they decided not to disclose what happened in the elevator, which I'm going to assume was only to save their own skins. An overnight stay is required in this district and…well…I'm so sorry, but I can't stay either. I have to go back and say goodbye."

"No Janice, don't say that. They can't go. We can get a hold of your judge friend now, or form a protest."."

With a doubtful look, Mrs. Minton asked, "And say what? The record of ownership goes back to the Brighams and they were legally dead nearly fifty years ago! The property was bought, sidestepping my office, and now belongs to H&G Investments." Mrs. Minton signed deeply and half-whispered, "Colin, it's *my* fault they're leaving. I-- I failed them." Unable to look Colin in the eyes, Mrs. Minton turned around, unsure what to do now.

"No Janice, you didn't fail them. You're the only reason they stayed so long." The sweet moment they shared in that room didn't last long.

Mrs. Minton turned back around. "How in the world do you know my name?" This came out a little snippier than intended. She didn't think anybody in town knew her name anymore.

Colin's sly smile was back. "Ah, that's easy. I talked with Kate about you. And as she recalls, the only reason Nora was such a wonderful babysitter was because she was one of the few people able to control the whirlwind that was Janice Darby."

It was unbelievable. Janice Minton never spoke with Katie, Helen, or any of the Brighams about life before the fire. How many wonderful memories did she miss out on sharing with them? And how else had she limited them?

"Mrs. Minton, can I at least call Katie?" The heartbreak in Colin's voice would melt even the coldest of hearts.

"I'll see what I can do. But I need to leave as soon as possible. I just wanted to let you know what was happening. Again, Colin, I'm sorry."

Without another word from either of them, she left. And there would be no phone call, Holt saw to that.

CHAPTER 41

The demolition trucks were already there when Mrs. Minton pulled into town late at night, ready for the next day's destruction. A pale morning dawned on a day Mrs. Minton hoped would never come and never dreamed would happen under her charge. Mrs. Minton took mental stock of her little town and how it had changed in the days since that sign was erected only months ago.

The flowers lining the main street, usually brilliant and life-giving, now wilted in their lack of color. The quaint downtown deserted of its normal populace, now overrun with unwanted vehicles of destruction. Their town's history and heritage now only mere hours away from being snuffed out permanently.

Mrs. Minton didn't bother to go home even for a quick change but instead parked in the south church parking lot where many other town vehicles were sitting. Complying with the Brigham family's request, no one petitioned the workers, but they did not abandon the family to face this condemnation alone. So great was the town's support that even the demolition crew looked as though they had second thoughts regarding this job.

"Minton!" came a voice above the crowd. It was Charlie. Always one to stand out, it did not take long for her to locate him. He reached her through the crowd and, slightly panting, said, "Oh Minton, I'm glad you two are back. Where's Colin?"

"What do you mean where—" Her question stuck in her throat. They didn't know? How did they not know?! Surely Colin would have called them immediately after she left him. How was she to know something else would go wrong?

Walking up to a shocked Mrs. Minton and startled Charlie, Katie didn't even bother to ask if something was wrong. "Where's Colin?"

"How do you guys not know? They took him."

"Who?" they both asked.

"Holt! Colin was making a scene in the office, so Holt had him dragged away and locked up for the night. They should have let him out by 8 this morning, but I expected him to contact you as soon as possible."

Katie all but fell into Charlie's arms. "Hey, it's okay. It's okay Katie. We're all going to be okay."

Katie didn't hear any of it. Her thoughts drowned everything else out. Katie didn't want Colin to go. She didn't want him to fight for her. At least, not like this. What good was someone fighting for you, when they couldn't be there when it mattered most? But above those thoughts was another voice that screamed at her, *"You're abandoned, again"*.

Such was not the case, but like everyone else, how was she to know? Colin raced with abandon towards that dot-on-the-map town that drew him to a new life just over a year ago. With a dead phone, and not wanting to stop a second, even to charge it, Colin was resolved to make it in time. He had to make it. He just had to…

CHAPTER 42

"Alright guys, let's roll them out!"
The signal.
The spark that brought all those vehicles to life.
And a family to death.
It was 10am. The large trucks and old-fashioned wrecking ball, Holt sure had a dramatic flair, lumbered towards the family estate. Many started booing at the approaching army, only to be silenced by Roy's dominating voice.

"Everyone, everyone, it's fine. We have all accepted this fate and have come to terms with it."
His words were spoken with more resolve than he felt. For every inch those large trucks moved closer to his family's home, he knew with more and more certainty that his life was soon to be extinguished along with his beloved wife and children.

Collecting his family one more time, Roy held his wife, looked at his sons, and faced his daughter. So much love for them welled up and spilled out of his eyes. "Helen, I got to love you deeper and longer than any other man has been able to love his wife. I know it feels cut short, but how blessed we are to have had so much time together. Boys, you both became men worthy of me to be proud of. I couldn't have asked for better namesakes. Jack, go home to Lisa and Luke. And Katie, I know lost love has made the decades unbearable at times, but not everyone gets a second chance. I'm glad you had one with Colin.

They all came together, a family one last time, and then they heard it; the release of the ball and chain, the sound of heavy machinery meeting concrete, wood and metal, and then…nothing.

A collective wail of sadness and terror rang through the crowd, for the Brighams, the immortal heart and soul of the town, were no more.

CHAPTER 43

As a group, they collectively felt the weight and warmth of each other; an incomplete family apprehensive of what to expect on the other side. And then, for Katie, there was no sensation at all…for three seconds. Those three seconds could have filled a lifetime. Her family, her café, her town, her Bill, and her Colin filled her mind. How she loved, how she hated. Her freedom to be herself; yet caged in such a small town. Her creativity, and the stifling monotony of the everyday. All of it, in three seconds.

Then she felt them. Others crowded in and pressed on her. And the sound, it was the sound of a waterfall, or was it an explosion? A myriad of voices?

Opening her eyes to the blinding sun, she was once again, in her small town. But this time it was only her. Those she held onto so tightly only moments ago were gone.

Just as stunned to see her as she was to see them, the crowd around her parted. Their eagerness to hold her and rejoice at seeing her was grossly outweighed by their fear of her reappearance. For they had all seen the entire family disappear for a span of three seconds, then in an instant she was again standing amongst them. Another face in the crowd.

Like an animal escaping its cage, Katie thrashed her eyes and arms around, looking for the familiar face of any other Brigham, but instead she was met with confused looks and fear. As any other person would do in that situation, Katie bolted from the crowd.

"They have to be somewhere; they have to be somewhere" were the only thoughts she could make out in her head. Another crash behind her sent her reeling around to see a nightmare. Her family home was in ruins. Chunks of her parents' suite were thrown down on the lawn. A large gap in the side wall exposed Charlie's kitchen and dining room. The other side of the building where her and Jack's apartments were located was no doubt under the same assault. None could escape this sentencing. None, but Katie.

"The store" she thought. Surely, they would be at the store. Or the café.

It was empty.

Desperate now, Katie ran with abandon to the brothers' shop. The lawn had been eerily cleared of the more unique creations it typically boasted; the small building also proved to be empty.

At this point, one would wonder why, for a town so involved in their goal to save the house and Brighams, the roads were now conveniently vacant of any help. At least, that was what she would have thought if Katie could think anything at all. Running up and down streets she knew would yield no fruit, there was only one place left to go: the cemetery.

Exhausted beyond the physical sense, Katie didn't even make it a step onto the lawn. She no more than looked at the tidy row of tombstones before falling to the ground.

There was not an ounce of doubt in her. Katie knew that if those graves were ever opened, they would reveal the family they claimed to hold for the last half a century. How she knew, she would never understand. But the feelings of peace and rest when she saw those cold, hard stones were beyond comprehension. Her family was finally home where they belonged, no longer chained to a town or house. They were free.

Katie's respite was too quickly over. Her parents, brothers,, and sister were where they should be. They were in their eternal homes. But she was not. Now there was only panic, devastation, loneliness, and hopelessness.

Unable to pull any air into her lungs, Katie clung to the sidewalk gasping. They're gone. They are, but she isn't. Oh god, she is stuck here all alone. "No, no I can't. I can't do this. I can't stay here," She cried. There is only one thing left in Katie's mind to do. Knowing the closest edge of town was at the end of Gunther Road, Katie feebly pulled herself up with all her strength and took one heavy step after another in an attempt to end all this madness.

Knowing he was too late, but praying he wasn't, Colin's disregard for all speed limit signs would have seen him spend a second night in jail if he had been caught. Rounding the bend just outside of town, Colin sped over the excessively high railroad track crossing, significantly damaging his Sunfire in the process, and slammed on his brakes to avoid running into Katie. Unable to believe she was still there; Colin flew out of the driver's seat and grabbed her in the fiercest of hugs.

"Oh my god, oh Kate, oh you're here," were the only words he could say, and he repeated them over and over while holding on to her limp form. It was at least a minute until he heard her soft whisper.

"They're gone."

"What are you talking about? You're-"

In a daze, Katie looked at Colin who was trying his best to interpret her expression of mental fog and misery.

"They're gone. They left me. I can't stay."

Katie took a few steps out of Colin's hands before understanding punched him in the gut harder than those security guards. Rushing to stop her, Colin grabbed at her again, but this time out of panic instead of relief.

"Kate, no! You can't do this!"

As if a switch had been flipped, Katie became almost feral at his objection. "Let me go! Don't touch me!" Still having some fight left in her, she clawed at his hands around her and kicked fiercely, giving everything she had left in her to escape. The struggle would have looked violent from the outside if there were anyone around to witness it. The lack of audience did not go unnoticed by Colin, and from her reaction, he could guess why no one was around. Although the struggle looked fierce, Colin did everything he could to not hurt the one woman he couldn't live without. It wasn't long until she finally gave up and collapsed in his arms as a flood of emotional carnage.

Easing her to the ground, it was now his turn to be stunned by the current events while Katie sobbed, holding nothing back. He wouldn't have considered everyone else's lack of sympathy something to be thankful for except that he and Katie were given privacy to grieve the family members they just lost. Though time was never an issue in the past, it was not very long before the two of them had to get out of the street to let some light traffic pass by. If they knew it was the crew that literally tore their family down, they would not have been so willing to let them by.

Katie resolved she would never allow herself to become another town oddity forever and eternity. There was only one way to be sure that would never happen, but she tried to get away from Colin before and only exhausted herself in the process. Now that he was finally here, finally here to stop her, protect her, comfort her, she wasn't so sure she wanted to leave after all.

"Come on, Kate, I know where we can go." Holding onto her hand to guide and because he was still afraid she would try to run, Colin began pulling her in the direction of the only place they could truly be alone. It wasn't far, and her feet knew where to go without any help, but Colin's hand never left hers.

The way there was muddier than either expected, but with the first of the lilacs coming out of their winter's sleep, it was well worth it. It was almost cruel how not even Living Color could outdo the beauty of that spot on this sad day.

On their bench, breathing in the calming lilac scent from the earliest blooms, the two sat a while in silence. Katie sat completely still, but Colin's jitteriness couldn't be controlled. He just lost his family too, and he wasn't even there to say goodbye. Then he saved his Kate just in time from committing an act of self-annihilation. Until he could guarantee her head was in the right place, he wouldn't be able to relax around her. But the silence was still nice. A calm amidst the storm. Not sure if he should break it, but knowing they had a lot to still figure out, Colin forged ahead.

"So, what now? I mean, we don't have to figure everything out, just…you don't even have clothes and a toothbrush, so I guess we can start there. I'm sure Mrs. Minton can –"

"Why didn't I leave too?" Katie's voice was just above a whisper, but she might as well have screamed it in his ears. That's what the voice inside his head was doing.

What could he say to this? It made just as little sense to him as it did to her. And like all the other questions they had over the years, could any answer be of any real help? It was safest for him to tell the truth without speculating.

"I don't know. But I don't think we're going to figure that out tonight, so let's get you settled down first."

His voice of reason won. Both still shaken from the morning's events, they made a plan to head back and raid Roy's store for some essentials and set up a makeshift bed on the couch for Colin while Katie stayed in his room, upstairs and out of sight for now.

Colin's foot slipped for the second time on their way back before he asked, "Did it rain here last night?"

"Yeah, it was a crazy storm. Jack... Jack said, 'Of course, it would storm on our last night'."

Colin knew that had to be hard to say because it was hard for him to hear. Clearing his throat a little, Colin said, "Well, watch out over here. It's still a bit muddy." He didn't really need to tell her that because he was still holding her hand and she was aware of every misstep he made.

"I thought the path was getting a little, Aahhh!!!"

Without warning, Katie's hand was ripped from Colin's, and he was just too slow to tighten his grip in time. Forget the path being muddy, the entire bank was eroded underneath them, and Katie had just become its victim.

"Kate? Kate!" Getting to her as quickly as he could, Colin slid down the muddy embankment and grabbed onto Katie, frantically checking to see if she was all right. She was mostly covered in mud but didn't appear to have any injuries, and what injuries she did sustain she assumed would be healed soon enough.

Rubbing her elbow, Katie did her best to reassure Colin. "Don't worry, it wasn't too high of a…fall." Seeing Katie turn white scared Colin more than her falling off the embankment. "What's wrong, what are you-"

Colin looked up to see what Katie's eyes were locked on. On the other side of a young tree that could not be more than twenty years old stood a red-marked post. "Kate, is that?"

"Uh-huh"

"And that means that you're?"

In barely a whisper Colin heard, "Yeah, it does."

"But, that doesn't… but you've come out here tons of times. Look, that marker's farther back from the park bench."

"Yes, it is." Without a second's hesitation, Katie jumped up and flew towards the opposite bank. Touching it, feeling the cool wet earth under her fingers, and the icy current around her legs was livelier than anything she could remember. She was on the other side of the city limits.

Uncontrollable laughter mixed with some lingering hysteria came from both of them at the realization that Katie could, and apparently has always been able to, cross the town line. "I can't believe it. Kate, you can leave!"

"I can leave? I can leave!" Pain laced its way through this joyful revelation, through her every being, and settled on her heart. Grabbing her chest and almost buckling into the water, Katie asked, "Omigod, could I have left this whole time? Could we all have left this whole time?"

Reading her mind, Colin had to put a stop to her toxic thoughts before they took root. He grabbed hold of her and drew her up onto their side of the river. Standing next to, but still on the other side of town limits.

"I don't know Kate, according to what you all said, no one was able to leave before. And with the house…you're the only one here." Beginning to believe himself, he kept talking. Instead of just cutting her thoughts off, maybe he had a point. "I don't think everyone else was allowed to leave, and if they tried, they would have disappeared even sooner. Unless…Do you feel any, well, any different? From before the house was…?"

Katie took stock of herself before saying, "No. And this doesn't make any sense. Colin, I don't know what's going on. Why the hell am I still here?"

That question brought her to her knees, easily accepted by the giving ground. On the verge of hyperventing and clutching her chest as question after question slammed into her with every breath, like a wave on the rocky shores she had never seen, Katie only calmed when she heard Colin say, "Don't leave her."

Turning her face upwards, she dragged the recollection of that phrase back from the recesses of her mind. The letter was always a mystery to them. It was always the outlying factor that didn't fit into the equation. So why did he choose now to bring up yet another thing they were unable to figure out? It aggravated her.

But Colin didn't bring it up to her, he was speaking to himself. And only after he realized she was no longer lost in her own misery, but focusing her anger on him, did he realize she heard him at all. But he didn't care so much that she was mad at him as he did that she was there at all. And Colin wanted her help, nay, needed her help, to find the answer to this final puzzle.

"That's what it said, right? The letter in the house, when you all came back? What if- what if *you're* Her?"

"But that's ridiculous. I can't be the *Her*. It was the house. Everyone vanished when they left or changed the *house*."

Colin knelt down onto the soft ground with Katie, unable to stop his thoughts from escaping his mind. "No, no they didn't. Everyone vanished when they were leaving *you.* When they moved away, or on with their lives without *you.* And the house was what kept you all here, safe and rejuvenated. So by changing it, why wouldn't they change as well instead of disappear?"

Katie thought she was incapable of shedding any more tears, but she was wrong yet again. The sting in her eyes could be heard in her voice as she asked, "You mean it's all MY fault!? I'm the reason they're all gone?"

Colin immediately realized his mistake in wording it that way. Thankfully it was also not true.

"No Kate, no, it's not your fault they're gone. There was a fire. They would have been gone anyway. So instead, is it possible you're the reason they got to stay a little longer?"

Decades should have taught her it was foolish to feel any hope in this situation, but she felt some anyway. Seeing that faint glimmer in her eyes, Colin stood up and pulled her up by the elbow. Katie was soon off her mud-caked knees, and back onto two wobbly feet, and the two of them made their way slowly back to town.

CHAPTER 44

Colin took Katie back to the apartment, but stayed away from the main road. It was hard enough to know your home was no longer standing without having to see it in shambles. Their clothes were still soggy, and more than a few places were coated in mud, but that didn't keep them from plopping onto the couch, too tired yet to raid Roy's store. But it was probably better this way. Katie was asleep within minutes of sitting, and Colin couldn't turn his mind off. He didn't want to leave her to take a shower, but he was able to quickly change and clean up at the kitchen sink before she stirred again.

Working with the abstract was never Colin's strong suit. Needing to get his thoughts out of his mind and somewhere concrete, Colin ransacked the apartment, finding it harder than he thought to locate a piece of paper and pen. He knew the next hour or so would not be fun, but after some consideration, he knew what had to happen next. Also, all of his research on G&H, as well as the accounts of the Brigham family fire were in Mrs. Minton's office. It was probably best for them to start over fresh anyway.

The night of the housefire was always hard to listen to, that was why Colin never wanted to ask for Katie's account, but something never felt right. And since she was the only one left to ask, he no longer had the choice but to hear the gruesome details from her point of view.

Katie was sitting up now, looking a little worse for wear. Since she wasn't much of a flight risk now that crossing city limits wouldn't obliterate her, Colin thought now was as good as ever to ask. Settling next to her on the couch and taking her hand, Colin began.

"Kate, I know this will be hard, and it's the last thing you want to do, but here's the deal. I love you. I've loved you for so long, and these last few months have been difficult for us both, but now that you're free from your Vernon, I want to take you out."

Shock brought those emerald eyes he loved to their popping point. Thanking God above, he did not need to quiet an interjection, he continued.

"I want to take you away from here. We'll go as far away as you want. Anywhere, everywhere! We'll cover every place on that list of yours...*but*."

He paused because he wasn't so sure he wanted to follow through with his own idea. How he would love to get up right now and just leave. Let the town think she crossed the line and disappeared. Let them think she went home with her family. Let them think he was just like his father; lost in heartache and fleeing from the aftermath. But he just couldn't.

"Before we can do anything, I need you to tell me everything you remember about the night you died."

He couldn't quite place the look she gave at his request. He thought she was going to fight him on it, but instead, she said something completely unpredictable. "But Colin, I've never been able to remember the night I died."

"How could you possibly not know?!" It was almost two hours later. Most of the time was filled with showering, finding something suitable of Colin's for Katie to wear, and cleaning up the muddied couch. However, Colin would not let this revelation go, and the more time that passes the more persistent Colin was in solving this mystery.

To make matters worse, the longer they stayed in his apartment, the more Katie wanted to leave. "I told you already, Colin. I don't remember what happened. And you playing Mr. Shrink isn't going to make me remember either. Now, for the last time. Let's just go." Katie's eyes swiveled towards the door for the umpteenth time, Colin couldn't take his eyes off her.

Colin put down his paper and pencil in defeat and asked with genuine curiosity, "But doesn't this bother you? You can remember details from decades ago about orders you had, birthdays, and weather patterns. Hell, you can remember everything about the day you opened the bakery, but this, the most life-changing, life-ending event, and you don't remember any of it?"

Looking back at Colin and taking note that he was no longer writing down everything she said, Katie replied, "No, I don't think that's weird. It was likely traumatic and over the decades of me pushing it away, I probably lost it forever."

Colin sighed as he leaned back in his chair and looked up at the ceiling. Then, he muttered, "But that doesn't make sense. Everyone else remembered."

"They did?" Katie's reaction startled both of them. This was news to her. Rarely did her family ever talk about that night. Even less than rarely. They NEVER talked about it. Katie, because she remembered nothing. The rest, because they remembered too much. But no one knew, because they simply kept the matter to themselves, even amongst their own family members. They only ever opened up to Colin about the night they died, and that was because he pried insufferably.

With genuine shock and anger, Katie demanded, "You asked them about dying in the fire? How could you!?"

"How could I not? Honestly, I don't understand why I'm the only one in this town who seemed to give a rip! Am I the only person who cares? It was one of the first things we covered. and sure, it was difficult on all of us, but after that was when I became one of the family."

"But you didn't ask me."

Colin couldn't see why that would bother her so much and frankly didn't care to. They were both tired and aggravated over the last four hour's traumatic experiences and she was getting off-topic. She needed to figure out what happened so they could leave.

"No, I didn't ask you, and I'm not sorry about it either," said Colin calmly. However, his curiosity got the better of him, and he asked, "Did you know they dreamed about it? They remembered sirens, smoke, the deafening roar of fire, and… it took them years before they weren't each haunted by it in some way, Kate. So, whether you were suppressing it or not, I'm glad I didn't ask you. Plus, everything involving Bill and you getting upset at all the questions I was already asking, it's not like I felt completely free to pry about that night."

Colin got up from his chair and sat down with Katie on the still-wet couch. With pleading eyes, Colin said, "I really need you to try and remember."

Katie glared at him. Standing up from the couch, Katie nearly shouted, "I can't believe you right now!"

With just as much energy, Colin called back, "That's fine, but c'mon, this is wrong! How can you think not remembering anything is normal? The night of the fire, the day or week before, can you just tell me *something* about it?"

Colin would not let Katie get by with saying "it was probably like any other time," and was starting to unreasonably lose his temper. In hindsight, this wasn't as important as he was making it out to be, but he couldn't ignore this pull inside that told him he needed to probe deeper and that if he didn't, he and Katie would never have any true freedom.

Nearly yanking her out of the door in irritation, the two made quick work of the stairs and locked the door behind them upon entering the back of the café.

Finding themselves in a dark, empty kitchen that should have been filled with the smells of baked goods, coffee, and dish soap this time of day, both were pained to see what used to be their whole world turned into such a dreary space.

"This better be worth it," was all Colin could think.

"Okay, it's the day before you *died*. What are you doing?"

With a look that echoed, *"This better be worth it,"* Katie decided to go along with and roleplay. Making a show of closing her eyes, she tried with everything in her to remember, but the desire to finally leave town kept invading her mind.

The exasperated noise Katie made was her way of throwing in the towel. "Nothing is happening, Colin. Can we please go now? I don't want to be here anymore. All I've ever wanted to do was leave and I finally can, so let's go!"

It was faint, but Colin heard it. A dry sob punctuated the end of Katie's plea to leave town, and it broke his heart. Colin knew he needed to concede. She was right. It was wrong, keeping her prisoner longer than necessary just because he couldn't let the mystery of it all go. She has been trapped here for decades. Who was he to deny her freedom any longer, and, worse, try to make her relive the worst time in her life? Why couldn't he just be thankful she was still there and high-tail it out of town like she had always wanted? Bill used to say Colin was the spitting image of himself, except Colin had a more stubborn chin and the personality to go with it. But stubborn or not, this crossed a line.

"Okay Kate, let's go. It just makes me sick to think there *had* to be something more that happened that night."

With no warning, Katie's memory came back. Not as a visual, or movie reel like you hear about or see in the movies, but in the form of a sharp stab to the stomach.

In all these years since the housefire, Katie and the rest of the Brigham family enjoyed perfect health. It helped that they regenerated to perfect health every morning, only being susceptible to the fastest of illnesses like food poisoning. Therefore, Katie never expected to feel ill, nor did she expect to be able to recognize the pain instantly.

After the unexpected pain, she was hit by a wave of nausea, sending Kate blindly fumbling around looking for any sort of handhold. A place to relieve her stomach was necessary after this most volatile of discoveries; her last day alive was not normal after all.

CHAPTER 45

The third time Colin called her name, Katie heard him. After throwing up for the second time what little was left in her stomach, Katie crossed the line between broken and resolved. Determined now to take this revelation to the end and finally know the *reason* behind her spectral existence, Katie stood up straight and marched into the café.

"Colin, you were right. Omigod, you were right."

Visually devouring the place, as if she could see the ghosts of decades past, Katie flew from surface to surface, moving a table here and a chair there.

Scared by her frantic behavior, Colin tried to stop her, but she would only push his hands away at every attempt. He decided to instead sit back and watch her work.

The café, now unrecognizable to him, made Katie even more invested in finding the truth.

"I was sick. I never got sick, even before dying, but I was sick for almost a week straight leading up to that night. Everyone was concerned for me, but I *had* to come to work. Why?"

Not expecting Colin to answer her, she walked again around the café; calmer now, but still seeking signs from the past. Colin had pushed her beyond her comfort zone to find the truth and now that same passion burned in her, begging her to remember. Imploring her mind to remember, Katie silently prayed for the answers that just wouldn't come. Then, as if a still, small voice told her to look, her eyes turned to the register.

"I couldn't leave because someone was stealing from me." Katie took a few tentative steps toward the modernized machine, but all she could see were visions from the past. "At first, I thought it was a miscalculation, but the books were consistently short, and I needed to find out who was doing it. Bill told me to inform the cops, but I didn't want to make a scene."

Hearing his father's name took Colin by surprise. The first few months he was in town, Katie could barely choke the name out in his presence. Nowadays, Colin noticed, she could say it with only a tinge of remorse. But now, seeing her dig up the past and not have tears in the back of her eyes over his father, Colin was both relieved and saddened that she was no longer pained by the past or resentful over Bill living his life. Colin couldn't help wondering. Could it be, now, that she finally accepted the fateful hand life dealt her and Bill? Or was she finally happy enough to just have Colin around?

Colin didn't want to make this about him, so he filed those questions away with the ever-expanding list of things to ask when everything began settling down. After all, all they had now was time.

Then Colin noticed what Katie had said. Justification for a wrong done was always Bill's way. It would make sense that his father wanted to get to the bottom of an issue as serious as thievery. Thank goodness that was a trait Colin had inherited along with his stubborn chin. Maybe, after all these years, they could still get justification for wrongdoing. Colin asked, "Who worked for you back then? And what does that have to do with you getting sick?"

Katie's forehead scrunched in an effort to answer. After a few seconds, she said, "I don't know, I just feel like it does. I started pulling money from the register right after my morning shift, but with days going by and nothing out of place, I focused on the afternoon crew. There was Maggie, she ran the register, but I trusted her fully and she worked here until she passed about 18 years ago. There were also 2 servers and a busboy."

"Wow, this place must have been really hopping back in those days," Colin said with a little too much surprise in his voice. Katie felt the need to educate him on years passed. "Jobs were more duty-specific then, you only did what you were hired to do. And don't forget, I wasn't dead yet. Naturally, we promoted the place more than we do now. Secrecy has a way of tempering things."

Colin mulled over these answers. He thought this place would be much busier if they were free to promote it. Actually, it could have been something really great. Another "if only".

Bringing himself back to the present, Colin asked, "Okay, it couldn't have been Maggie. Who were the other three people?"

"It doesn't matter who the servers were. I always suspected the busboy. That's another reason I didn't want to get the cops involved. He was such a teenage punk and too old to act so childish, but his father... I knew the only reason he worked so much was to get himself and his mom out of town and away from him.

"I didn't want to bring any charges against him without hard proof too, or they would all suffer under the father's wrath. And...I had it! Oh my goodness, I had it! I was getting ill only in the afternoons, and on the days I went home there was always money missing. Then, one day I pretended to go home, and I saw him pocket money through the kitchen door!"

"This was the day before you died?" Colin couldn't keep his excitement at bay. They were finally getting somewhere!

Katie had to concentrate to answer this question too. Caressing the modern cash register, as if hoping it would help answer for her, Katie said slowly, "No, but almost. I gave him a choice. I told him he had three days to repay me the money he took and resign from his position, that way we could both save face and keep his father out of it, or he could keep the money, take his mother, and go. But, I said, if he didn't make any decision at all, I would have to inform the police."

Katie sat down in the nearest chair, her head reeling from all the memories that now seemed determined to never leave her alone again.

"Then what happened," whispered Colin.

Katie gave a little shrug and said, "The three days never came. I got really sick the next afternoon and went home earlier than ever before. That night, the fire happened."

"And the busboy?"

"I wanted him to take the money and run, so I assumed he took me up on the offer. That is, if I had *remembered* giving him the offer at all, that's what I would have assumed. "

"So, you don't know if he ever paid you back or kept the money and left town?"

"No. I mean, I don't even know when they left. And I didn't care about any of that anymore. Bill was gone, I was dead. What was a couple hundred dollars? Everything else, compared to what I permanently lost, seemed so pointless. Besides, all I really wanted was for him and his mom to get away from his father, so, in my mind, there was no more problem concerning the café'."

"So, we know why you had to come to work, but do you think… Did you ever get sick after that? After the busboy left?"

"No, but I don't even know if he *did* leave town. Like I said, I wasn't paying attention to that stuff anymore. So, I don't know, maybe whatever it was just couldn't *get* me sick anymore. I know I'm not invincible because I've had food poisoning more than once over the years, but the little common colds or flu don't bother me like normal people. And I would wake up feeling almost as bad as when I went to sleep, so whatever made me sick premortem probably disappeared like a lot of other things."

Neither Colin nor Katie was satisfied with that answer, but there wasn't much else to go on. The consolation prize of Katie's last day no longer being a mystery would have to suffice. But there just *had* to be more.

Getting up from his seat, Colin began to slowly make his way back to the kitchen. It didn't seem right to walk away after coming so far, but a deal was a deal. Once they entered the kitchen, Colin innocently asked, "What did your afternoons look like? On days you weren't sick. Did you stay back here in the kitchen?"

Katie smiled a little at the memories. She was really going to miss this place. "I've always been the only one in the kitchen, well, until now. I've stayed back there more in the past decade than I used to, but only because I'm not supposed to be seen as much. Until the last twenty years or so I was back and forth between the customers, drinks, and kitchen."

They made it to the stairs, beginning to climb them to collect the few things Colin had and for him to take a much-needed shower. "Did you ever eat or drink on the job?"

Katie scoffed. "Yes, but we all did. And all of it was either made here or brought from home. I had a strict policy on what type of outside food was allowed in my café. Food items were kept in the back, but our personal mugs used to be kept on the far corner of the counter. You know, where that muffin basket is now. I had this vibrant, oversized mug

Bill gave me for Christmas the previous year. It had orange and teal-”

"Did it have a lid?!" Katie was a little put off by the interruption.

"What? No, none of them did. They didn't have travel mugs back then, and why would that matter?"

Colin stopped on the stairs, Katie at the top landing. She couldn't understand why he looked so dumbfounded. "Are you kidding me, Kate?! You were being poisoned by the busboy."

CHAPTER 46

"Poisoned? But that, that… is *exactly* what he would do." Katie's eyes were huge, and they looked deadly. "Oh, that devil! He's the reason I went home so early and had such a hard time waking up."

Katie began pacing the landing while she continued to rant about the hard mornings and painful experience when Colin reached out for her arm and said, "No Kate, I mean… I don't think you woke up at all. Everyone said the fire started around 4:30. You would have been here, at the café, by then, right? I think you died before the house fire."

"So, so they're not all gone because of me?" Katie looked close to tears at the mention of her family. It was still hard for both of them to think they were all gone.

Clearing his throat from the emotions that were stuck there, Colin said, "No Kate. If anything, I think they were allowed to stick around to help you with all of this. Unfortunately, you all never talked about it, so how would you know?"

"Holt."

"What?"

"The bust boy's mother. Her maiden name was Holt. He must have changed his name to his mother's after moving away. I can't believe I didn't see it until now."

Like a floodlight on a stage, illuminating the main character for a monologue, Colin could see the old man's smug, sneering face as he said, "Oh no, I know exactly what I'm doing to them." One more time.

His white-knuckle grip on the stair railing didn't go unnoticed by Katie. "He knew, Kate. Clinton Holt knew you were attached to that place, and he wanted to get rid of you. All of you. Why now, I don't know, but damn him, Kate. I know it's not much, but at least we finally know what happened and, in the end. And that fire would have happened with or without you, and you got to spend all those extra years with your family. But you're free now, so let's just go. We'll disappear. I'll keep my word and we'll go anywhere you want now. Every place on your list. Okay?" Colin tried his best to change the subject.

Katie thought for a few seconds. They could go anywhere? Do anything? She knew exactly where to start. Stepping down, towards him, Katie couldn't bring herself to look him in the eyes as she asked, "Hey Colin? I don't really have anything anymore, so I need to run down to Roy's. Why don't you go upstairs and take a quick shower while I grab a few things? I'll be back in about 20 minutes."

Not thinking anything of this, and desperately wanting a shower, Colin asked, "You want me to come with you?"

Katie gave a sweet smile and said, "No, I won't be long. And I want to look around for a little bit. See Dad's store one more time."

"Okay, Kate. Then you can tell me where you want to go."

Once Colin was inside the apartment, Kate descended the stairs and left out the back. She knew exactly where she wanted to go, and it was exactly where Colin would never take her. Knowing she only had a 20-minute head start, Katie ran as fast as she could to her brother's place. It had been decades since she drove the car, but it rode so smooth that remembering how to drive it came to her like riding a bicycle.

Katie had the address committed to memory and, fueled by hatred, it was easy for Katie to grab the keys to her brother's black '67 Corvette and race down Gunther Ln, not even looking back at her hometown prison once she crossed city limits. She did feel a tinge of guilt, leaving Colin behind, but she needed restitution. Clinton Holt had a debt he needed to pay.

CHAPTER 47

Time crept by for Colin. Believing Katie was just as anxious to leave town as he was, he couldn't understand why it was taking her so long to grab a few items and come back to get ready. Then he remembered it was her father's store. Her now gone father, who ran it with her now gone mother. Wanting to respect Katie's loss, Colin waited half of the twenty requested minutes before grabbing an armful of his favorite clothes and stalking down the stairs, taking care to lock the apartment for likely the last time.

Calling her name without any response should have been concerning enough, but when the door to the store proved to still be locked, panic set in. "No, no no!"

Colin couldn't explain how he knew, but somehow, he knew exactly where she was going. He also knew she had no idea how dangerous her decision was. No longer the bullied teenager, Clinton Holt had status, thuggish protection, and a deadly cold heart. If Clinton knew he was willingly re-killing an entire family by taking away their home, what would he do if one was found to still be alive? Dropping the clothes, Colin sprinted down the road to his abused and abandoned car, praying it would survive the breakneck speed needed to make up for time lost waiting.

Katie was thankful for the many road signs guiding her through the backwoods roads. She was completely unprepared for how many cars now traveled the interstate. Seeing so many was both frightening and exhilarating, but the fear won out and she never turned onto the onramp until she had reached I-75 outside of Flint.

On her slower drive, Katie kept thinking back to the many vehicles flying by, her focus turning to the people inside. Everyone on the road with a different purpose, a different destination, a different story. She couldn't wait for hers to soon be a happier one.

Even though this was an impulsive decision, she was still smart about it. Keeping at the speed limit that was much faster than she had ever driven before, Katie wanted there to be no reason for a cop to pull her over, demanding papers that didn't exist for a driver who had been long dead. Thinking about what a ridiculous position that would put her in made her chuckle a little, then sober up once she saw her first state trooper on the side of the road. As comical as it sounded, her position still put her in danger of being experimented on by some freak scientist. That was, if she didn't wind up in a looney bin instead.

If her goal wasn't so serious, it would have been a wonderful drive. Stopping at a gas station, Katie observed families while pumping her own gas for the first time in decades, taking care to follow the directions exactly. Once that experience was over, she walked inside and, seeing the baked goods wrapped in cellophane made her think of her own treats being sold at the nearby gas station. That made her heartache. Leaving them, she went with a brain-freeze-inducing, shaved-ice beverage and a half-stale, not-so-soft cinnamon pretzel.

In another speck-on-the-map city less than an hour from Detroit, Katie found a secondhand retail store. Back on the road, cleaned up, and in a new, flattering outfit, she resolved not to stop again until reaching her destination.

Poor Colin had to stop two times as well. The first was by a state trooper who seemed most unconcerned about why this man was going twenty-eight miles over the speed limit and would have given him a second ticket, if he could, to prove that point. The second was at that same gas station just off the interstate, now more than thirty minutes behind Katie. This stop did not involve a frozen beverage or pretzel, but coolant for his abused car. Hope was sparked when he inquired about the Corvette and the worker remembered it. Colin was on the right track. This time, he was going to save Katie and take her away from all of this.

CHAPTER 48

It was dark when Katie arrived at the skyscraper. Parking across the street, she decided to camp out and watch… until a security officer by the name of Curry knocked on her window.

"Is everything okay, ma'am?"

Not exactly sure how to answer that, Katie thought honesty was the best way to go.

"I'm trying to find Clinton Holt, of Greene & Holt. He tore down my home this morning and I would like to confront him about it."

"Oh, um…" Poor Curry really was a good guy after all, and he struggled over this information. At first glance, Curry thought Katie was as sweet and lovely as ever, yet here she told him she wanted to confront one of the biggest real estate sharks in the state. The poor girl would be chewed up and spat out, and he knew it. And if it was ever discovered he helped her in the process…

"Look, ma'am, you seem like a very nice lady. Surely you would prefer a lawyer to talk with Mr. Holt instead? Or, since he tore down your home and most law firms are closed now, I could help you get a list of hotels for the night and you can see him in the morning?"

Katie gave him a small smile tainted with sadness. "No, Mr. Curry, I would really like to speak with him. That's all. There's also a previous debt he still owes me from a while back and all I want to do is remind him before being on my way."

Grabbing his neck with one of his hands, Curry consented. "Oh, okay. Well, if you would like, I think the lobby is still open. However, I don't suggest you leave a car like that out here." Looking around, unsure of what he was doing or why, Officer Curry made a decision that, unknowingly, caused the first domino to fall. "If you want, there is a parking garage for the building just around the corner."

Just like that, Katie found herself in a most fortuitous position. She was tired from the drive. Tired from the heartache of loss. Tired of running from the shadow of affliction. But most of all, she was tired of the life she was forced to live day in and day out for nearly half a century, all because of the selfish act of a teenager who never received the consequences for his actions. Katie knew she had to find Clinton, and had to finally confront the man who ruined her life so long ago.

Then a thought brought her to a crashing stop in the middle of the lane. She didn't even know if Clinton was still in the building. She didn't know what he looked like, what he *was* like. And if he wasn't here, she had no possible way of finding him. On the brink of despair, Katie let her head drop back on the headrest. Deep, long breaths turned into shallow, rapid breathing until Katie found herself not crying, for she was done with crying, but letting out her rage and ferocity in one barbaric scream.

She was close. So close. Too close! Her goal was to come and confront Clinton Holt, and she'd stay damned if she didn't.

Then, Katie noticed the parking plaques bolted into the parking garage walls, the ones that reserve a spot for the more distinguishable employees, and it dawned on her. She didn't need to find Clinton Holt, she just needed to be in the right spot for him to come to her.

CHAPTER 49

Clinton Holt swaggered toward his car, victorious. His kingdom growing ever bigger from the rubble of other's lives gave him a power trip most only dreamed of. The faint heartbeat of a conscience-on-life-support stopped bothering him years ago. Despite his real age, he sauntered on with the energy and carnal drive of a 40-year-old, trying to decide where he should pick up his celebratory lady of the evening.

Seeing a most attractive figure of a woman leaning against an equally attractive car, Clinton thought he needed to look no further than this siren, and waited with bated breath, lust growing with every step, for her to turn and look at him.

Unlocking his car while only three steps away, Clinton figured this little minx was purposefully looking away from him, and he fell for the bait. Walking around to the passenger side, mere feet from his interest, Clinton leaned back against his new Porsche 911, as black as his soul, crossed his arms, and waited for three long seconds before making his move.

Katie knew it was him instantly. Forty-six years may have gone by, but there was no mistaking that king-of-the-world demeanor, that swagger, that arrogance. He was a long cry from the kid he used to be, but apples really don't fall far from the tree and this apple grew into the father he once despised. Disgust and hatred exploded in her heart; she couldn't even get herself to look at him. How in the world did she forget about this man for so many years?

But he was here now. Clinton Holt was here, and every fiber of her being was terrified. What was she thinking? Why did she come? More importantly, why did she come alone? She hated this man with every fiber of her being. She wanted him to know exactly what kind of terrible person she knew him to be, unleashing her fury on him, but she also wanted to be rid of him forever, getting as far away as she could. The internal tug-of-war wouldn't stop. Praying he would go away and praying for the chance to rip his eyes out at the same time fought within her until she heard him stop next to his car, behind her, and felt his eyes rake over her from behind.

Katie wanted to jump on him, claw him, scream at him, throw something at him; anything to cause fear and pain. This man ruined her life, her family's life, and the lives of everyone else she loved, and she wanted nothing more than to ruin his right back. But she couldn't take him in a fight and expect to come out victorious. No, she was at a disadvantage there, she knew that, but she did have the element of surprise. And she would keep her face turned, biding her time, for that element of surprise to be just perfect.

Clinton couldn't believe he had to wait so long for anyone to pay him attention. It angered him, and he liked it. He also knew the best way to get what he wanted with the fairer sex was to play the nice card until he had them how he wanted them.

Clinton's voice wasn't loud or demanding, but he spoke with the seductive resonance that had never failed him in the past. "A pretty little thing like you shouldn't be out here all alone. Are you lost?"

"No," Katie said without turning her head around. Bewitched by his desire to dominate, Clinton couldn't let her get away now.

Dropping his voice a little lower, Clinton spoke with slow, perfect cadence, hoping to finally catch his prey. "Well, I know every person of interest who should and shouldn't be in this parking garage, and I know you don't belong here. If you're not lost, then is there anything I can do for you?"

"Why yes, Clinton, there is." Perfectly executing her words with her turnaround, Katie faced the man, fire burning in those eyes that still betrayed every emotion. Her surprise paid off.

"Jesus Christ!" If his heart were in any less condition, he could have possibly keeled over there. Acting appropriately as one who literally just saw a ghost, Clinton not only fumbled away but searched for sanctuary on the other side of his car. Once Clinton had both hands out to steady himself against the hood, and it was apparent Katie did not desire to chase after him, Clinton demanded. "How are you here? I got rid of you all!"

"Oh, poor Clinton." Katie spoke in the same slow cadence to mock Clinton. She was thrilled her scare tactic worked. She was going to have him begging for forgiveness on his knees before the night was through and relish every moment of it. Shaking her head and slowly walking towards him, Katie put on a bold face and played her part well. "You didn't get rid of me, you set me free. And now it's time to pay me back."

Everything was going perfectly. Katie stopped in front of his car and looked at Clinton's hand frozen on the door handle. She would say her peace, give the threat to haunt him forever unless he admitted to murdering her all those years ago and the attempt to get rid of her just this morning, then leave him cowering by his car, treasuring that memory forever.

Narrowing her eyes at the trembling man, Katie dropped the act and began speaking with unrestrained emotion. "Why did you do it, Clinton? Why did you kill me all those years ago, and try to kill me again? I gave you a choice. All you had to do was leave, and none of this would have happened."

Clinton's face drained white. That was all the proof she needed, but Katie wanted more. More fear, more conviction, more closure. "You didn't succeed in getting rid of me the first time and now... here I am! Free, forever."

"But you can't! You can't be here! I destroyed the house! And you crossed the line! How are you even here?" Clinton's voice was much higher than before, and void of all power and authority. For the briefest second, Katie saw him for the pitiful man he really was, and it sickened her.

"Trust me, Clinton, I am very much here."

"But, the house?"

"The house kept me trapped in Vernon, but it's gone now. You did that. Again, Clinton, I gave you a chance to walk away and you didn't take it. Why did you kill me?"

In an instant, his fear was replaced by something else. Katie noticed it, yet didn't know how to interpret this change. At first, he was scared witless, literally trying to run from her. And now he looked like a child who didn't get his way; an unattractive look on any adult, but a dangerous look on him. Then, she heard it in his voice. "Stop saying my name! I'm Mr. Holt, and you will not address me like a child anymore! I am not some kid working in your café!"

Anger burned on both sides. For Katie, Clinton did not deny killing her but he also would not admit to it; condemning her to being a perpetual secret in that small town; trapping her, and her family, and taking her greatest love from her. Katie called him by his given name because she had no respect for his position of authority.

And Clinton? He was an even bigger egomaniac than his father; demanding, harsh, and always getting what he wanted by any means necessary, even violence. He hated Katie as a child, who was loved by parents, siblings, friends, and strangers alike. Always taking their warmth for granted. And despite how beautiful she was or how she ended up at his work after all these years of being dead, he hated her now. She haunted him for years! Knowing he had accidentally killed her tore at him at first, and if she had approached him shortly after the occurrence, he would have been on his knees begging her forgiveness and admitting his actions to all.

But she didn't. She literally let him get away with murder. And the taste of that power, that power absolute, enslaved him. And he was more than happy to serve this master. His heart was bitter and hard, and no ghost was going to move it.

Katie wouldn't give up though. Not now. Enraged, Katie screamed, "I said, Why Did You Kill ME!? I gave you everything you needed, and you killed me! You stole from my cash register, and you poisoned my drinks! Then you trapped me! You trapped me and my family in that small town for decades, lost and afraid in the never-ending sea of time, always afraid of when our secret would finally be discovered, and we too would be ripped away and disappear from existence. Then, for no good reason at all, you had to go and kill me again! But it didn't work, Clinton, because now I'm no longer trapped in that town, I'm here, and I will never, *ever* stop haunting you." By the end, Katie was nearly deranged, but that didn't seem to bother Clinton Holt.

Standing up straight, Mr. Holt's face as stone cold as his heart. It was his turn to take a step towards Katie and her turn to take a step back in fear. In this exchange, neither of them heard a car door shut half a level below them.

In a cold steely voice, Clinton Holt said, "You never did listen to me, did you? Never paid attention to what I wanted, never saw me. I didn't want to work for you, I was forced to. You knew why I needed a job, why I needed to get away and you *dared* to make me nothing more than a clean-up boy! Is that all you saw me fit to be? A trashman, forced to hide in shadow and take orders from everyone around? Do you *think* you gave me a choice? I didn't need to leave, all I needed was to be seen. Be seen as something more than a punching bag, a scapegoat, a trash boy."

Clinton was now standing at the front of the Porsche with Katie backed up against the hood of the Corvette. Her thoughts were going a mile a minute, processing everything he was saying. *"He did this because of his pride? Because he didn't get what he wanted? He killed me…over nothing?"*

Colin interrupted her thoughts, now inches away from her face, an ugly sneer on his face. "But you see me now, don't you? Everyone does. And if you think the loss of your poor, pathetic family is going to make me cower at you, or anyone else, you're wrong!"

"Kate! Kate, get away from him!" Colin's voice sliced through the air, catching Katie by surprise.

"Colin?" At the sight of Colin, racing towards her in a flurry of panic, eyes locked onto hers, she finally snapped from her haze of revenge. This man killed her for no reason when he was a teenager and tried again just because he could. What would he do now? What has she done, seeking her own revenge? What---?

She didn't have time to search for the answer. Shattering the silence, a shot rang out, vibrating off the walls and cars. Only thirty yards away and closing fast,

Colin saw the gun being drawn from Holt's jacket, raised to sight its target, and recoil upward. Despite the deafening sound and horrifying sight of Katie's body succumbing to gravity's pull, Colin bulldozed Holt to the ground. Incapacitating him with a few hard blows, he didn't waste any time before turning to his Kate.

So much blood, a crimson stream flowing downhill. Colin grabbed her limp body.

"Kate! Kate, Kate, no. No, you can't die. Please, don't die." His cries and pleas reverberated off the cold, cement walls, getting no sympathy in return.

It was such a damned lucky shot, straight to the heart. Right where Holt would have wanted.

She was gone. No more words, no more waiting to live, no more anything. Kathleen Brigham, 26, of Vernon Michigan breathed her last in the arms of the second love of her life.

Colin held her in his arms, tears unrestrained. While kissing her brow, his first romantically physical act, his pain flowed faster than her blood. She was finally free, free to be his and his alone, and now she was gone.

CHAPTER 50

Autumn leaves crunched underfoot, a familiar sound no matter where in the world one found them. Whether in the biggest of cities or smallest of towns, all could share in its melody, its serenade of another year closing.

It's amazing, the changes and wonders one year can bring. Colin's altered point of view on life, death, love, and self was one no one outside of Vernon would have noticed. Well, maybe his money lenders in California and a few ex-girlfriends, but besides them there really was no one else. Vernon and Katie took the broken and empty canvas that was Colin's life and added color, excitement, and opportunity, and Colin valued it more than any masterpiece could hope to be cherished.

It was late October, just over five months since Kate's permanent death. Colin didn't stay in town for the prosecution. He didn't even stay in the country. Shortly after giving his testimony, he heard G&H Realty was going through a reconfiguration and change in branding, but that was expected when parking lot surveillance footage convicts its owner of first-degree murder.

Colin only went back to Vernon once. His task was to lay his Kate to rest next to her parents. His prize was an old, handwritten cookbook in the middle drawer of the kitchen island. Just inside its cover was a letter.

Dear Colin,

If the love I have for you is mirrored in any way, I know the torment you are about to put yourself through. Don't. I love you, you love me, but you are not bound and shackled here or to your past.

Out there is a giant world full of adventure and beauty. If I could grant you anything, it would be the freedom to go and enjoy that world with a clean conscience knowing this truly is my desire for you. See what I never could, Colin. Being here, with you, I've lived more since being dead than most get to in their entire lifetime. And even though the thought of being apart from you breaks my heart, I am ready. I'm ready to go and that's okay. You're going to be okay.

Don't be afraid to love again. Don't be bitter by fate's cruel hand. Give generously of yourself to those who need a little help. You never know, they could end up changing your life like you changed mine.

Thank you for changing mine. Thank you for coming to Vernon. To me, you are the world.

Your Kate

He couldn't count how many times he opened that book just to see her tidy, curvy script. Mrs. Minton had caught him on the way out of town to sign some papers he didn't even bother to look over. Since then, he received several voice messages on his phone from her, likely wanting him to go over some more legal documentation.

Who knows, maybe she just wanted him to make good on that dinner date they never had.

Keeping her promise, Katie left Colin everything. The café, he gifted to Bree. He understood his father a bit more, for he, too, could never go back to Vernon.

Colin never checked his bank account after that first time. There would never be a need for him to worry over his finances again. Feeling obligated to pay her back in some small way, Colin kept an eye out for others in need and generously donated his finances, time, and abilities.

The only thing Colin would never part with was his father's watch and Katie's book, which he carried with him everywhere. Not that he baked anymore. He hadn't darkened a kitchen since leaving America. Working his way through Katie's list of places to go, he was currently in France.

Following the Seine up the D6015, a sign caught his attention just outside of Port Villez. Vernon, 4.4 km. His pulse quickening and fingers grew cold. Colin never dreamed he would see that name here.

Driving through the small town, new images brought back a myriad of memories. The Old Mill, if painted an obnoxious purple would match the empty storefront across Katie's Café perfectly. The turrets, though tall and demanding, never received the attention they longed for. To this day it still stands vacant. For all Colin knew, most of the town was vacant these days.

Parking next to a church near what he assumed was their version of downtown, Colin found a Tourist Office not too far away. Thankfully there were English translations, and he saw Claude Monet's House and Gardens were not even 10 minutes away. The abundance of foliage and color reminded him painfully of Living Color and Dually's unmatched fascination for the plants.

The pamphlet informed him the town was known for producing engines. Jack and Charlie would have had a blast getting ahold of spare parts. With their tinkering minds, the creations would be endless.

Walking up and down the ancient streets until he found himself at the end of a block constructed of touching buildings of mismatched sizes and colors, he dwelt on the idea that this was the kind of place Katie belonged all along. Her Vernon was small, secret. This new Vernon, all made possible by her parting gift to him, was vibrant and expressive.

Lost in thought, Colin's mind came back to earth when a door not too far away opened and a young woman nearly fell out, coughing from the smoke that pursued her and contaminated the clear, clean fall air. Her hair caught his attention first. Unmistakably the most vivid, mahogany red found in nature, it was cut just above her jawline and flipped out at the ends. What caught his attention second was her petite, yet shapely, frame. When she stood up to her full height, she barely came up to his mid-chest. But what caught his attention and held it captive was when she turned and looked at him. Her hair perfectly framed her face in which were set two large, wildly green eyes the deceitful color of new spring grass. It was a lovely counter to the approaching winter and dead, crunchy leaves that littered the ground on this chilly fall afternoon.

A corkscrew tightened in his chest. She was nearly identical to his Kate when he saw her the first time. His feet, heart, and mind battled in the milliseconds between seeing her eyes and her next expulsion of smoke from her lungs. His body wanted to run, his heart wanted to grab this woman and hold her tight, and his mind told him doing either would ensure the cops were called. Seeing her cough again, Colin's feet instinctively moved forward to help while his heart put up a feeble barricade.

"Hey, are you all right?" Not knowing anyone was there, Anne wasn't sure if this large stranger coming towards her was a welcome sight or not. Until she was able to take a few clearing breaths, her hand came up to halt him at a comfortable distance.

Looking up at his strong jawline that led to a stubborn chin, and halting green hazel eyes, there was no denying he was handsome, but she felt as tiny as she looked next to his tall frame. She didn't like always being the small one, always feeling tiny. It gave her a sense of helplessness. Having to make up for her 5'2 frame, her feisty personality tended to rub people the wrong way, even when she didn't want it to. Not wanting him to sense any uneasiness, Anne composed herself and instantly closed off her emotions. Colin saw the change immediately; it was in her eyes.

"Miss, I asked if you were all right. Would you like me to get some help? It looks like there's still a fire inside."

His genuine kindness and offer crumbled her wall as easily as if they were made from the charcoal biscuits sitting on the countertop. There was no fire, just smoke; the byproduct of her every attempt in the kitchen.

With an Irish lilt Colin didn't expect to find here in the middle of France, yet matched her look perfectly, Anne said, "Aye thanks, but it's all for naught. The baker is all fluttered, and I'm up to 90."

"Um…" He didn't understand any word she said other than 'thanks', but she sure was cute saying it. Well, that wasn't all. He also realized that she needed a baker. He was a good baker, thanks to Katie. Holding Katie's book a little tighter, Colin wasn't sure if he was ready for what he said next but he said it anyway. "Would you like a hand in the kitchen?"

Sticking her chin into the air in a way that was all too familiar, Colin saw this captivating stranger wouldn't let him in that easily. Like a little dog in front of a Great Dane, she needed him to know she was no one to mess with. "Don't act the maggot with me, I'm no chancer."

Colin laughed in surprise while he shook his head in confusion. "What? No, I'm being serious. I even have my book with me. Look, I'm only passing through town, but I can stay if you need some help, and if you're not happy with my work you can kick me out and I won't bother you again."

Glancing towards the cookbook in his hand, there was no hiding her desperation. And right now, she didn't have the energy nor the financial resources needed to refuse his offer. Calming down a bit, her English became less jumbled for Colin, "What can you make?" Showing her some favorites but making sure the recipe was kept covered with his hand, the young woman was indeed impressed. Colin could tell in her eyes.

"All right, I'll let you help out, but in the kitchen only. How long can you be staying?" Colin noticed her accent wasn't quite as pronounced when she was calmer, but the lilt was still very present.

"Well," Colin sighed, quickly thinking it over, "I've only been in town for about an hour, but I'm not really on my way to anywhere else. I can stay as long as you need me." As long as she needed him. It was both freeing and binding to stay. He had the freedom to go anywhere or stay put for any reason. Another thing to add to his growing mental list of gratitude.

With raised eyebrows, Anne asked, "So you can do it as a nixer for me?"

Colin could only shrug at her question and said, "I have no idea what that means."

Looking him up and down, it was the smoke seeping through the crack in the door that made up her mind. "There's a room above the kitchen. I need you now, but I'll give you till the end of the hour to settle. Tomorrow, be ready by 4. If you have a car, the parking lot is around the back."

That gave him less than an hour. Less than an hour for his life to change, again. With a half-smile, Colin nodded and turned back towards his rental car.

The young woman called out to Colin before he got very far. "I'm Anne, by the way. Anne McDermott." Her voice, slightly brighter, registered in Colin's ears. She already seemed to soften towards him, giving Colin some hope that she wouldn't be as hard of a boss as Katie was his first week.

Colin thought that was the perfect name for her. Turning back towards the young woman, a full smile on his face, he answered back, "I'm Colin Warrington. It's nice to meet you, Anne."

He didn't know how long he would stay, how or if this would work out, but he was free to go anywhere, try anything. Thanks to the Brighams and his Kate, Colin's life became something so much more, so much bigger than himself. And to think, none of this would have happened if he had chosen to go anywhere but Vernon.